Circulum

IMRE ZSOLT BALINT

Copyright © 2020 Imre Zsolt Balint

All rights reserved.

Contents of this document, whether whole or part, may not be reproduced in any way, shape, or form without explicit written permission from the author.

Any references to characters, names, events, locations, organizations, businesses, governments, etc. are a result of the author's imagination and is a work of fiction. It is pure coincidence if any such details resemble real people (dead or alive), actual events, businesses, governments, aliens, etc.

DEDICATION

To my Mother and Father, and all the science fiction lovers on Earth.

CONTENTS

Chapter 1   1

Chapter 2   4

Chapter 3   10

Chapter 4   17

Chapter 5   22

Chapter 6   25

Chapter 7   31

Chapter 8   36

Chapter 9   41

Chapter 10   47

Chapter 11   53

Chapter 12   60

Chapter 13   62

Chapter 14   70

Chapter 15   74

Chapter 16   78

Chapter 17   82

Chapter 18   84

Chapter 19   91

Chapter 20   97

Chapter 21   104

Chapter 22   111

Chapter 23   117

Chapter 24   120

Chapter 25   123

Chapter 26   129

Chapter 27   135

Chapter 28   141

Chapter 29   149

Chapter 30   157

Chapter 31   163

Chapter 32   170

Chapter 33   176

Chapter 34   184

Chapter 35   190

Chapter 36   198

CHAPTER 1

A swift jab to the ribcage on the right. Followed by another to the left. The final blow straight to the stomach from a fist that felt more like a brick.

The two heavies that held up Trent, one on each arm, let him slip from their grasp and crumple in a heap like a plastic wrapper to a flame. Trent's butt plopped to the ground and he cumbersomely folded his arms over his midsection, his back to the wall, knees bent haphazardly. He lowered his battered face, and an animal-like grunt escaped between his clenched teeth. His brow was screwed up, eyes shut tightly, and a trickle of blood escaped from a cut on his lower lip. *Fuckers. I hope this blood washes out of my shirt.*

"Trent. My good man. You missed your deadline... twice," Harold said as he took a handkerchief from his pants pocket and started wiping off the blood on his hands.

Harold was the right-hand man to a local drug dealer in the area. He was a large guy in his fifties, short-cut graying hair, rough skin, but in damn good shape. He liked to look the part of a businessman, but his cheap suit made him look more like a cut-rate old timey door-to-door salesman. Trent met Harold several years ago after being laid off from a small software development firm that went under. He came across a job ad for a "Security Programmer" and decided to apply. Not because he had the knowledge and experience as a software developer, but because he was desperate for cash, and frankly found the poor wording on the posting comical. He thought to himself, why not?

"Nothing personal, Trent. You know. The Chief's not patient and he just wants the gear installed for his client. The guy's paid good money. You're paid good money. Minus a late fee this time 'round." Harold glanced to his left and right down the apartment corridor and pursed his lips, tossing the bloodied cloth away without much of a thought.

Trent reminisced about the time he first met this bunch. The moment he walked through their office door on interview day, was the day he wished he hadn't done that. That part of the city hadn't changed much over the past fifty years, hidden in the shadows of elegant skyscrapers that could tickle the soles of clouds. The small few hundred square foot retail space featured worn carpets, a scent of mold and casinos, water stained ceiling tiles, and rickety shelves stocked with third rate, but affordable, security related products and anti-spy equipment. To most, it was a typical nerdy outlet. An aging door behind the counters at the rear, desperately aching for a fresh coat of paint, hid a tiny nondescript office where Trent's interview was held, along with an equally puny and putridly kept washroom, and a storage area about twice the size of the retail frontage. That storage area guarded the real goods of the business. Trent was none the wiser to this detail then. He just sat anxiously in an uncomfortably shoddy office chair, eyeing his future employer, the Chief, and his "business associate", Harold.

A young couple with giggles and sparkles in their eyes exited the elevator a few feet away from the foursome. Harold and the goons synchronously turned their heads and stared at the couple expressionless. The lovebirds froze in their tracks, eyes darting to each figure, smiles fading, with adrenalin and heart rates rising. The girl's eyes locked onto Trent and didn't flinch for a moment as her boyfriend grabbed her by the arm and pulled her back into the elevator. The doors seem to shut in a hurry.

Harold turned back to Trent and the goons returned to casually scanning the apartment hallway. "Tomorrow you do your thing, Trent. The Chief likes your work. Our clients like your work. Tomorrow, I know you'll be back to your usual self, and you'll get this project back on track. Ain't that right, Trent?"

Trent slowly dropped his arms by his side to steady himself. He raised his head upward to look at Harold, his head bumping gently against the wall, the thud quietly reverberating down the hall. His eyes were glazed over, vision blurred. His breathing was returning to normal, but still sputtering like an engine starved of fuel.

At first Trent didn't think twice about the projects he got. Install a security system here. Upgrade another one there. Work on some in-house machine learning security system software that could analyze and alert owners to suspicious activity. But it's not like Trent was completely oblivious to his environment. The plastic grins and façade kindness from the home owners. The swanky upscale, immaculately kept residences that always seemed to have security personnel lurking in the corners. The hot wives and expressive cleavage. Areas off limits and silent answers when curiosity welled up. Trent liked to stay out of trouble for the most part and took to the cues quickly. After all, the work he did wasn't shady. What it was used for, well that's another question. He'd report most of his pay to the taxman. And ultimately, did he really care about what these people did? But he still couldn't help but wonder what his family would have thought, that is, if they were still around.

Harold looked up, but at no one in particular. "Gentlemen, Trent looks tired. I'm sure he's had a long day. Let's let the man rest. He's got a busy day tomorrow. Goodnight, Trent." Harold buttoned up his black suit jacket and headed toward the elevator. His associates followed close behind, being nice enough not to step on any splayed out digits or legs. Only Trent's eyes lazily tracked their movements, while he took deep laboured breaths. A few moments passed and the elevator returned, yawning open to collect its temporary guests.

Trent remained sitting on the worn out carpet, recalling his day. He'd been interviewed for a data analyst position at a stock trading firm by a pleasant HR lady in her fifties, Caroline. She smiled sweetly and tilted her head as he thoughtfully explained his past experience, skills, and strengths. She'd nod every so often, her bangs bouncing hypnotically as she did. There was an elegance to this woman. Trent recalled the band on her finger, but couldn't help think she was somewhat smitten by his company. Maybe she wasn't satisfied with her spouse? Or maybe she liked younger guys? Her hand seemed to linger a second too long when they shook after the meeting. Those bright blue eyes burrowing into his. Then again, maybe Trent was just imagining all this. He had been single for several years.

He took a deep breath, scrunched his face together, and slid himself to a stand using the wall for support. Reaching the top, he exhaled loudly and rotated on his shoulder to face his apartment. With a nudge of his arm against the wall to get him moving, he trudged toward his place a few doors down. He wiped at his lower lip with his sleeve and gasped suddenly as the pain of his cut lip sliced into him. Trent grumbled.

CHAPTER 2

Early the next morning, Trent faced his bathroom mirror in his gray boxers assessing the butchery bestowed upon him. Droplets of clean cool water dotted his face and hung on to day old stubble. He hadn't slept particularly well. No surprise. The aches and pains from his encounter last night pestered him throughout. Bruises were disclosing their whereabouts like ink soaking through a cloth, left eye going a tad black. The cut on his lip was crusted over with dried blood, but still oozed a bit. His gaze lowered to his ribs as he explored them gently with outstretched fingers. His lips curled slightly at the touch. Nothing broken, but this would hurt for a few days.

With arms straightened, he placed both palms on the edge of the sink, fingers dangling down, and leaned in. He thought how lucky he was to have interviewed with Caroline yesterday. He smirked as he imagined her seeming him in this condition. He doubted she'd be smiling.

Trent's mobile rang aloud and startled him. The device whirred restlessly against the bathroom counter to his left. He reached for it and scanned the caller ID. He swiped at the screen with his thumb.

"Jeff. Hi."

"Hey, Trent. Did I wake you? You sound stuffy."

"No, no. I just woke up a few minutes ago. All good. How you doing, man? Haven't heard from you in a while." Trent grabbed a facecloth off the rack and soaked up the last bit of moisture from his face and neck with his free hand. He dropped the cloth on the counter and started toward the kitchen.

"I'm well. Yea, business is a bit slow. The big corps in town are snatching up all the small businesses and they don't need us much. All their hiring is done in-house. But anyway, let me get to the point."

Trent poked a finger at his cappuccino machine and it started up with a buzz. He slid a small white cup under the spout and responded, "Ok."

"You'll be happy to hear that I have a position that suits your talents. I deal with this mining company, Irradiance, and they typically need admin and sales staff, but this time they're looking for a developer who specializes in robotics. They had some sort of a failure at one of their facilities and production has come to a stop. The mining equipment can't be restarted, and they've got no one at the site who can do anything about it. That's where I'm hoping you'd come in. They also requested a specialist to fix the hardware, so you might assist there with your background, and they mentioned a geologist is heading to the place to do whatever they need them to do. The latter is from the company who's tagging along for the ride. There's an urgency though. I need to find someone like now. The bus leaves on Thursday. Can you meet with me in a couple of hours?"

Trent pondered the new info for a moment before responding. "This sounds nice and all, Jeff, but doesn't sound permanent. I just had an interview yesterday for a fulltime job and I'm waiting to hear back from them soo—"

"The pay is worth it. I mean really worth it. I doubt this will take more than a week or so, but you'll be making what an AI developer earns in a year. And no, I'm not pulling your leg."

"Now this sounds too good to be true. If they need software, I could do this remotely. That way I could still grab this other job. I have a feeling they'll be calling me back."

"Yea. About that. You'll need to work on site. By the sounds of it, remote wouldn't work, as the equipment's really gone to shit."

"Where's this mine at?"

Jeff's hesitation was barely audible. "It's not on Earth."

Trent furrowed his brow and his eyes unconsciously focused on a photograph of his ex and daughter. "Shit, man, you know I don't do off world work."

"Trent. You got to get over this. It's been years my friend. Look, come down. Meet with me. This job will hold you over a little while. Give you some time to look for something else. Come to think of it, forward your calls to me. If that other place calls, I'll tell them you had some sort of emergency, but are still interested in the position. You know I can be convincing. There's also good money in this for me too. C'mon, help me out too."

Trent puffed out a long breath of air. He flicked his head up to the ceiling and straightened his back but regretted it instantly. He recalled the beating, the faces, and those callous words. Trent stooped in the form of a cane, fingers on his free hand kneading his wounds. *If the money is enough, and the analyst job comes through, I might just be able to get into a new place and out of that low life's hands. It's a gamble, but might give me a chance to disappear and let things cool off too.*

"You there, Trent?" Jeff interrupted his thoughts.

"Yea. I'll come down. I can be there in about an hour."

"Good! Coffee's on me." Jeff hung up.

Trent's gaze returned to the photo for a moment. He then remembered his cappuccino. He skidded his mobile onto the counter top by the quietly hissing machine, opened a cabinet door to grab a couple of pain killers, and returned to wash it down with the dark nectar. He dragged his feet over to the sliding door that lead out to the balcony and butted the glass gently with his forehead. The coolness of the window gave him some comfort as he starred out at the bustling urban landscape.

This feels wrong. Shit. I feel wrong. Trent's heavy breaths fogged the glass in gentle waves. *Then again, Jeff's probably right, you got to get over this. How long am I going to hide from this?*

He shut his eyes for a few long seconds, straightened up, and shook his head slowly. He turned and started to pace around his coffee table, narrowly missing its leg with his right foot. His eyes were locked in thought, his breathing becoming sharper, lower lip being chewed. A one-eighty later he paced back toward the coffee table, but on its opposite side closer to a small sofa. This time, his right pinky-toe hit the mark.

"Fuck!"

Trent stumbled forward and splayed out on the sofa. He sat up quickly and nursed his self-inflicted injury, heaving a few grunts while he was at it. Then he froze, inhaling slowly and exhaling quickly through his mouth. His eyes flicked up as if someone was watching him. He sat face-to-face with the photo. His face relaxed and his mouth sealed up. His daughter's youthful joy lifted his spirits no matter how down he felt. He still loved her dearly. What father wouldn't? Trent released his foot, and slowly eased back into the sofa. He thoughtfully folded his hands in lap.

No more sitting on my ass. Let's see what Jeff's got to say.

Trent made it downtown in about forty-five minutes, the time now 8:50 a.m. He strode out of the mildly packed light rail car, his eyes darting from figure to figure. He doubted the Chief's heavies would be out looking for him this early, but later, well that question already had an answer. A little extra vigilance never hurt anyone. The air was warming up, even though the sun was far from overhead, its rays slicing through the narrow spaces between the skyscrapers. May was often gray and wet, but only a few pillowy clouds randomly dotted the bright cyan sky. People hustled by each other, consumed with their own thoughts, briefcases on a mission, and mobile devices and techware zombifying their hosts. A few lumbering Hynafol with their reflective sienna craniums, broke the monotony of the masses, their height and slow moving bulk towering above all.

Kul'ahnntac Plaza glimmered exquisitely. The ninety story Too'ndehrrehk constructed skyscraper held a mixture of small and large businesses, along with scores of upscale residential condos. Its cathedral-like lobby always impressed Trent, even though he'd seen it more than a dozen times. The rose marble floors were imported from their homeworld and glittered richly with numerous shades of quartz, and the beautifully designed mosaics that loomed overhead told the condensed history of the species up to the point of first contact with humans. But neatly concealed behind the adorned façade was the inexplicable efficiency of the Too'ndehrrehk.

Trent gave a quick nod as he passed by the information and security desk manned by a couple of humans and a Kezdari, who could easily be mistaken for a human, and gave him a quick greeting nod. Many Kezdari worked on Earth or even called it home. They didn't feel as incongruous here compared to the other inhabited worlds of their region of space, the Ty'kape Empire. Trent reached the elevator bank and joined the small herd awaiting migration to a higher level.

On the twenty-sixth floor, Trent eagerly retreated from the crowded glass-clad elevator and shot down the hallway to the right. The chrome lettering of Miller & Associates Staffing, Inc. emerged, contrasted by the wide dark wooden doors it was affixed to. He grabbed for the wide brass handle that ran the width of the right-hand side door and swung it open.

"Good morning Trent," greeted Kol'tia. The slim, early twenties Too'ndehrrehk receptionist flashed a smile as she turned toward him from behind an elegantly arcing wooden counter. Her jet-black shoulder length bob cut hair swayed playfully as she moved, and juxtaposed vividly against her pearlescent white skin. Her cool blue eyes could pierce an inch thick steel plate, and they darted around Trent's face, exploring its recent history.

"Morning, Kol'tia, nice to see you." But before Trent could ask how she was, Jeff hurriedly materialized from a hall to the right holding a tablet in his left hand. The mid-fifties man of Jamaican descent wore a simple but stylish suit and black leather shoes to match. His thin gold framed glasses sparkled against his bronze skin, and his short curly black hair with flecks of gray was well groomed.

"I thought I heard your voice. Let's grab that coffee—" Jeff offered his hand for a shake and then froze. "Well that's a new look for you. Looks like our conversation is about to get more interesting."

Trent and Jeff got out of the elevator on the third floor and strode into Jasmine's Café, a classy hangout that would host live music on Friday and Saturday nights. The two weaved across the mostly vacated set of tables and chairs, out to the patio area. They claimed a small table near the corner that overlooked the busy sidewalks and avenues below. Two foot high glass barriers kept the warm breeze and urban clamour subdued. A human waiter took their orders and departed to prepare them.

"Is it too cliché to tell you that you look like shit?" Jeff started the conversation with a smirk.

Trent shook his head and lowered his eyes to the table, "Yea I know. Feels like it too. They also busted up my ribs, but I don't think anything's broken."

"I shouldn't have to tell you to stop working for those guys. I know coming up with money is hard these days, but even if it's working for less elsewhere, at least you're not going to get your head knocked off your shoulders." Jeff eyed Trent thoughtfully and continued, "This contract might just help push you in the right direction."

Trent sat up straight, entangled his fingers in front of him on the tabled and asked, "Speaking of which, what are the details of this job? And where off Earth are we talking about?" He scrunched his brows, slight screw to his lips,

"So as I mentioned, Irradiance needs a software developer specializing in machine learning and AI, as they had some critical fault in their equipment. They have technicians at the mining facility, but they do general maintenance, keep the machines oiled and that's it. They haven't got a clue what caused it and they're not qualified to fix it. There's physical damage to the feeders and conveyor systems, but I got a guy for that. He's a Salapernean by the name of Dvenoor. Seems all right, haven't met many of his kind. They always give me a bit of the heebie-jeebies," he shuddered, "Anyway, he's taking care of that and is well qualified for it; good references. But back to you. You need to get those machines going, because they aren't responding to any commands. These are mostly drillers, blasters, and movers. Oh, and parts of their refinery are down."

The waiter returned to their table with a dark roast for Jeff and double-shot of cappuccino for Trent. They thanked him and he retreated. Jeff tipped a bit of cream into his cup and added a couple of sugar cubes.

"They have code for you to look at, so it'll give you something to do on your trip there."

"So… where is there?"

"Ah yes. This place is in the Nyomor system, a rock called Circulum."

"Nyomor?" Trent squinted in the brightening daylight as he looked off into the distance, brow furrowed. "That's way the fuck out there."

"Only a few days travel by boat. Your buddy Phil's the pilot." Jeff sported a wide grin.

"Really? It's been a few months since I've last seen him. Last time we spoke he said he'd be cruising between Kezda and Hyna for some big shot Hynafols." Trent twiddled with his cup as he recalled meeting Phil a few years ago at the staffing agency. Phil was an outspoken extrovert who struck up a conversation with Trent while he waited to be interviewed. Both had an interest in engineering and sciences, so it didn't take long for them to become good friends.

"Yup. He's finished that contract. Messaged me a short while ago that he'd be looking for new flights. Good timing. So anyway, this job suits you, no?"

"Yea. I know my way around the bots," Trent sighed. "You said this pays well. How well?"

Jeff held his stir spoon between his right index finger and thumb and tapped it on the table to the syllables of his words. "They're offering 290,000 credits."

Trent's eyes bulged and jaw dropped, as he straightened his arms against the table and reeled himself back into his chair. He looked around and returned his stunned expression back to Jeff.

"You weren't fucking kidding me! That's close to a year's worth of good pay for a dev." Trent shook his head then locked eyes with Jeff. "What are you not telling me? This doesn't sound normal. Not one bit."

"I'm telling you everything I know, Trent. What Irradiance isn't telling me, well that's another question. But I have a feeling there are a couple of reasons for this urgency and expenditure. One is that there is a significant quantity of heavy element alpha and uranium on the planet. I've been told there are several hundred kilos of it and tons of uranium, both easy to extract from the ore. Apparently this is unprecedented and a one in a billion chance they've found such a place. A gram of element alpha goes for about twenty million credits. And two, it's the Nyomor system. It's far out there and hasn't been explored much. That's about all I know. Phil on the other hand might know more about the region and planet. You can grill him when get on your flight. Which is two days from now." Jeff snatched up his tablet and slid it across the table to Trent. "I need to get back to Irradiance by this afternoon."

"Uranium. Great. I'll be glowing in the dark when I return. Save me some cash on the power bills."

"You'll be writing code in a cozy office area, not licking the walls of the damn mine." Jeff let a quick chuckle escape.

Trent lethargically eyed the tablet that rest before him for a moment, biting down on his lower lip. He reached for the device, his eyes darting from side to side as he absorbed the details. *What's up with this? That much money for something that doesn't seem all that complicated. Or maybe that's it, something is being concealed. I trust Jeff. I don't trust this.*

He was just about to set the tablet back down when his mobile intoned. He shifted the pad to his right hand, swiftly withdrew the phone with his left, and read the message to himself. "Trent ur late to wrk. maybe u didnt get r msg last nite."

Trent glanced up momentarily. Jeff raised his head slowly and elevated his eyebrows, and after a moment, his straight lips curled up and face relaxed.

The mobile now replaced in its holster, Jeff had his left thumb and right middle finger on the signature line of the tablet. The device chirped to confirm his acceptance.

CHAPTER 3

Clouds gathered from the west as a chilly breeze disturbed the pleasant start to the morning, their shadows seeping into the urban landscape. The sun's light no longer provided warmth, yet Trent's face was tinged with perspiration. With every few steps back to his apartment, now about a block away, he scanned the area for the Chief's thugs, eyes wide and twitching. The occasional pang from his midsection jarred his motion. Although Trent believed he was being surreptitious, hands in his pockets while he hurried down the sidewalks, passing denizens couldn't decide if this man was ill or high on the wrong kind of meds.

But Trent's mind wasn't solely fixed on the heavies. He was already considering the suggested itinerary Jeff passed along from Irradiance during the remainder of their meeting, and was eager to examine the code and other pertinent details of the operation that would be sent to him via email soon.

Trent stopped on the corner by a small convenience store situated across the street from his apartment, face flushed with heat and his heart rate picking up the pace along with his breathing. The entrance to his building was centered on the block, just close enough to recognize faces, but far enough away not to be noticed too easily. Harold and one of his associates stood side by side with their backs up against the wall. Each held large disposable coffee cups, sipping at them occasionally. Harold sported one of his usual cheap suits, and his associate had loose fitting sweats with a dark baseball cap, several large rings glinting against his thick fingers. *Shit.*

Trent inhaled deeply and exhaled forcefully, puffing up his cheeks. He rounded back behind the corner and dropped his arms to his side. His left hand caught on the mobile case attached to his belt. Remembering the text message, Trent quickly extracted the device and punched in a reply. "Got msg. In hospital. You broke my ribs." Send. He peered around the corner.

A few seconds passed and he could see Harold react. The gruff swapped the coffee cup into his left hand and reached into his inner jacket pocket to pull out his mobile. He entered a few strokes and paused for a moment to examine it. After uttering something to his associate, who responded with a few quick nods, Harold appeared to glower and tapped on the device again.

Trent's mobile chirped to indicate message received. "Sry 2 here which hspital u at? well bring flowrs." Although the air was heavy, he found the poorly constructed message amusing. The sidewalk bristled with activity and Trent watched the figures glide by his field of view, yet his eyes were distant. Then he looked down at his screen and typed a reply. "Come find me." Send.

Rolling over on his right shoulder, Trent once again spied on his opponents from the relative safety of the corner. Harold and his buddy had shifted their weights to their feet, both surveying the surroundings more actively. The associate tossed his cup away from himself, receiving a few nasty glances and words from passersby, ignoring them as if nothing were said. Harold glanced down in response to his mobile and again mouthed something. He handed his cup over to the heavy and fidgeted with his phone for a few moments. Harold waited a moment before raising the device to his cheek. His mouth murmured every so often, same expression throughout. After no more than about fifteen seconds, he replaced it into his jacket pocket. Harold launched himself into a stride and motioned for his associate to follow, who on command tossed the cup against the entry doors to the apartment and began trailing his leader.

Trent watched as the two took off in the opposite direction from him. They disappeared to the left around the building. With a deep breath, Trent lurched around the corner down the sidewalk, and took a quick right into the convenience store, where he'd spend the next few minutes browsing snacks and killing time.

Chewing contently on his purchase, Trent walked down the sidewalk toward the main entrance to his place, still keeping a vigilant eye on his surrounding environment. He hustled through the coffee splattered doors and toward the small bank of elevators in the lobby, jabbing at the call button. A few moments later the carriage arrived, doors gaped open, and he nestled into the back corner. The doors started closing. With less than a foot of space to go, a hand suddenly clutched the panel on the left. Trent jerked against the walls with a thud. Eyes wide open, assessing the hand. He gasped through his nose, energy bar held tightly in his mouth.

"Oh thank heavens! These elevators can take forever some days," said a middle-aged female tenant a little out of breath. She poked a finger with bright red nail polish at the number eight button, then rummaged through a large purse pulling out a key card. She looked over at Trent. "I'm sorry! I didn't mean to startle you, hon."

Trent still wide eyed and molded into the corner began to mumble, then realized he still had the bar held between his lips. He removed the bar with a bite. "That's all right. All good." And smiled wearily.

The elevator released its female passenger on the eighth floor. She flashed him a quick smile on her way out.

On the thirty-second floor, Trent walked down to his apartment on spaghetti legs. He examined the door and lock, but it appeared free from intrusion. His hands still trembling, he swiped his key card over the sensor. With a swift motion, he squeezed through an opening just large enough for him and quickly shut and locked the door. With his left shoulder leaning against the door, Trent stood awkwardly as he caught his breath.

The rain gently pattered on the balcony, and the heavens sporadically lit up Trent's small flat with a deep growl reverberating a few seconds later. Light from Trent's tablet cast a glow on his face that flickered with every gesture of his fingers as he leaned over his kitchen counter, propping himself up by his elbows. The screen displayed his itinerary, listing schedules for the flight and a few key meetings. Also included were documents on what to bring, what not to, and some information about planet, Circulum. Trent yawned and stretched his arms slowly into the air. He ran his hands down his ribs slowly, groaning at the pangs. His arms straightened against the counter, he peered outside at the gray skies and considered his choice. *No going back now, Trent.*

As if on cue to remind him of his decision, his mobile piped up on the countertop. He used his right index finger to rotate the screen toward him and read the message. "Ur not at any hospitl. We need 2 tlk. Better be at ur place." *Shit! I knew this would happen. I gotta pack quickly. They're coming here!*

Trent already had his two large suitcases thrown open on the bed. One empty, the other with a few items of clothing. He rushed to his closet and snagged a few more shirts and pants off the hangers, haphazardly folded them, and tossed them into the cases. He grabbed a couple of reusable cloth sacks from the dresser, placed his work boots into one and shoes into the other along with a pair of slippers, dumping them into the emptier case. Laptop and tablet was next, with a couple of his backup drives that contained archives of past work and personal projects that might come in handy to fix the mining bots. Next up, Trent scurried into the bathroom to grab a couple of towels to wrap the laptop and drives into for cushioning, and a bar of soap just in case. Now the electric razor, comb, toothbrush, toothpaste, and some deodorant, the latter of which he squeezed into a resealable plastic baggy. *Socks, boxers, t-shirts, belt, jacket, check. What else do I need? Sunglasses. Where the hell are my sunglasses? Hat. Do I need a hat? Shit. I should've read about the damn planet. I have no idea if it's hot or cold. Fuck it. Hat, scarf, gloves. Ok.*

Trent secured the clasps on the suitcases and inspected his apartment. The cappuccino maker was off, monitors unplugged, heat turned down, patio doors locked. With what little he had, there wasn't much to do. Until the buzzer sounded. *They're already here? What the hell!*

Snatching his suitcases off the bed and extending their handles, Trent rolled them to the door as the cases fought back, lurching from one wheel to the other a few times. He tugged on his sneakers and unlocked the door, briefly peering out to scan the hallway. Empty. Trent leapt into the corridor, grunting as his bruises didn't agree with his sudden motions, and pulled his suitcases along, one to each side of him. Leaning back, he grabbed the door handle and slammed the door shut. Bolting to elevator, the bright ice blue readout indicated the elevator was on floor nine. A surge of heat enveloped Trent as his adrenaline spiked, sending his heart into his throat. Fighting the queasiness, he took a couple of deep breaths to stabilize himself. The elevator passed eleven.

Trent looked down the hall and the neon red glow of the exit sign caught his eye. The emergency stairs. He stomped toward them, and before arriving spun one-eighty to depress the locking bar with his hip. After entering, he leaned over the edge of the bannister and peered down, a hint of vertigo striking him. With much strain and a lengthy groan, he curled his arms up to raise the cases and trudged down the stairs as quickly as he could.

The elevator doors on the thirty-second floor revealed Harold and the same two associates that provided assistance to deliver his message a day ago. Harold marched out of the elevator and toward Trent's apartment. He thrusted his meaty left middle finger against the doorbell button, while his right hand was clenched in a tight fist. After a moment, he raised his fist and hammered against the door, causing loud deep reverberations down the hall.

"Open it up, Trent! Your delivery's here." boomed Harold. He laid down another hammering.

The door to Trent's nearest neighbor's apartment swung open and a mid-twenties man stepped out, mouth frowning and brow scrunched together in annoyance. But his expression was short lived and morphed into bulging eyes, a raised eyebrows, and a mouth wide open. It was the same man who witnessed Trent's first message delivery, minus the girlfriend.

"Mind your damn business!" said an associate as he made a gun sign with his index and middle finger, pointing it harshly at the man.

A hesitant nod later, which looked more like the shakes, the man sprung back inside and slammed the door shut.

"It's too quiet. He skipped out of here," said Harold. He turned his head left and right, and spotted the staircase. The door hadn't shut completely. He motioned with his head, "There! You two follow him. See if he's headed that way. I'll grab a ride down and cut him off if I see'em."

The heavies bolted into action and lumbered their way quickly down the hall, punching through the staircase entrance. Harold marched back toward the elevator and jabbed a finger at the lower call button.

Trent huffed hard at the twenty-seventh floor and paused. There was no way he could carry the cases down another two floors, let alone all the way to the bottom. He caught his breath for a couple seconds and careened through the staircase doorway, suitcases in tow. A clone of his own floor materialized and he headed toward the elevators. He pressed the call button, and after a few moments the panels split open. He quickly entered and paused for a brief second. *Parkade. But I can't use my car. They'll know it's mine. Phil. I could call Phil. Maybe he could pick me up?* He pushed the P1 button and the panels mated. The carriage lurched. But not in the direction Trent hoped. His gaze shot up to the readout. Twenty-eight. Twenty-nine. Shit! Shit! No! Down damn it! Thirty-one. Thirty-two. Pause.

It seemed to take a lifetime for the doors to start opening. Trent held his breath. The panels began to part. Before him he saw Harold. He was looking down at is mobile. The doors parted completely and the bell tolled. Harold raised his head and started to express something. Trent didn't wait to hear what he wanted to say. His adrenalin powered his body as he raised his foot and connected it with Harold's gut, while releasing a fear induced roar. Harold folded in half and his backside connected with the wall behind him. He slide down to the floor, the wind knocked clean out of him. He groaned in pain and gasped for breath, his mobile resting several meters from him from an uncontrolled toss.

Trent was bewildered at first, but quickly regained his composure. He hit the P1 button frantically, and the doors began sliding shut.

"I'm out. Find someone else to do your work."

Fury across his face, Harold cradled his gut with his right arm. He grimaced and tried to lift himself up off the floor, but the elevator doors sealed before his glaring eyes and clenched teeth.

The elevator descended this time around. Trent bent over, placing his hands above his knees, arms straightened. Blood started to refill his head as he took long deep breaths to keep as sane as he could under the circumstances. After a few moments he stood up straight and wiped his hands across his face to clear away the sweat. He glanced up at the display. Nine. Eight. He was nearly at the parkade.

The panels parted. Trent was slinked up against the side wall of the carriage as if walking a thin ledge on a cliff side. He cautiously peeked out and scanned the area for any movement. Satisfied it was clear, he recovered his two suitcases that he had shoved up against the opposite side wall. The doors were about to shut behind him, but he stepped back to stop them. Quickly slinking back inside, Trent pressed several random floor buttons and jumped back out into the parkade. *That should slow him down.*

Trent looked around for anything or anyone suspicious. He had a feeling Harold was not alone. His small dark green sedan was three rows ahead and near the wall to his left. *I might be able to get to my car after all and get the hell out of here. I'll call Phil later and maybe I can crash at his place.* He darted ahead, dragging the suitcases behind him that clattered loudly on their tiny bouncy wheels, which echoed noisily throughout the concrete garage. He flashed a quick cynical gander at one. When he stopped for a moment to reorient the cases in his grasp in order to slip between a couple of parked vehicles, silence fell promptly. Trent decided he'd carry them for the remainder of his run.

The rear hatch to his car popped open and Trent threw in his cases, the muscles in his arms burning. After a quick adjustment he shut the door, and that's when he spotted two figures invading his peripheral vision. One of them pointed and both started running in his direction. Trent skittered around to the driver's side door, pulling on the handle, but it was still locked. *Shit!* He fumbled with his key FOB to unlock the door. He gave the handle another tug and the door released. Before leaping in he checked the location of the heavies and they were just over a row away. He activated the vehicle and pressed the icon to drive.

"Please buckle your seatbelt for safety, and enjoy your trip," said the car's computer with a simulated, but pleasant, female voice.

"Damn it! I won't need the damn belt if I'm dead you stupid car!" Trent fumbled for the seatbelt clip and latched it in securely. He hit the icon again and floored the pedal. The sedan heaved out of the stall and Trent made a hard left toward the exit that was down on the other end and to the left.

The two thugs now stood side-by-side, occupying the middle of the driveway about twenty meters ahead. Trent refused to let off the acceleration and the sedan charged. He could make out the goons scowling faces. They started to yell. Trent guessed they wanted him to stop. *Get out of the way! C'mon! Get out of the damn way!* The electric motors whirred with a higher pitch as his vehicle's speed increased. The thugs faces transformed into neutral expressions of wonderment. A moment later their eyes widened and they yelled at the top of their lungs, arms outstretched with hands and fingers flaying frantically in the air.

Trent depressed the horn forcefully with his palm and held it down. A high pitched yowl reverberated throughout the garage. The thug on the passenger side leapt out of the way, coming to a rolling stop on the cold concrete floor, but the heavy on the right moved too late. The driver's side corner of the bumper caught his right chin hard. The bone snapped in two and his body slammed against the pavement. Trent glanced into his side mirror and noticed the additional kink in the associate's leg.

"Damn it. Still... serves you right, you bastard."

"Collision detected. Please confirm if vehicle is safe to operate," said the synthesized voice.

"Yes. Yes it is. Everything's just fucking fine." Trent struck the confirmation button. The exit to the parkade was mere meters away, and Trent backed off the accelerator. A piercing squeal shrieked from the tires as they struggled to maintain traction. *Hurry up!* Trent's patience wore thin as he pulled up to the garage door that automatically opened when an authorized vehicle approached. He slowed to avoid hitting the barrier, but the moment it was high enough, he sped through the opening. Coming up from the ramp to the street above, Trent was forced to come to a sudden stop, as a few pedestrians in no hurry strolled by before Trent could hit the road. When he did, he kept driving for almost an hour.

CHAPTER 4

The rain pattered on the roof of Trent's car at the rear of a mall complex parking lot far on the opposite end of the city. The grayness of the skies muted the colors around him, and the windows of his quaint cabin lightly fogged up. Trent watched rain drops slithering down the windshield creating highways of distortion, and after a few moments he tapped at his mobile screen and held the device to his cheek. The line rang several times before connecting.

"Buddieee! Long-time no hear. How you doin?"

"Phil, good to hear your voice, man. Jeff told me you'll be taking me on a field trip, so I had to call you and let you know."

"No way! Are you kidding me?" Phil could be heard gasping comically. "I can't believe it. Are you pulling my leg?"

Trent's lips curled up. "No, no. I accepted the contract and have my bags packed. Actually they're right here in my car. I'm as ready as I'll ever be."

"That's insane. Wait. You're in your car? Bags in your car too?"

Trent hesitated a moment before answering, "Yea."

"Kay. You know we're leaving on Thursday morning. Not Tuesday. You're a tad early and I can't clear you for boarding yet. You know, check boarding pass, sign forms and waivers so I own your soul. Why am I thinking something's up?"

Trent let his head fall and he shut his eyes. "You read me like a book," Trent sighed aloud. "I, umm, have some bad company at my place and needed to get some fresh air if you know what I mean. I'll get to the point. I was hoping you wouldn't mind if I crashed at your place."

"What do you take me for? A charity? Fuck, man. You know it's all right!" Phil chuckled. "You can crash at my place. Better than crashing in my ship. You owe me some beer. It just so happens I'm out of it. Tell you what. Get some beer. Get to my place. And make yourself at home. I bet I know what this shit is about, so we'll have a chat later. I can buzz you in remotely, so send me a text when you're there. I'll be working on the bird quite late. I'll probably head home around seven-ish. All right?"

"You're the best, Phil. But you already know that. I'll stock you up, and yea, I've got stories to tell."

"Looking forward to it. Kay, I gotta run, folks are waiting for me. See you later."

"Yea, see ya." Trent hung up. He sucked in his lower lip and scanned the area for a liquor store.

The burnt umber couch was comfortable. Real leather. It squeaked quietly as Trent crossed his right leg over the left. He held his tablet with a hand on either side, but his gaze observed Phil's condo. Ahead of him was a large screen monitor, bordered by two shelving units with various models of ships, plaques of recognition, and awards in standing frames, along with a few knick-knacks. The oak wood accented the pale cream walls, on which a few medium sized photographs hung, each displaying a different type of ship. *Phil loves'em.*

A click at the door snapped Trent out of his curiosity. He uncrossed his legs, placed his tablet on the glass topped coffee table, and stood up. The contemporary metal door revealed Phil as he stepped inside, and with the flick of the wrist he thrust the door shut.

"Hey, Phil." Trent walked over with a big grin and held out his hand.

"I see you made it." Phil firmly grabbed his hand and yanked him forward into a man-hug with a quick few fist pounds against each other's backs. Trent reversed and headed toward the kitchen counter, grabbed a beer, and twisted off the cap. He held it out for Phil, who had slipped off his shoes by the door and unzipped his bomber jacket.

"Atta-boy! Thank you. Best kind of fuel there is." Phil took a swig of his beer as he reached the counter. The stout man placed his drink down on the glossy dark granite surface and shook off his jacket, tossing it semi-neatly onto the puffy armrest of the couch. He straightened his back and ran the palms of his hands against the buzz cut sides of his head. "Oh, that was a long day." He eyed Trent's new makeup. "Seems I ain't the only one."

Trent sat down on one of the bar stools and let out a sigh. He grabbed his beer off the counter with his left hand and clutched the cool bottle against his thigh, thumbing the condensation on its side, with his right elbow braced against the countertop. "Yea. I don't think I can do those jobs any longer. I don't want to see or know about those people anymore. That's not my crowd." Trent ran his hand through his hair from his forehead to the back of his neck and held it there for a few moments.

"Long story short. I played hooky on a contract for the Chief and instead interviewed for a position yesterday; stock trading data analyst. I think I have a good chance at it, went well enough." Trent paused a moment as he recalled Caroline's warm smile. "But he sent his guys after me and they did this number on me," he motioned lazily with his right hand, "right outside my apartment. Then I got the call from Jeff this morning about the mining bots gone haywire. So I met with him. Got the details. Almost didn't take the job. I mean something still seems off, but whatever at this point. Anyway, got back to my place and the fuckers were there waiting for me at the entrance. I replied to a text he sent me during my meeting with Jeff, about me not getting the message–"

"You never do. You're a bit slow," teased Phil, glued to Trent's recollection.

Trent couldn't help a wide grin, "—ok, where was I? Oh yea. I told them I had to check in to a hospital and to come find me. That got them out of the way for a while, but the assholes came back. I packed my bags in a hurry, rushed down a few flights of stairs, back out to the elevator, and would you believe my luck? That stupid elevator took me back up to Harold!"

"No shit." Phil took a long swig of his beer, eyes locked on Trent.

"I don't know what came over me, but I kicked that son-of-a-bitch right in the stomach and watched him keel right over. So down the shaft, into my car, and if things couldn't get any worse, I actually hit one of his thugs on the way out. I think I broke his leg pretty bad too. And yea. Now I'm here." Trent took a big breath and a couple of gulps of his malt.

"If you were followed, I'm gonna fuckin hurt you boy," taunted Phil, his eyes wide as he pointed at himself and then at Trent. "Shit, buddy. So really, how are ya?" he jutted his chin at Trent and took a few chugs of beer.

Trent reacted silently, his shoulders hopping up and down, grinning from ear to ear. "They haven't killed me yet."

The two cracked up. Phil's loud bellow reverberated in the condo.

"I'm bushed, buddy. I'm gonna take a shower and hit the sack. Did you get a chance?" asked Phil, motioning loosely with his arm toward the bathroom as he got up and disappeared into his bedroom.

"Yea, thanks. When I got here. I've been working my way through the code Jeff emailed me ever since. You sure did put in a long day. Everything all right?"

"Oh yea. The schedule's tight, but we'll manage. This morning we replaced the nav circuits, they were cutting it close to their maintenance lifecycles... well, we have one left, which we'll do tomorrow." A rustle of clothing could be heard as Phil paused for a moment. "After that it'll be some QC and diagnostics and a shitload of paperwork. Then we should be ready to go. How 'bout you? Fix up the code already?"

"They didn't send me what's the in the brains of the machines. This is the code that would normally operate them. I guess I'll know more when we get there and I have access to their memory. There's going to be a Salapernean there to do some hardware work, so I'm hoping he'll know how to perform a memory dump. I'm a bit rusty with that. By the way, who else is coming? Aside from the hardware guy, Jeff told me about some geologist, a PM from Irradiance, said he seemed liked a nice guy, and that's about it."

Phil returned to the living area and headed toward the bathroom. His bulging arms showed signs of grease and grime, with a few scuff marks from the activities of the day. He had changed into a pair of light-gray sweatpants, stood barefoot, and had a white t-shirt slung over his right arm. Pausing by the door, he turned to Trent. "Ah, yup. Sounds about right. Except for the PM. Jeff just sent me a message before I left the hanger. Apparently he's got some sort of family emergency to deal with, so he's being replaced with some other guy. We'll also be transporting four additional passengers, some miners. Haven't personally met any of'em though." He shook his head slightly and pursed his lips. "I just care about getting everyone there and back again in one piece."

"What's the planet like? I take you haven't been there before."

"Correct. This'll be a first." Phil leaned his shoulder against the bathroom doorframe. "Pretty much all my flights have been in and around this system and Ty'kape. Mostly Too'ndehrr, Kezda, Medenza, Hyna, and some of their natural satellites. And I haven't been to Salapernia yet. This Nyomor region hasn't been explored much, so I don't know a hell of a lot about it, other than how to get there. The planet, Circulum, is obviously habitable, but only on a thin band around it. It's tilted mostly toward its star and tidally locked so one side is blazing hot and the other is freezing cold. That in-between part is where we'll be."

"That sounds a bit messed up." Trent scrunched up his eyebrows and his mouth hung slightly open, concern weighing him down as his shoulders slumped.

"Didn't you read about the planet yet? You nerds are all the same, it's all about you and your code." Phil shook his index finger at Trent and shot him a teacher's dirty look.

"Sorry. You know, I should have. The code…" Trent struggled to organize his words, his eyes seems to hunt around the room for them. "…it takes my mind off this… I guess I've been avoi—"

"Dude." Phil raised his left hand, fingers extended, palm toward Trent. "I know what you've been through. It'll be fine. Really. It's just a planet like the thousands out there. It's another job and I'm sure you've worked on similar projects. There's going to be camp setup and you'll have your cabin to work from. I'll be nearby if you need to talk, but I bet you'll be busy keeping the hardware guy in check. There's like fifty people at this mine. Nothing to worry about."

Trent dropped his head for a moment and managed a weak smile.

"Thanks, man. Sorry. I should know better. I'll get over it."

Phil nodded calmly and said, "I know you will, buddy. Time to lay off your tablet. I'm not the only one bushed here. Get some rest. And I'm taking my shower now so I can get some sleep too. Oh, by the way. There's some medigel in the bathroom cabinet, feel free to help yourself to it." He loosely circled his face with his left index finger, then keenly glided into the bathroom and closed the door behind himself.

Trent was chilled to bone. The location unfamiliar. The wind howled around him, with the swirling mass of air tearing at trees with enormous leaves. He couldn't see far. A thick musty gray haze limited visibility to a few meters. His feet felt like they were on a billowing air cushion. He stumbled often with no set goal, his hands digging at the spongy moist ground. He wiped his hands onto his dirt encrusted clothes and noticed that the dark crimson fluid wouldn't come off. He yelled.

A tall diluted ragged shadow of a figure scrambled by. Then another. And another. Trent's eyes hunted for the shapes, but they seemed to play in his peripheral vision. Haunting screams from a distance echoed endlessly in his ears. The sound emanating from all directions. He spun his body as quickly as he could to catch sight of these elusive specters.

As he sought his unknown pursuit, a familiar voice called. No words, but yet beckoning. A voice in the mind. A trail mysteriously emerged, familiar, as if once traveled. Trent's legs felt heavy, but he willed himself to trudge along the path as fast as could. He saw a haunting gaping mouth formed by rock, trunks, and mossy branches. The dark specters still whispering their presence around him. He inched closer. Then a figure coalesced from the mist. A young girl in tattered clothing. A specter on each side appeared like predators on the hunt. Abruptly, each form thinned, engulfing the girl in a tornadic helix. "Daddy!"

Trent gasped loudly as he leapt up into a seated position on Phil's couch. Beads of sweat hung heavily on his face as he breathed quickly and raggedly. He searched the darkness for the fading image of the girl. A few moments passed by and a tinge of composure returned. Trent used his t-shirt to dab the moisture from his face. He sat up with his knees bent, forearms perched on the caps, and fingers interlocked. He'd stay like this until exhaustion coaxed him back to sleep.

CHAPTER 5

"Your hacker almost fucked this up, Koorehg." Maksim Malaki flared his nostrils and forcefully exhaled through them. "But we've been keeping tabs on the hiring process and we might be in luck. It appears they've employed a *competent* being to get the mine working again," he snickered.

The exoplanetary research director for the Cronos Corporation stood tall in his expensive custom fitted lustrous black three piece suit with matching black silk tie. His hands were cupped behind his back as he strutted slowly around the Hynafol's office in his equally pricy and shiny black leather shoes, chin held high. Ocean waves of dark walnut hair, professionally stylized, topped the man's clean shaven angular features, along with dark eyebrows to match. His piercing blue eyes had an evil glow that could chill the soul of anyone in their sight. An enormous gold signet ring, set with a large beveled rectangular obsidian stone accented with sparkling pure white diamonds on either side, occupied his right index finger.

"Yessh, but the tashk hash been completed nonethelesh. No need the attitude," rumbled Koorehg.

The Hynafol were the least human looking species in the Ty'kape Empire by far. They stood just over seven feet tall, but their arcing hunched over bodies measured almost ten feet in length. The heavyset beings were almost as wide as two people abreast, with large bulging arms, and legs that resembled those of the terrible lizards that once roamed Earth millions of years ago. Each hand had five claw-like digits, two of those situated further back like a pair of opposable thumbs. Their powerful grasp could easily crush a human's skull. Their mammoth sized hooves were drawn-out and wide, well suited to their ancestral nature of plodding through bogs and marshes. The semi-gloss sheen of their thick sienna tinted skin, added to the Hynafol's foreboding appearance.

But it was their shiny large bald heads that made many take a step back.

Or two. The hairless creatures had no nostrils, instead they breathed unnaturally long slows breaths through their mouths. Two pairs of cavities on opposite sides of their heads collected sound with remarkable directional accuracy. A pair of elongated solid black eyes oozed horizontally from the front to the sides of their heads. And the piece de resistance were their mouths that almost split their skulls in two. The loose, yet thick, skin along the edge of their maws could ripple and contort gruesomely, and tens of gargantuan flat teeth, over an inch wide each, along with a thick heavy dark violet tongue, occupied the rest of the large cavity.

Kooregh Minosfehg Goorrehssh was scarcely any different than the rest of his kind, except for deep gash of a scar that careened down the right side of his face, even tearing through his tough eyelid, albeit, it did save his eye. He wore a common loose fitting garb, armored and ornate. Two large ceremonial blades were sheathed, a sign of his faith in the ancient Soh'kash.

Maksim turned toward Kooregh and gestured with his right hand as he spoke, left still tucked away. "I'll be implanting one of my specialists to keep a close eye on things. In fact, he should be getting ready as we speak. This prize is also far too lucrative for me not to get involved directly. We can't afford any more fuck ups. I'll be taking *Hyperion*. It should arrive in a few hours."

"How are the weapon upgrade-sh performing?" rumbled Kooregh as his head raised.

"Beautifully! A few Kezdari transport vessels were kind enough to lend their element alpha to us. We're not just the most powerful ship in the region, now we're the fastest too. Hell, we're going to be in Nyomor before the fixer upper crew." Maksim continued his slow strides around the office, brow furrowed and lips pursed as his eyes examined the room. He uttered under his breath, "There are no colors anywhere… everything is stained in shades of shit."

Kooregh mostly ignored his comment, shaking his head slightly, eyelids closing for a few seconds. He took his time to inhale through his slightly parted lips, sounding like a wind howling through a haunted mansion. A thunder rolled up his throat, "Nyomor ish not void of life, and we have jusht as musch of an interesht in thish ash you. Shtay out of shight. Exshpediently recover the ore and return."

"Of course, Kooregh. The ship is in good hands. When have I ever let you down?" Maksim faced the large being with a toothy grin as he held up his palms at shoulder height, then eased his hands together, fingertips coming to a steeple before his chest. "Seriously though, who wants to vacation in that rundown shithole of space anyhow? Speaking of which, if I stay in this room any longer, I'll need therapy." He let out a quick puff of air. "Would it kill you to add some house plants? A few paintings?" Maksim turned on his heels and strode toward the door. "We'll be in touch. Order some of that fine champagne you folks make, what it is called now? Ah yes, peh'shgoush. Something to celebrate with." He tapped at a glowing symbol by the door with this index and middle finger extended and the large panel to the room slid up. Without looking back, Maksim vanished down the hall and the door slid shut with a gentle hiss.

Kooregh released a deep throaty rumble. He took heavy lumbering steps toward a trapezoidal window overlooking an expansive supercity and centered himself in front of it. The two ornamental daggers sung with a metallic resonance as they were freed from their lavish scabbards. The Hynafol held them up in front of his face, points downward and edges overlapped in an X. He began chanting.

CHAPTER 6

At five in the morning, Phil's alarm triggered. A male voice shot out of the speaker with enthusiasm, announcing a brief schedule of what listeners could expect in the next few minutes. The news, traffic report, and the weather forecast. But as abruptly the voice had started, it stopped with a subtle slap. Trent had slept poorly again, but wasn't haunted by any nightmares like the night before. His eyes snapped open and examined the dark ceiling that was gently lit by the various pinpricks of light emanating from the various electronic devices scattered around the living room. A few seconds later the ceiling brightened up with light scattering from Phil's bedroom, angular shadows contrasting around dividing walls.

Trent breathed in deeply through his nose, and sighed out of it too. He swivelled from his lying position and dropped his feet to the floor, elbows on his thighs, face dropped into his hands while massaging the lethargy out of himself. He wished quietly to himself that it was still Wednesday, which had passed uneventfully. Phil took off for work early that morning and Trent continued to digest the thousands of lines of mining machine code. His mind still wondered and wanted to know more about the planet, but the brief informative summary proved elusive.

After a few fibrous sounds of clothes brushing against skin, Phil popped into view as he tapped the lights on with his hand.

"Up so early? Looks like we're ready to get going. Well, I gotta take a piss, so I'm going first," said Phil, striding toward the bathroom.

"Thanks for the info." Trent chuckled.

The bathroom door shut, but Phil's voice rumbled through it. "I get to use you while you're still crashing my place, 'cause you're technically here for another thirty minutes, so go make some wake-up juice."

"Yes, boss. On my way, sir," chuckled Trent as he grinned from ear to ear and got up to fulfil the request.

After about half an hour of bantering, shaving, scarfing down coffee, last minute packing, and close to an hour on the road, the men reached Refuuloushehg exo-port, a Hynafol owned and operated facility. The imposing main terminal jutted from the landscape with its jagged spires and angular construction. Smokey mocha tinted windows sat flush with the outer walls and conformed to the shape of the trapezoidal exterior walls, nearly blending in with the similarly shaded matt exterior. Over two dozen sizable hangers stretched out from either end of the elongated terminal in a compressed *V* shape.

Taking up the central zone in front of the terminal and between the hangers were six large octagonal pads for launching and receiving incoming vessels. Some were only a couple of hundred meters in diameter, with the larger ones spanning just over two kilometers each, and all were arranged in a logical triangular formation to effectively use up the territory. Each pad was also connected to the other and to main taxiways, which led to either hangers or passenger loading areas.

Being one of the larger exo-ports in the region, thousands of travelers from a mix of all known races hurried in and out of the facility. Hynafol had a thing for doors that slid open upward. With all the commotion, it appeared like the complex was eating up and spitting out its hosts. Hynafol security guards straddled the access points, while others paced in pairs one after another, all with dark amour sporting pyramidal textures and shiny gold outlines.

"I swear most of their cities look like this." Phil motioned his left arm toward the port. His hand grasped a subway sandwich they picked up along the way, and he dragged a large suitcase with the other arm.

Trent walked by his side, his grub long devoured before their arrival. He was tugging along his cases that still acted drunk.

Phil continued, "The rest of the planet isn't too bad. There are some protected zones with greenery and fresh water lakes, but the cities… feels like you're going colorblind. Anyway, hanger Yosherr twenty-two is where the bird is."

The pair located an autonomous personal transport vehicle, APT, and got in. Phil vocally commanded the unit to head to the hanger. The machine acknowledged the order in its dry Hynafol designed robotic voice and the pudgy vehicle lurched into motion. The APT's chassis and seats rumbled suddenly, along with Phil and Trent's bodies and ear drums, drowning out all other sound, as a massive human-built cargo vessel launched from one of the pads. The men turned their heads to view the impressive sight lift into the troposphere and propel its bulk to surprising speed as it tore upwards through the air. Within thirty seconds, only the electric motors of the APT and general aspects of life hummed around them.

A few minutes later, their ride jarred to a halt and drearily announced their arrival. Phil and Trent stepped out, retrieved their cases, and eyed the medium sized hanger, which stool over three stories tall and was at least forty meters wide and long.

Phil glanced at his watch. "All right, let's get inside. Just past seven, we're doing good. The passengers should be here no later than seven thirty, and then I'll debrief everyone on the flight." His identification had already been authorized remotely as he approached the door, but all flight personnel were required to perform a retinal scan. Phil leaned into a recess on the wall and a tangerine glow warmed his face for a second or two. Another dry synthetic voice acknowledged his access and the personnel door to the hanger slid up. "Follow me, buddy. There's probably already someone here who'll get your paperwork straightened out."

"All right." Trent followed Phil, glancing back momentarily to watch the door slide shut. *No going back.* Mice in his gut ran circles and he suddenly felt a warmth flush across his body and face. He could hear his heart beating in his ears, and the handles of his cases became slippery from his sweaty palms. He eyed Phil and hoped he could stay as level headed during travel as him one day. Then again, this was his first trip off world since that dark event. Trent surreptitiously took a few deep breaths, which calmed his nerves a little and focused ahead as they crossed through what appeared as a parts and supply area.

Regardless of his anxious state, the sight through the next doorway would send his neurons into a frenzy. Before his eyes in the cavernous hanger perched an impressive ship that took up most of the volume. Trent's pace slowed to a crawl as he almost strained his head upward to see the upper decks of the vessel. The engineer in him was always fascinated by the technology, even if the travel aspect didn't sit as well.

Trent studied the wide body of the ship and its stubby length in comparison. Four large winglets, two on each side and about six meters long each, extended outwards from the fuselage. The two toward the bow were angled slightly upward, and downward for the pair at the aft end. Each thick winglet also housed several small maneuvering thrusters. Further caressing the ship with his vision, he inspected the four large engine pods situated at each corner of the ship. Each pod could be rotated to provide propulsion in almost any direction, even sideways. The aft engines had the ability to creep up the side of the ship, which permitted the thrust from the bow pods to pass by freely when the vessel cruised along. A wide cargo ramp was lowered, its glowing lights beckoning passengers to enter. Trent couldn't quite make out the bridge, he guessed it was the projection in the upper forward position.

"Great. We have some guests," rung Phil's voice in the hanger. He was now almost on the starboard side of the ship and shot a glance back at Trent. "Hurry up slow poke."

Trent snapped back to reality and focused ahead. He picked up the pace to catch up, his suitcases fervently teetering behind him. A few seconds later he caught up and noticed a small group of people. Phil was expressing morning pleasantries to them, as well as expertly engaging in small talk, a skill he was quite gifted with. Three passengers sat in the three available chairs, while the rest stood.

One of the maintenance workers approached Phil. He informed him that the passengers' baggage had already been loaded and motioned if he could also take his and Trent's. Phil acknowledged and the worker sprang into action. He grasped Phil's large suitcase and both of Trent's, skilfully positioning them back to back with the handles against each other to roll them at once. Trent nearly rolled his eyes when he noticed how obediently his suitcases followed their new handler.

Trent nodded at the group and greeted them. He quickly scanned across the new faces. The four furthest from him were all Kezdari. Three males stood, while one female sat, and all wore the same Irradiance branded overalls. *Probably the miners Phil mentioned.*

In the middle seat sat the Salapernean. He was short, typical for their species, had light-gray skin flowing with darker gray veins, gray irises, and startling teal sclera. His short charcoal hair shimmered with tinge of turquoise. Trent guessed he was wearing an outfit common to his species, which appeared to be comfortable light gray overalls with red accents. His outfit had several pockets and some loops where a belt would normally be, which held various electronic devices. His shoes matched his getup and looked more like durable versions of sneakers than work boots.

But when Trent's eyes met the last member, he was taken aback. Time seemed to slow as he studied the Too'ndehrr. Her captivating wide set large eyes with long smoky eyelashes and deep pupils, featured hypnotic iridescent irises with spokes of cerulean blue and rays of a yellow sunrise on a brilliant white canvas. Dark chocolate eyebrows gently angled and arched over each eye. Her straight shoulder length auburn hair glimmered with golden strands as it parted in the middle and elegantly framed her firm but delicate features. A slim nose with a slight upturn, rested between a pair of high prominent cheekbones. Her slender carnation lips tastefully contrasted with her doll like pearlescent white skin, and her jawline tapered gracefully into her chin.

A typical Too'ndehrrehk long slim neck joined up with her tall lean body. Trent figured she was more than his height of six feet. She sat with perfect posture, wore a functional khaki jacket over a lightweight off-white body hugging sweater that accented the curves of her modest but attractive bust. Even apparent from under her beige corduroy pants, endless slim legs extended from her shapely hips. Her elegant hands were casually crossed over one another on her legs, with elongated fingers that matched the rest of her body. A pair of light gray hiking shoes completed her outfit. A subtle tilt of her head caught Trent's eyes, only to be met directly by her gaze. *Oh no! I'm staring. Look away. Now! I didn't stare too long. Did I? She's… beautiful. I wonder what her name is.*

Trent beamed sheepishly and quickly turned his eyes to the ship as if that's all he'd been admiring for a while. His face turned a warm shade of crimson, and he started to slowly pace toward the front of ship to take a stroll around the perimeter. Trent figured this would help him avoid awkward introductions and small talk, something he wasn't skilled with.

"All right everybody. We're missing one passenger. We'll give him a few minutes to show, after which I'm going to debrief everyone on this flight and then we'll get going. We're still on track for an eight forty-five departure." Phil keyed some details into his tablet, then turned toward the ship's ramp and scurried off.

At about seven forty-five, a pudgy man in his early fifties rushed through the hanger access door, rolling his large handbag style luggage by his left side. Trent sipped on his water from a small disposable cup he'd gotten from the water cooler as he watched the man approach. He figured this was the replacement project manager sent to oversee the operation, and eyed the business casual outfit strained by the man's tubbiness; white shirt, dark blue jacket and pants, and black leather shoes. It was apparent that a think covering of gel held his black thinning hair in place, loosely concealing a bald spot. The man's round head with chubby cheeks, stubby wide nose, and full lips, was accented by a well-trimmed goatee. His green eyes were alert, cradled by slight bags and bushy eyebrows. *Typical management. Whatever, be nice. Smile.*

Phil hopped down the ramp and headed toward the PM, hand outstretched. "You must be Michael. Good morning."

"Good morning, sir. My apologies for my lateness. I had to contend with some unforeseen circumstances, but came as fast as I could," replied Michael while he firmly grasped Phil's hand.

"That's all right, we're not too late." The two released their grips and Phil took charge. "Ok, please gather around the ramp folks. I'm going to provide you with a flight debrief." He marched to the ramp, took a few steps up, and about-faced waiting for the crowd to gather.

Trent, still lingering by the water cooler near a corner of the hanger, disposed of his cup and started toward Phil. The other passengers had just arrived before him, so he took up a spot behind the miners, with the Salapernean front center, Michael to his front-right, and the Too'ndehrr left-front. He couldn't help shift his eyes to flowing locks, admiring her profile. His attention snapped back to Phil as he clapped his hands together and began speaking.

"If you're here to fly to Lanzeedia's Recreational Theme Park, you're in the wrong hanger." The group chuckled. Phil could always lighten any moment. "Kay. As you've guess by now, I'm the captain and pilot, Phil Sykes, just call me Phil, and this is our ride into the Nyomor system, *Ut'ahhziik*. Our journey to the planet Circulum should take three days and seven hours, so we should arrive on Sunday afternoon, around four o'clock Earth local time. This ship is equipped with a fully stocked galley, head with a standing shower, small commons area with some resistance workout equipment, and two sleeping quarters for passengers with soundproof bunks. There's also a cargo area, but we're only hauling your luggage for this excursion. So cargo and maintenance are on level one, level two features the sleeping quarters and head, and level three has seating, the galley, and commons area, along with access to the bridge. Aside from me, the only other crew member on this vessel is Sheh'geetch, our friendly robotic assistant. She's currently busy prepping the ship, but you'll get to meet her soon enough. Fantastic cook too."

His comments spawned smiles and a few giggles. "Three hearty meals a day will be served, starting with an early lunch today shortly after we launch. Now in the case we have an emergency and we need to abandon ship, which we certainly hope won't happen, there are six escape pods, with room for up to three folks each. Lighting will activate and direct you to them, but they're accessible to the port and starboard side of the passenger seating zone. The bridge is a restricted area, but I can always be reached through any of the comm-panels. Kay. Before we have a quick question period, let's roll call."

Phil held up his tablet and begun calling out the names on his roster, tapping beside the name he called upon hearing a response. Trent listened carefully and caught the name of the Salapernean. Dvenoor Captiosve. Michael Simmons was next, then another miner. He gave a thumbs up when Phil called his name. Another miner. Then her name. Anamara T'unnusalia. *A beautiful name to match the looks.* The rest of the names were a haze to Trent.

"Good!" Phil dropped his right hand to his side, and swung out his left, tablet in hand, gesturing for everyone to board. "There's no assigned seating, so take your pick. No squabbling for seats or you go straight to the brig." Laughter erupted as the passengers hiked up the ramp, Trent pulling up the rear. As he walked up the skinny staircase to the first level of the ship, his heart skipped a beat as the ramp rose off the hanger's concrete floor, clanking rhythmically as the locking mechanisms engaged.

CHAPTER 7

It was eleven o'clock when Phil announced that lunch was served. Sheh'geetch prepared dishes appropriate for the assortment of species on board, cooking up individual meals for Dvenoor and Anamara. The robot auto-balanced on a pair of dinner plate sized pneumatic wheels about a foot and a half apart. In place of legs, the machine had a stylized rigid rectangular enclosure with most of its control and power systems, on top of which sat an agile humanoid torso that could swivel and bend similarly to a humanoid. Dexterous arms and hands, along with a few hidden tools folded away within the machine's paneling, allowed the robot to clean, cook, and assist with numerous ship related tasks. Being a Too'ndehrr creation, its blue-white color scheme and stylized smooth head somewhat resembled the species.

The aroma from the various foods mingled cooperatively in the air, and the casual buzz of activity settled Trent's nerves. Standard procedure for compression travel required all passengers to keep buckled in during the jump event, and seated for twenty minutes after until the effects of the space-time crunch normalized. Trent didn't feel inconvenienced much and had been examining the code from Irradiance on his tablet that he retrieved from his case earlier. He clambered out of his seat in the backrow to retrieve his meal, placing the tablet on his seat and stretching his back after rising.

"Pardon me everyone. I just spoke to our gracious captain and at two I get the floor to formally introduce myself to those hired to work on the mining equipment, and that includes our geologist too. Enjoy your lunches. Thank you," announced Michael as he aimed his words at Trent, Dvenoor, and Anamara, while his hands stabilized his full plate. The members of the new team nodded their heads and thanked Michael.

A few minutes before two, Michael asked the team to converge at the front of the seating area. The large comfortable chairs where paired up in six rows. Trent got up and strode to the front, but the first two spaces were occupied by Dvenoor and Anamara. Without skipping a beat, Trent backed up against the galley counter. His teammates noticed his arrival, Dvenoor initiating a slow bow, and Anamara flashing a courteous smile. Trent nodded quickly and said, "Hi."

"Great. Thank you," proclaimed Michael. "First, please let me quickly introduce myself. My name is Michael Simmons and I've been reassigned as the lead project coordinator for this particular mining facility, at least for the duration of this trip. From what I've been told, Derek Heiman, who is normally head of this unit, is currently unavailable due to a family emergency. I generally accept contracts, and have had my expertise utilized by Irradiance for the past three and half years. My past work history includes similar positions, especially those involving contingency planning and disaster relief, to keep operations running smoothly. Now, I'd also like to have each of you introduce yourselves, as I haven't even had a chance to review your files in much detail yet. Let's start with this young lady on my right." Michael motioned with his right hand toward Anamara.

Anamara smiled gently and rose to her feet. She angled herself to face the others. Trent noted that she was indeed taller than he was.

"Good morning. My name is Anamara and I'm a geoscientists for Irradiance. I have been with the company for over three years. My education is from the Academy of Maunsalman, Ty'krattama territory. In comparison with human educational terminology, I would hold a PhD in this discipline. My task during our stay on Circulum will be to assess the mineralogy of samples taken from various sites of interest, and assess further opportunities for mining on the planet." She returned to her seat.

Trent couldn't help admire her soft, yet strong voice. An unconscious smile crept into his expression.

"It sounds like we have a very talented geoscientist with us." Michael smiled and motioned to Dvenoor. "Sir, you're next up."

"I am Dvenoor, but please call me Noor," he said, rising to his feet as well. "I consult as a specialist in the fields of exobiology, geophysics, and various disciplines of engineering. In the past few years I've been primarily focused on nano and geotechnical applications. I am tasked with repairing the hardware aspect of the mining equipment that has failed." He quickly sat back down.

"Excellent. Thank you, Noor. And last but not least." Michael turned his gaze to Trent, who already stood, and raised his eyebrows in anticipation of his introduction.

"Thank you. My name is Trent. I'm an engineer with a specialization in mechatronics. My undergrad degrees are in computer science and mechanical engineering, but I also hold Master's degrees in software engineering and industrial engineering. Specifically advanced software design for the former, and robotics for the latter. I'm hoping to solve the software problems affecting the mining bots. Looking forward to working with you all." Trent nodded and gave an awkward smile.

"Great. I believe we're in capable hands, and I will be relying mostly on your expertise to ensure this mining facility is brought back into action, and that there might be further opportunities to mine this planet," said Michael as he swiveled his head back to Anamara. He brought up his tablet closer to his face, hands clasping each side, and continued, "Ok. Here's the story as I've been told. About a week or so ago, the mining bots malfunctioned. It says here these issues were minor at first. The machines would drill at the wrong speed, miss their targets by a few centimeters, and drive off their intended paths, but shortly thereafter make course corrections. However, as the day went on, drill bits were broken, the machines drove into walls and continued to power into them without taking corrective action, and one ran over a worker."

The team glanced at one another in surprise and Anamara asked, "Is the individual all right?"

"Yes. I was told his leg was broken, but there are medical staff on site and they've patched the worker up." Michael cleared this throat and continued, "The machines also stopped responding to commands, and they were taken offline using their emergency shutdown procedures. The facility staff are capable of repairing hardware aspects of the machines, like welding a broken drilling arm or replacing bearings on a conveyer belt, but they are not trained on computer hardware or software aspects. That's where you two come into play." He pointed to Noor and Trent, and let his left arm dangle by his side along with the tablet.

"So, Trent. You're our resident software expert. Have you considered a plan of action to get these machines up and running quickly?" asked Michael, stroking his goatee a few times.

Trent momentarily widened his eyes and took a deep breath, holding it in for a second or two. *Sure. Planned this out from day one. Shit. Think fast, Trent. Not the first time you've done debugging. Let's start with the usual.* Before speaking, he noticed a slight tilt of the head from Anamara.

"Well, I've been analyzing the code provided by Irradiance and nothing unusual has jumped out at me yet. So I'm thinking that something has affected the systems of these machines in the mine. Maybe it's the abundance of various radioactive elements, especially radium and radon gas, for example. Radiation can damage and corrupt memory cells if they aren't protected adequately. Or maybe the heavy element can cause some issues. Don't know, not my expertise there. But I expect that with a bit of help from Noor, we can establish if there's anything wrong with the memory, perform a clean install of the code, while saving the code in the machines for analysis later, and fire up the bots to see if that corrects the issue."

A strange silence seemed to waft into their meeting. Everyone was focused on Trent, his eyes the only part of him in motion, anxiously scanning the faces of his new teammates. Noor suddenly jerked his head toward Michael, expression unchanged.

"Michael, I believe Trent's assumptions are correct. Mining equipment also endure substantial physical stresses from their regular operations, especially in the form of vibrations. The hardware should be protected from such use, but possible manufacturing defects and poor maintenance can cause problems to develop." Trent's shoulders relaxed and he quietly breathed a sigh of relief that Noor agreed with his impromptu plan.

Noor adjusted his seating position and continued. "I intend to run an offline scan on the devices for any immediately noticeable issues. If none are found, then the control interfaces will need to be disconnected from the components so that I can activate the various systems in a virtual environment. This will allow me to run detailed diagnostics and simulations on them. I have various tools at my disposal to repair or completely replace the circuitry."

"And I've packed some advanced systems for live testing once the original or modified software has been installed," added Trent, giving Noor a friendly nod. Noor curled his thin lips upward.

Michael nodded. "Nice. Very nice. You two seem to be well rooted in your fields. Now I need something from you both. Put what you've told me in writing and send it to me, but include some timeframes. I'd like to have a schedule and Gantt chart going before we reach the planet so I can keep track of our progress. Our deadlines are tight. Anamara, run your goals by me." Michael turned toward her and raised his head in anticipation of her response.

Trent watched as she leaned back in her seat. Her fine threads of hair caught up to the rest of her, hypnotically oscillating for a moment before settling. She rested her elbows on the armrests and intertwined her long fingers on her lap.

"I will be descending into the mine with Noor and Trent on the morning after our arrival, but will be escorted to a new section of the mine to evaluate the attributes of the area. I will collect various samples and readings for further analysis. This process should take most of the day. My following activities will consist of examining the twenty-six samples taken at various locations throughout the planet, and reporting my conclusions regarding their viability for future mining operations. Of those sites, three have been deemed high priority, thus I will be personally visiting those locations to investigate them further. Would you like me to provide you with a written timeline of events, Michael?"

"Took the words right out of my mouth. Yes please. Excellent. I think we're off to a good start. I'd like to get those write-ups by dinner time, and for now I'm good. Do you folks have any questions for me?" Michael looked at his subordinates and widened his arms, palms and tablet upward.

Trent raised his right hand to about chest height and paused.

"Yes, Trent," Michael responded and pointed at Trent.

"Have you been to this planet before?" asked Trent as he lowered his hand.

"I have not. This will be a first for me. Seems like quite a strange world, but that's what'll make this job a bit more exciting." Michael flashed a quick toothy grin.

Trent managed a quick nod and pursed his lips in a haphazard smile.

"Any other questions?"

The team paused for a few moments, after which everyone indicated they did not have any further questions.

"Ok. You know where to find me. Usually by the kitchen." Michael patted his belly and chuckles sounded off. "Thank you. I'll keep you folks informed if I have any further needs."

Anamara and Noor stood and shook hands with Michael, and Trent stepped in a moment later to do the same. Michael then headed off to a lower level of the ship.

"Nice to meet you both," said Anamara, turning her head toward Noor and Trent. "Although I won't be working with you directly, I hope to converse with you at some point later. It seems we have similar interests and backgrounds."

"Likewise," answered Noor.

"Sounds good," Trent followed up. *'Sounds good?' Really? How about, 'I'm looking forward to discussing your research, Anamara. Maybe you can tell me more about element alpha.' I have no hope.*

Anamara briefly looked at Noor, but met eyes with Trent before she slightly bowed her head, pivoted around the row of seats, and glided toward the slender stairwell to a lower level. Trent lost in thought, hadn't noticed the subtle amusement cross her face. Her lips widening ever so slightly, eyes beaming just a trace.

"I believe this spot is as good as any to draft my strategy." And with that, Noor sat down and began composing.

"I'll leave you to it, Noor. See you later." Trent shuffled back toward his seat. On his way, he paused for a moment and glanced through a small porthole. Although *Ut'ahhziik* was tearing through space at over a thousand light-years per hour, stars far in the distance appeared virtually stationary. Only the occasional ones nearby, a few parsecs away, would drift slowly across the field of view. The compression effects from the engine caused the vista to ripple feverishly like a river bed viewed through swift currents. Trent noted the similarity this had to the way he felt.

CHAPTER 8

Trent rushed to complete his plan for Michael as he sat hunched over in his right rear seat, his face lightly illuminated by the screen of his tablet. His restless right leg urged him to stop proofreading for the umpteenth time and just hit the send icon. The fact that another aromatic meal wafted through the air wasn't helping him either, his stomach gurgling its feelings. But before Sheh'geetch notified all on board that dinner was served, Trent managed to poke the symbol. He had but a moment to sit back in his seat and release the tension from his muscles.

An unconscious nod overcame him as he wiped the corners of his mouth with a napkin, as licked the last remaining flavors from his lips. He held his plate steady in his right hand, maneuvered himself free of his seat, and headed toward the galley.

Sheh'geetch detected movement and turned its head to face it. "Trent, I can take that for you. Did you enjoy your dinner?"

"Yes I did, Sheh'geetch. Compliments to the chef. I'm already looking forward to breakfast."

"Thank you. I am glad you enjoyed it."

"Hey, Trent. You have a moment? I'd like to run something by you," asked Phil, peering from the doorway to the bridge.

Trent took a beat to locate where the voice was coming from and noticed Phil standing at the entrance, arms outstretched and propped against the frame. "Sure, yea," Trent acknowledged, then changed course to head toward him. Phil took a step back and behind the frame to Trent's left, his right hand hovering above the icon to close the door. As soon as Trent took a few steps onto the bridge, Phil thumbed the icon and the pocket door panel slid shut.

Trent's nerd within kicked in, accelerating his pulse and honing his vision. His jaw fell open in slow motion and his lips mouthed a silent, "Whoa!" His arms were by his side, but his fingers were stretched out to grab nothing in particular.

"Yea. You get why I became a pilot? Behold my lair!" Phil swung his left arm with palm up in an arc out from his body and across the bridge in majestic fashion.

Trent laughed aloud, but suddenly grabbed his mouth with his right hand, speaking through it. "Oops! That was loud, sorry." His eyes darted to the doorway.

"Relax. Soundproof," Phil chuckled. "Come on, co-pilot, take a seat." Standing to Trent's left, he slapped his back and jutted his chin to the right in the direction of the co-pilot's chair.

Trent took a couple of steps toward the comfortable high-back bucket seat located in front of a sweeping console panel with various screens and indicators lit up in several colors. He tenderly swivelled the chair to face him, then backed himself into it, steadying himself using the armrests. The cushions let out a satisfying hiss of air as his body weight was embraced by the material.

The view through these windows looked quite different than the scenery through the portholes on either side of the vessel. A large unwavering dome-like extension projected beyond the nose of the ship, visible merely by virtue of the lens-like distortion it created. It superficially magnified the stars and other celestial objects in the galaxy ahead, making it seem like they were just outside of one's reach. As the spherical field receded back toward the ship, fluctuating ripples appeared gradually and washed into the chaotic distortions Trent saw earlier, essentially the spacetime wake of the vessel.

Phil watched Trent with a wide grin, like a parent watching his child take their first bike ride. "Cool, eh?" he asked as he slinked into the captain's seat to Trent's left.

"Sure is."

"Ok, now watch this." Phil expertly tapped at various icons on his console panel. In a fraction of second after he struck the last one, a holographic heads-up display materialized in three dimensions around the far edges of the consoles and onto the panoramic windows. Phil continued, pointing as he spoke, "So dead ahead you'll see our destination indicated by that small circle with the crosshairs. The outlines are the borders of various regions of space. That thicker blue one represents Nyomor. The thinner green contours are objects like nebulae and star clusters and other points of interest. Then you'll see the names of nearby stars, and the usual info, fuel levels for thrusters, compression status, temperature levels, relative speed, and so on."

"Yup," nodded Trent, "I'm impressed." His eyes fed on the display and he bit his lower lip.

"So… the new guy's kinda cute. His stripes make him look taller. I always find those couples with big height differences *adorable*," quipped Phil, lingering on the last word with affection and straining to hold back the giggles.

"Shut. Up," chuckled Trent, shaking his head.

"Buddy, you got the short end of the stick. No pun intended." Phil laughed heartily, his belly emphasising his sounds.

Trent swivelled his chair to face the console and retorted, "Ok, I'm just going to start randomly pressing these buttons. Hmm? What does this half-moon icon do?" He feigned jabbing at the symbols on the display.

"All right, all right. That was good. You know, even if you were working with the pretty toonie, you'd still have the height difference, but she'd be the one with the edge. I noticed she gave you a good long look before she took off after the meeting this afternoon."

Trent furrowed his brows and frowned slightly. "But you weren't at the meet—"

Phil quickly tapped a few symbols on the console with his left hand. The holograms instantly provided a live video stream of several sections of the ship.

"No fucking way. You dirty bastard. New fetish?" jibed Trent.

"Man, the things I've seen. You couldn't even begin to imagine." Phil raised his right hand to his head and gestured as if his thoughts were exploding from it. "Seriously. I need to know what's going down on my ship. Hey look, I can even take a look outside." With another dance of his fingers, the holograms displayed fore, aft, port, and starboard views.

"Damn. That's cool." Trent paused for a moment as leaned in to inspect the unique sight, but his mind quickly wandered. "She's quite something though. Seems smart as hell. And she's really beautiful."

"You should have a chat with her."

"The Salapernean has a better chance of chatting with her than I do."

"She barely threw the guy a glance. She has her eyes on you. You're taller. And have healthier looking skin."

"Funny. Man, I never know how to start a conversation." Trent's hands rested on the armrests of the chair, his fingers picking at the synthetic leather-like material.

"May I remind you good sir? You had a hot wife—"

"Really, dude."

"—yea really. Hear me out." Phil extended his left index finger and shook it at Trent like a teacher emphasizing a learning objective. "I remember you telling me how you met Vivian while you were out grocery shopping for some weird toonie or kezi veggies. Out of the blue she appears asking you how you cook up the stuff, and you said you rambled on and on about how it should be prepared. Somehow, just being who you are, kept her there listening to your veggie tale."

Trent leaned to his left. His elbow rested on the armrest while his hand cradled his chin, fingers curled before his mouth. His lips gently arced upwards. As he continued to listen, his eyes peering beyond Phil.

"Look where that landed you. You got married. You had a kid."

The floor took over Trent's view, his expressed numbed.

"Don't think of the—" Phil's voice had increased in volume during his story telling, but he caught himself to think a moment before expressing potentially uncomfortable words. He took in a breath and continued with a more relaxed cadence, "—look, remember the times you made your woman happy. You pulled it off then and there's nothing stopping you from pulling it off now. And I'm not saying get married with her. Hell, maybe she's just bored and needs some hardware installed."

Trent's teeth were now showing and silent giggles convulsed his body, eyes peeking up at Phil.

"Ok, I'm betting you tech geeks have better terminology for this. But hey, it's not that hard, man. I admit, I get bored on my travels too. Although I have do have the advantage of being a pilot. Chicks love pilots. And look at these." Phil engaged his bodybuilder pose and flexed his biceps. "And if you think these are big…"

Trent pinched the bridge of his nose and chortled, "I though steroids made them smaller?"

Phil noticed Trent easing up and continued egging him on. "You know, toonies ain't that hard to impress. Well maybe Anamara is. But for a species that comes off kinda stuck up, they can get pretty friendly fast. You know there's also a Kezdari lady on board. She's in nice shape. They put up a good fight."

Trent leaned back in his seat, head tucked into his shoulders, eyes on the ceiling. He nearly lost it, but managed to sputter, "So how are those Hynafol gals?"

The wisecrack caught Phil off guard and his mouth gaped open in surprised. He mock gagged and leaned over the side of his chair to feign spit on the floor. "You, turd. You, monster. My best friend thinks I'm an animal. Oh that's nasty!"

Both men lost it. Trent slapped his knee and Phil roared, seizing his armrests to steady himself.

"I needed that," said Trent as he wiped away the tears collecting in the corners of his eyes.

"You have a dark side, man. Holy cow." Phil spotted an icon on the console in his peripheral that ebbed and flowed in brightness. "Shoot. I need to run my maintenance cycle. Ok, mister, out with you." Phil comically swung his right arm out, pointing at the door.

Trent, still giggling to himself, got up and rubbed his hands together. Phil followed closely behind and gave him a friendly slap on the back with a strong squeeze to the nape of his neck. He thumbed the same icon as before and the door slid open.

"All right, buddy. Take it easy. We'll chat later," said Phil.

"Yea, you bet. Later, man." Trent gave Phil a lazy salute and headed into the commons area.

Sheh'geetch was nearby and noticed Phil look over. The robot lurched into motion and sailed past him onto the bridge to assist with the cycle, the door sliding shut behind them.

The commons area was occupied by two of the Kezdari miners working out on the resistance equipment. Trent made a mental note to try out the gear sometime tomorrow. He made his way around the seats and toward the slim staircase that led down to the second level where the sleeping quarters were, grabbing his tablet on the way that was tucked into a side compartment of his seat.

He peered into the first bunkroom and noticed Noor working busily with some hardware scattered on the small table in the room. Trent figured he was most likely assembling something that will be used at the mining facility. One of the bunk units was sealed with the privacy shield activated. Slinking past, he entered his assigned room. The other two Kezdaries, a male and female miner, ruled over the small table in this room. Trent observed them playing some sort of card game with a couple of large multi-faceted dice that were engraved and painted with colorful symbols. They noticed Trent had entered and they enthusiastically greeted him. Trent returned the greeting with a hearty smile and nod, and the Kezdari quickly returned to their game. He couldn't understand what they were saying, but he could tell they were quite engrossed by the action.

Trent extended his personal storage compartment and swapped his tablet for another one with a larger screen and additional control surfaces. He figured he'd examine a few more sub-routines before calling it a night. He shut the compartment and glanced over at the two Kezdari laughing it up and twirling the dice on the table. *I ain't moving these two and it's too noisy to stay in my bunk.* His thoughts returned to the first bunkroom. *The gray's busy and I'd probably just be disturbing him. I don't want to listen the workout session upstairs either.* Then it dawned on Trent that Phil probably wouldn't mind him quietly working away on the lower deck. With that, Trent turned on his heels and headed toward the cargo area.

CHAPTER 9

"Spirit envelopes my essence. Peace shrouds my mind. Focus brings me clarity. Strength tones my body. I have purpose. I have will. I am one with the divine." Anamara whispered a set of mantras in her native language from her faatausia practice, which were masked to all but herself from the hum and rumbles of ship's inner workings.

She faced the stern of the ship. Her slender arms were outstretched at an angle, hands on the floor and next to each other, with thumbs closed up and fingers straight. Her head was tucked in between her upper arms, eyes shut, hair limp around her. Matching the angle of her arms, her back arched into her buttocks, from which her thighs angled back toward the floor; knees locked, feet together, and toes bent to support her weight. Her body formed the contour of a triangle with the textured metal beneath her. Having practiced faatausia, a Too'ndehrrehk yogic marital arts form, for almost a decade, her toned muscles held her as still as a statue of fine marble.

A set of feet, then legs, and the rest of a human materialized down the stairs, unbeknownst to Anamara. Having reached the bottom, the pair of feet jostled against the metal floor, causing one of the floor panels to clink.

Anamara's eyes shot open. *Someone's here.* She dropped her knees to the floor. In a swift move she straightened her back, flung her hair back, and twisted her upper body to face the visitor.

"I—I'm so sorry! I didn't see you, realize you, or anyone was here. I—" Anamara mused Trent's genuine response. His eyes were wide, eyebrows raised, and mouth hung open, posture uncertain of moving back up the stairs or staying put. He held his tablet in his left hand slightly out toward his side, right arm half-extended toward her, hand apologizing with spread fingers. She could feel his eyes curiously exploring her body. The Capri skin tight faatausia wear accentuated Anamara's curves and contours. The pant legs extended just beyond her knees, leaving her firm pearlescent calves and feet exposed. She knew humans well enough, but felt no ill intentions from this one.

"Trent. It's quite all right." A relaxed expression embraced her face, along with a gentle smile.

"I should have been paying attention. I was buried in my code. It can, uh, take a hold of me like a spell." Trent massaged the back of his neck with his free hand, turning a tinge of pink in the cheeks. His muscles has eased up, dropping his shoulders to a more comfortable stance.

Anamara stood as if light as a feather and the ship's gravity field decided to release her from its grip. Her hair mystically undulating as she moved. She edged toward Trent a few steps. Glistening droplets of sweat on her face and neck, like tiny jewels, were now visible to Trent.

"There's a fair amount of space in this section, seeing as how little cargo is on board. This allows me plenty of space to train."

"Yea, nice and quiet here too. You know, I can find a find a spot upstairs to continue my work."

"Actually, I wouldn't mind a rest. Why don't you sit with me for a while? I wouldn't mind some company. Michael has been preoccupied with his duties, and I feel Noor is not much for conversation."

Anamara looked to her right and gestured with her arm toward a crate they could sit on together. She noted that Trent hadn't turned his gaze from her eyes since they started conversing.

"Sure. Sure, why not." Trent nodded and his smile widened.

The two paced over to the large olive heavy-duty polymer crate and sat down. The crate protested against their weight with a few muffled groans. Trent had his legs slightly apart with his hands resting in the middle, clasped onto the sides of the tablet. Anamara had crossed her legs at her ankles. Her arms were straight by her sides, palms on the crate, fingers dangling off the front.

"You said you were studying some code. How is your work progressing?" asked Anamara.

"It's all right, I guess." Trent signed. "I just have the feeling all I'm really going to do is wait until Noor checks out the hardware on the machines, tells me they're ready to have the software installed, and then that's all I'll have to do. See, the code I got here, well this is the original system software. Apparently this has done its job for months straight, so whatever has happened is doubtful to have come from this." Trent gestured at his tabled with his right hand, fingers flexed as if holding a ball. He continued, "Whatever has gone wrong is locked into those mining machines. Until I see that code, I'll have no clue what's going on or what I might need to correct for. I haven't spotted anything unusual yet." His brow crunched up.

"Well you seem passionate about your work, so I have a feeling you'll discover the cause of this failure."

Trent turned his head to Anamara and asked, "So are you looking forward to exploring this strange new planet? Have you been to many worlds?"

Anamara shifted her right arm back to face Trent more easily. "Yes. Actually, I am quite excited about it. For a planet to have naturally occurring heavy element alpha is unique. Incredible really." Her hair bobbed almost weightlessly as she spoke with the nuances of her movement. "As you already know, my task is to determine where more of this element might be found on the planet. I have to admit that I'm also curious as to its origin. My theory is that a nearby supergiant star that went supernova a few hundred million years ago, expelled this element, among others, and it peppered this young world. The whole region we're entering is engulfed within a nebula, so I believe there is some merit to this idea."

Trent slid himself further back onto the crate so he could rest his back against the wall. He screwed up his lips for a moment and asked Anamara, "So how safe is this place? I mean there's a lot of uranium apparently, and Noor mentioned radium and radon gas."

"We will not be in any significant danger. This mine was constructed to extract element alpha, not uraninite ore. Our health will also be monitored continuously, and I'm certain the medical staff are qualified to handle the hazards of such an environment." Anamara mirrored Trent. She raised her legs up on top of the crate, bending them sharply at the knees, wrapping the long fingers of her left hand around her left shin. Her right shoulder lay against the wall as she faced Trent. She continued, "My visits to the other sites will help determine where to mine for the ore. Sightseeing is the best part about my job. This will be the loneliest place I've been though. On my other trips I enjoy exploring nearby outposts and meeting the inhabitants. I've made many lifelong friends. Have you travelled often, Trent?"

"Ah, no. Not really. Most of my work has been on Earth."

"May I ask, do you have any family?" The moment Anamara finished her question, a pang of hurt welled through her system. It almost startled her. A near silent gasp faintly parted her lips. *Such an innocent question to most. What happened to you, Trent?*

Trent took a quick breath and shifted his gaze to the back of the cargo bay. "My parents live in a small town. They're both retired. I have an older sister, Eva, and older brother, Jim."

Anamara brought her lips together. Her brow crinkled little, and she tilted her head.

"Used to be married. Divorced many years ago," Trent started.

She felt it again. *What happened? This was a major event. Can't just be the divorce.* There was a subtle tremble in Trent's lips. "Had a beautiful daughter."

Oh, you poor being. What must've happened? Anamara pulled herself upright. She reached out with her right hand and gently wrapped her fingers around Trent's shoulder.

"Had?" Her voice was a mere breath.

Trent took an uneasy breath, but continued, "She passed away on a trip. An accident."

"I'm very sorry for your loss, Trent." Her fingers tenderly squeezed his shoulder, and her expression relaxed as Trent's muscles loosed up.

"Thank you. It was many years ago."

"I can understand why you wouldn't enjoy such travel."

"This is my first time off Earth since I lost her. But I guess it's also a way to heal. It's ok."

Anamara adjusted her position, sitting more upright and resting her hands one on top of the other on her lap. She took a deep breath.

"I admire how you feel for your child even after all these years. The Too'ndehrr government took me away from my family when I was quite young. My parents, from what I can piece together from memory, were immature. They didn't even bother appealing their decision in order to take me back. I was adopted after a short stay at the child welfare facility. My adoptive parents took reasonably good care of me, but their expectations were much to bear. They were... are wealthy, so at the least I did have the pleasure of attending some of the finest educational institutions Too'ndehrr has to offer. But even a slight deviation would enrage them. I was more a showpiece than anything else." Anamara's expression took on a chill. She sensed Trent's sympathy, which helped her regain her composure. "A child without love, with no one to hold them, to play with them..."

"I know. I'm sorry. Seems we've both had some darkness in our pasts." Trent raised his left hand off the crate momentarily as if to console Anamara, but he solemnly replaced his hand.

"But I prevailed. You learn to adapt. Of course you have little choice unless you want a diminutive life. But I've strived to succeed and I'm faring well. I've excelled in my education and thus far my career is holding strong."

A lopsided smile adorned Trent's face. "Speaking of strong. May I ask what I interrupted tonight? Looked kind of like yoga."

Anamara appreciated the change of topic. She unconsciously looked over at the spot she was performing her faatausia routine. Her eyes brightened.

"It's called faatausia. You mentioned yoga. I've been around humans long enough to have picked up on some colloquialisms and one comes to mind. Faatausia is like yoga on steroids. Although it has some graceful moments, as you saw," Anamara perceived a warmth within Trent and her heart fluttered a moment, "but it can be quite physically demanding. In fact, I would say it becomes more similar to martial arts, helping to enhance ones reflexes, strength, and mental awareness. I've even earned Kee'alo rank, the highest possible for those practicing faatausia. This also grants me to the right to teach the tradition."

"I'm impressed," said Trent, with a wide smile across his face and admiring eyes.

"Perhaps I could introduce you some basic skills."

Trent nodded. "I'd be up for that."

Anamara slipped back into her original seating position on the large crate, legs dangling off the side, arms propping her up. She nearly had her back to Trent, but she turned her head to the right, giving Trent a profile view.

"Thank you for keeping me company, Trent." Her voice had softened, a gleam of drowsiness.

Trent slid himself off the polymer container and onto the ground. Anamara watched him as he took a few small steps toward the staircase, then swiveled on a foot to face her. Her head remained in the same position, but her eyes found his.

"Pleasure was mine, Anamara." Trent took a few paces in reverse. "And I'm going to hold you to that training."

A warm smile etched itself across Anamara's lips. "Good night."

"Good night," Trent replied as he returned to face the staircase and worked his way up.

Anamara sat motionless on the crate for what seemed like a minute, but was likely only a few seconds. She then sprung to her feet, stretched her legs, body, and arms, rotating her head around in circles to relax the muscles in her neck. She paused, wearily eyeing the room in which she now stood alone. The unusual silence sent a chill through her spine. In a flash, she darted up the stairs, two steps at a time, and headed off to take a shower.

Trent strode onto the first level and directed himself to the cupboard. A quick glass of water before turning in would cure his thirst. The two Kezdari who occupied the resistance machines were gone and replaced by the female miner who was working out her legs. She flashed him a quick smile as she puffed with every exertion. Trent gave her a friendly wave.

Having reached the cupboard, Trent swung open the door, and removed a cup. He was just about to hit the tap to fill it when a near silent hiss and motion caught the corner of his eye. Trent straightened up and turned toward the entrance to the bridge.

There stood Phil, thumb on the inner door panel, with a grin from ear to ear, and eyes about to pop out of their sockets. He gave Trent a mighty thumbs up with his left hand and mouthed the word, "Nice!"

It took Trent half a second to process the situation. His eyes started bulging too. Mouth gaped open in shock. He quickly shot a few glances around the room to see who else might have seen this. Luckily the Kezdari miner was too intertwined with the resistance machine to notice what was going on, and everyone else had retired to the second level. Trent snapped his gaze back. He started pointing with this free hand and begun mouthing the word, "You!" just as Phil jabbed at the panel and the doors slid shut with haste.

Son of a… I need to have a chat with him about that. Shock morphed into silent giggles as Trent started filling his cup.

CHAPTER 10

A few small droplets of water fell from Trent's damp hair and pattered against the floor mats as he stood before his bunk. He snatched his towel off his mattress and gave his hair a quick once-over to soak up any leftover spots he missed after his shower. Although disordered, his hair took on a nice sheen and fluffed up, erasing traces of the day's troubles. He stowed his towel in the compartment under his bunk after folding it in half and rolling it up.

Trent was ready for bed. The excitement of the day had been enough for him. He wore his baggy sweatshirt and sweatpants as pyjamas, and was glad he remembered to toss his slippers into his case during his speedy escape from his apartment. He scrutinized his sleeping pod for a moment and couldn't but help think that they reminded him of coffins. They were nice coffins though, with their interiors bathed in pleasant shades of light beige. At about four feet in height, three deep, and at least seven feet long, they were roomy for a human and suitable for a Too'ndehrr. The inner lighting could be customized and an adjustable tray could drop down to support tablets or other devices. Even the headrest could be elevated for added comfort. The sound proofing was apparently quite good too. Trent was curious how much of the ambient noise would be blocked by the privacy screen that would slide over the opening, and how much of any internal sounds would be retained. *I hope enough air can still get in here.*

Trent ducked down, rolled himself into the sleeping pod, and clutched the soft blanket. He pulled it over his body, lightly gyrating with his feet to get it into position. He shot a glance out of the large opening with its rounded corners, peering across the room where two of the miners had already activated their privacy screens. The third miner, who appeared to be reading something on his tablet with a serious look on his face, claimed the bunk at the back of the room, which was situated high above the small work table. Its collapsible metallic ladder was extended and hadn't been stowed into its cubbyhole. Shuffling sounds came from above Trent's pod. He guessed the female miner was preparing herself for the night too.

Michael, Noor, and Anamara occupied the other sleeping quarters, and Phil used one of the pair on the bridge. Trent wished he was in the other room, but his aversion to socializing led him to instinctively follow the four miners into this one. He figured the miners wouldn't have much in common with him and leave him be, which, excluding a few pleasantries, was the case. But his chat with Anamara made him consider moving his belongings over. At this point, he figured it might come across awkward or strange. Then again, maybe he was wrong.

The small control panel directly above his chest glowed with various thumbprint sized icons, and Trent poked at the indicator for the privacy screen to activate. It quietly shushed up within a few seconds, and indeed choked the rustles, hums, and activity of the ship. *Cool. Works quite well.* The shield also became deeply opaque, dimming the view and light from intruding. One could still make out some details peering through it from within, but viewed externally, the screen appeared milky, completely obscuring the contents inside. With another poke, the lights dimmed to darkness. Trent took a deep breath, followed by another long one. He could feel the slightest air current confiscating the heat from his breaths as he exhaled. *Good. I might just wake up in the morning.*

Trent awoke to a deafening silence. He looked over at the darkness that cloaked the sleeping quarters. He could just make out that the other pods were empty and that none of the privacy screens were active. Including his. He lay still. Not a sound. No engines. No clothing rustling. No voices. His heart picked up the pace and was the only sound pounding in his ears.

He cautiously crept out of the bunk and scanned the room.

"Hello?"

He waited, but no answer.

"Is anyone here?"

Nothing. Trent approached the doorway and looked to his right, but only a bulkhead greeted him. He looked left down the staircase and heard whispers. Treading carefully, he inched down the steps and saw an empty cargo hold. No luggage, crates, or supplies. But the loading ramp was lowered. His thoughts were fuzzy. Had they landed?

Not even his footsteps made a sound as Trent descended the angled platform. The whispers became louder, but he couldn't make out any words. The disorienting murmurs came from all around him. He couldn't see beyond the ship, as if a void had enslaved the vessel.

A damp slosh sounded as he took his first step off the ship. Trent looked down. Mud. He snapped his gaze back. A murky forest surrounded him. He spun one-eighty. The ship had vanished. Trent roared in fear and frustration. Yet his voice didn't carry.

He turned around to face the way he left the vessel and began to trudge as quickly as he could through the greedy soil that refused to let him go without a struggle. Densely packed moss laden trees faded into view through the dark gray haze.

Then a painful wheezing gasp made Trent freeze in this tracks. He instantly spun himself toward the plea for much needed air. A clearing materialized into view and he could barely make out three figures. He lurched toward them. As he did, a dark slimy rocky cave etched itself into view. Trent took a few more steps and the beings became crystal clear.

Noor sat on the left, legs crossed. Child-like. In the middle, a tall thin unrecognizable form stood. Its gangly elongated legs, torso, and arms appeared hideously inhuman; its head enveloped by a flaming charcoal blaze. To the right, held by the throat by the being's outstretched lanky arm, was Anamara. Her eyes were rolled back in their sockets. Mouth hung open struggling to inhale precious oxygen. Her body and limbs limp like a ragdoll.

Noor took notice of Trent. His curious expression locked onto him. Then his mouth suddenly sprung horridly wide open as an ear-splitting resonating growl shot from his being. At that moment, one of the giant's huge digits sprang to the side of Anamara's head and snapped her neck ninety degrees down to her shoulder with a thunderous crack.

Trent released a haunting wail as he jolted upright in his sleeping pod, only to be met with a firm cushion to the forehead that cut his fear induced reaction short. His head slammed back down into his pillow and utterances of protest left under his breath. He brought his hands to his head, palming his forehead. He groaned a few times as his heart rate returned from its fight or flight state and his breathing calmed. The lights in the pod automatically activated, bathing the small environment in a soft warm glow.

Trent finally opened his eyes and blinked a few times. He brought his hands down over his chest and hesitantly shifted his eyes to the side. He scanned up and down the length of the pod. Satisfied the privacy screen was in place, he let his head turn to take a better look. The other sleeping compartments appeared occupied. The control panel indicated a time of two thirty-eight a.m. A quivering hand rose with Trent's middle finger bumping the icon to retract the shield. With a near silent hiss the screen descended.

The hum of the ships inner workings was a relief to Trent's ears and state of mind. At this late hour, no voices permeated the air, but that meant everyone was fast asleep. Trent uneasily worked his way to the edge of the pod and set his feet firmly on the floor. He wiped the sweat off his face using the sleeves of his shirt, then stood, still on a shaky foundation as the adrenalin hadn't receded yet. He placed his hands on his hips and let a few moments slip by, taking deep breaths to further calm himself. That last cup of water before hitting the sack needed to escape, and Trent realized he was thirsty again. A quick trip to the head and then to the galley for another drink would be needed before he could slink back into bed.

It was mandatory that passenger vessels always had the lights on in corridors and key decks, a safety requirement. Trent's eyes took a moment to adapt to the brightness beyond the sleeping quarters, but he could see fairly comfortably by the time he finished in the loo and reached the first deck. He headed toward the galley to fetch a cup, but a shuffle made his heart skip a beat.

Trent stalked cautiously around the perimeter of the row of seats, angling his head into each one. *Empty. Empty. I know I heard something.* Then he peer around the first row.

"A good evening, Trent. Or would it be good night. Yes, night it is still," greeted Noor. He sat at an angle toward Trent in the port-side row holding various electronic gear in his hands, with the seat to his right filled with even more circuitry and small equipment.

"Oh. Noor. Hello. Sorry, I didn't realize you were still up. You're sure working late," Trent said with waning quiver in his voice. He leaned on the top edge of the seat next to him.

"Ah, yes. Sleep. An interesting concept. One I can hardly imagine. Salaperneans do not require sleep. Quite fascinating how so many species have evolved similar brains that need a rest period. Salapernean brain structure is substantially different. Even the Mammalia, Aves, and such on our homeworld forego this peculiar activity."

Trent wrinkled his forehead and gave a quick puff of air through his noise in amazement. "Well that's something I did not know. That's incredible. I suppose it's hard for me to imagine what it would be like not be tired and to just keep working throughout the day. How would you even feel that a day passes?" His eyes wandering around the room looking for invisible answers.

"I understand your perspective. For us that's irrelevant. Do you know the basis for Salapernean time?"

"No, I don't," answered Trent, his eyes glued to Noor's.

"About twelve-hundred years ago, Salapernia updated and standardized the method used to keep time. Our technology had advanced rapidly during that era and we had a much better understanding of atoms and physics, but our species used three different methods of time keeping. Strange times in Salapernia's history. None were easily relatable to another and they did not contribute well to the sciences. Thus, with the advent of technology capable of analyzing the behavior and properties of atoms and sub-atomic particles, it was decided that one billion cycles of a neutral hydrogen atom would be considered a single unit of zitula, our second if you will. I believe humans know this electromagnetic radiation as the hydrogen, or twenty-one centimeter, line. One hundred zitulas makes a ka-zitula, a minute in your terms. One hundred of those a ma-zitula, an hour. Ten ma-zitulas gives us our ha-zitula, or day, and our luzaga, month, has ten ha-zitulas. Finally, there are ten luzagas in our gudina, year."

Trent hardly breathed as his absorbed this fascinating new information.

"Compared to human time, our zitulas are about seventy percent of a second. But since we have more in a minute and hour, they do add up. Let's see." Noor rested the electronics he held on the seat next to him and detached a small hand-sized tablet from a belt around his waist, dancing his fingers rapidly across the screen. "Ah, here we are. Salapernean time in human units. Our minute would be one-minute ten seconds, an hour almost two human hours, short a couple of minutes. A single day for us is a substantial eight days and three and a half hours for you. A month would be eighty-one and a half days, and a year almost eight hundred and fifteen days."

"That's incredible. So I'm guessing that the light and dark periods on your world are not related in any way to your time?"

"That is correct," Noor answered as he reattached the device to his belt and took hold of the gear he set down a few moments ago. "Unlike for most other species, it's irrelevant to us whether there's a morning, afternoon, or night. Our year end or beginning does not coincide with the revolution of our planet around Aliatia, our star, either."

"That's wild," Trent grinned while nodding to himself. "So what are you working on?" he asked, jutting his chin at the circuit-like boards scattered on the seat and in Noor's clutches.

"Ah. A few of these shall be useful to repair the mining equipment, if need be. And I've also brought along some other projects I've been working on."

Trent considered the Salapernean as he snatched up a small pointed tool with a miniscule display. He asked, "So what are these? What do they do?"

"Some of these will be used to interface with the electronics of the mining equipment," said Noor without making eye contact.

Trent waited a moment, but Noor kept toiling away, jabbing the tool against various locations against the board. He pressed on, "Cool. What kind of projects are the others for?"

Noor was about to take another jab at the piece but froze for a fraction of a second. "Those would be for another client. However, I must adhere to a confidentiality agreement. I'm sure you understand." Noor's gray eyes with those bright teal sclera flashed up at Trent for an instant.

Trent gestured with his right hand in understanding and responded, "Oh, of course. No problem. I gotcha." A yawn unexpectedly overpowered Trent, and he courteously turned away, placing the back of his hand near his mouth. "Excuse me. I think I better have that drink I came for and get back to sleep. Still a few hours to go. Well nice chatting with you, Noor. Don't work too hard now."

"Indeed. Rest well. See you in the morning," Noor responded with a faint smile, eyes focused on his work.

After fetching and downing his water, Trent traipsed back to his sleeping pod. Gravity seemed to be pulling down on his eyelids with greater force, and the bunk looked warm and inviting now that his nightmare woes had worn off. His mind replayed the conversation he just had with Noor as he slipped back into the pod and fumbled with his blanket. He wondered if maybe he should have taken Noor's hesitance to answer as a sign to stop asking questions. It was nothing more than curiosity after all. Then again, maybe it was just how Salapernean's behaved. If fact, aside from the rare greeting, Noor was the first he had conversed with for any meaningful amount of time.

A gentle blip responded to Trent's fingertip and the privacy screen slid up, cloaking the distractions of the ship, as well as his thoughts. He took a few deep breaths and his eyelids fluttered shut.

CHAPTER 11

The next couple of days would be uneventful. Trent's nightmares hadn't returned, which he was quite thankful for, and he had finished examining the code. As he suspected, there wasn't anything erroneous with the original software. The answers to whatever happened to those mining machines was tucked away in their memory cores. He had run into Noor a couple of times after their chance encounter during the first night, but aside from a few pleasantries, they hadn't spoken much. Luckily, Phil satisfied that void. They spent a few occasions bantering on the bridge, and Trent even assisted with a minor repair to the ventilation system. Phil exclaimed he could become an expert HVAC repairman if the software gig didn't work out for him. Michael kept Trent occupied during a few one-on-one meetings. He wanted to become better acquainted with the processes he'd employ, the objective being to create contingency plans for any risks during those tasks.

Trent's reclusive sanctuary during meals, the last pair of seats on the first deck, was no more, as Anamara decided to keep him good company. Between bites, they would exchange bits and pieces of their working and personal lives. She even managed to convince Trent to try a basic faatausia routine, a series of stretches and warmup practises for beginners. His ribs protested a little, but he managed to wince himself through the contortions.

"Good afternoon, everyone," announced Phil as he stood in the doorway to the bridge, his outstretched arms braced against the door frame at shoulder height. "This is your captain speaking. But if you didn't already know that, you should've been paying better attention three days ago." Everyone chuckled. Phil had become well acquainted with most of the passengers during the trip, and it was likely he'd keep in touch with a few.

"Kay. In a few minutes we'll be disengaging compression and performing landing maneuvers to get us settled on Circulum. At this point, your devices and trays should be stowed away and your harnesses secured. If you feel a little disoriented coming out of compression, just close your eyes for about ten seconds and you'll be back to normal quickly. As a reminder, this is a strange world. The habitable zone of the planet is situated in a band around the equator about a thousand kilometers wide, as the planet's axis is tilted eighty-three degrees, nearly facing the star. This means the star will appear to dip and rise just below and above the horizon in more or less the same spot each day, which in Earth time is twenty-one hours and thirty-eight minutes long. Since the world is tidally locked, the side facing the star gets to about five hundred Kelvin, with the opposite side going down to about a hundred and twenty Kelvin. So lots of sunscreen or layers depending on which side you're out for a hike on." A few nervous laughs could be heard during Phil's pause to emphasize the extreme range of temperature on the world.

"The habitable zone is quite comfortable though. But if you are going to explore the mining facility on the surface, be aware of the weather. It can apparently change in a heartbeat and strong winds in excess of a hundred kilometers an hour can whip up within minutes. Bottom line, if it looks nasty, seek shelter immediately. The facility is built to take the punishment, so you'll be fine in your cabins or in the main structure. Speaking of the facility, the whole area is fenced in. I'm told no one should venture out on their own, as there are some potentially dangerous wildlife and insect species.

"Considering the planet's size, about eight thousand seven hundred kilometers in diameter, it's got a strong magnetic field, along with a dense ozone layer, so cosmic radiation is a non-issue. And it shouldn't take anyone too long to adapt to Circulum's gravity. It's about 90% of Earth's, 85% of Too'ndehrr's, and around that range compared to Kezda and Madenza. All right. Any questions?" Phil had taken a couple of steps toward the passengers, who were now all securely fastened in their seats. Trent could see Phil scanning faces for any uncertainties, but no one replied. Phil nodded his head slightly when he came across Trent.

"Good. Now I get the best view in the house, but lucky for you, I'm not selfish. So once we pull into normal space, we'll activate the screens on the back of each seat, and the folks in the front row can view the show on the monitor on the wall here." Phil gestured toward a large screen next to the bridge entrance. "Thank you and I'll see you on the surface."

Phil turned on his heels and strode onto the bridge, reaching behind him with his left hand to secure the door. A few minutes passed and Sheh'geetch's voice signalled over the ship's intercom. "Attention. Re-entry into normal space in five… four… three… two… one."

Trent couldn't quite remember how this felt from his trip many years ago. He braced himself for the moment the vessel would lunge out of compression. He counted the last few seconds with Sheh'geetch, then mentally did zero on his own.

A bizarre hollow metallic ping radiated throughout the ship, drowning out all other sound. It endlessly echoed for several seconds and branched off into multiple phases, each with a Doppler shift of its own. The wall to the bridge abruptly launched away from his location, stretching the floor, walls, and ceiling along with it. Within an instant it appeared to be tens of meters away, but in the next moment it began homing in on its original location. As it did, a wave undulated through the ship, from bow to stern, which warped the remaining portions of the interior away and toward the approaching wall. The portions joined up with the bridge wall as it dropped back into normal spacetime. As suddenly as the event occurred, it ended. The normal hums, shuffles, and activity of the ship resumed as if nothing had happened.

Trent felt like this process had taken minutes, when in fact it was no more than a few seconds. After the decompression, he felt immeasurably different, but couldn't conclude what it was that changed. He stared slightly to his right, but not necessarily at anything. His fingers wound tightly around the armrests of his seat. A cool gentle sensation on his left hand jolted him out of his stupor.

"Are you well?" Anamara asked softly, her hand resting on Trent's.

Trent turned his head toward her and responded, "Yea. I'm ok. I'll be adding this to my list of reasons why not to travel." His shoulders relaxed and a wavy smile added to his expression.

"You get used to it. But I fear it's this next leg of the journey that will cause you some further discomfort."

At the comment, Trent's lips formed a line and his eyes sharpened, then his head snapped straight ahead as the monitors on the seats came on and displayed the foreboding yet mesmerizing sight. *Ut'ahhziik* had entered normal space about a hundred and fifty thousand kilometers from the planet, tearing along at nearly half the speed of light and decelerating rapidly. Trent spied Anamara in his peripheral vision being just as enthralled by the spectacle as he was. The main engines could be heard through the vibrations in the hull as they faced directly forward and fired at full power to reduce their speed.

Circulum's star facing hemisphere loomed prominently on the monitor. A grayish burnt umber circular region blasted by the perpetual rays of the star's direct radiation seemed to be etched in pain. The minute details of ancient mountain ranges and fissures lay dreadfully barren, with ghostly indications that vast bodies of water once filled and ran through the cavities. Surrounding the pupil were several colossal spiralling cyclones and billowing storm systems, more analogous to those seen on gas giants than on rocky worlds like Earth or Too'ndehrr. *Ut'ahhziik*, now down to about a quarter of the speed of light, swung under and around the planet, still quite a distance from it. Circulum had rolled from being center-left to predominantly at the top of the display, as the ship's topside was parallel to the surface of the world.

Toward the direction of the planet's equator, and in great contrast to the barrens of the pupil, the storm systems pacified and even evaporated above the landscape, revealing vast stretches of brilliant light and dark greens and tendrils of blue crawling across the landscape, akin to the details of an iris in one's eye. The surfaces of large lakes, and an ocean that materialized into view, glistened in gold sparkles as the star's rays hit the surface at a drastic angle. Heading further across the landscape, Trent mourned the loss of detail beyond the terminator, as it washed away the light and bathed the opposite side of the world from the star in everlasting darkness. The occasional flickers of lightning provided glimpses of structure to the clouds, and the contour of the dark side of the world could only be perceived by the subtle glow of the atmosphere arcing around it, and how the planet's shaded body obstructed the view of expansive filaments of nebulae far in the distance.

Circulum appeared to make a loop on the monitor as it went from being on the top half to the bottom, as *Ut'ahhziik* made a barrel roll to position its bow toward the surface of the planet. The vessel was now down to about one twentieth of the speed of light, and also drew closer to the world, leaving only a slight curve to the horizon visible on the display screen.

"Attention everyone. We're on our final approach to the mining facility. The ride's gonna get a bit rough as we descend into the atmosphere, as ground control has notified us that there's a moderate storm in that area. Please stay calm and buckled in your seats until we've landed and I've given the signal that it's safe to begin departing. Thank you," announced Phil over the intercom.

Trent leaned back in his seat and expelled a long breath of air that puffed up his cheeks. He threw a quick glance at Anamara. She gave him a smile and tenderly wrapped her fingers into his hand.

"Don't worry. I've been on many flights where we had to endure landing during a storm. Remember, these ships are designed to withstand forces far greater than what the winds of a powerful cyclone can generate. Yes, we'll experience some turbulence, but it'll be over quickly," Anamara informed Trent.

"Great. I hate long drawn out deaths."

Anamara grinned widely, rolling her eyes and shaking her head. "You know what I mean."

The roar of the engines became progressively audible from the exterior as the ship descended into the upper layer of the atmosphere, where the density of the air was enough to carry sound and buffet the vessel. Control thrusters started firing to help keep the ship steady. *Ut'ahhziik* had now almost completely rounded Circulum and faced nearly the direction it came from. Trent watched the screen as the ship altered course, a slight bank to port, placing the terminator more to the right edge of the display. The thermal shielding produced a barrier a few meters thick between the hull and the air surrounding the ship, making the searing air glow and undulate around its exterior. Seeing the visuals alone caused tiny beads of sweat to form on Trent's forehead, and it didn't help that his restless right leg kicked in. The speed indicator now displayed just over forty thousand kilometers per hour.

The storm system Phil cited earlier crested over the horizon and the ship was almost level with the peak of its clouds, about fifteen kilometers up. It reminded Trent of the supercells on Earth with their anvil formations, except this one dwarfed anything he'd seen in his lifetime. Within a minute, the ship plowed through the wall of the storm, now traveling under a thousand kilometers an hour. The video stream on the monitored turned a dull gray, but occasional flashes lit it up. As warned, the vessel lurched and jolted unexpectedly. Although the inertial reduction system kept the g-forces manageable, Trent was thankful for the seatbelts. With the thermal shielding deactivated, the powerful turbulence swept and raced across the hull. Shrills and whistles forced their way through the sound dampened bulkheads, chilling Trent to the bone.

A deafening sudden thud reverberated in the cabin, catching everyone off guard. Trent jerked in his seat and gasped. He even felt Anamara's hand tighten around his.

"This is your captain again. Please do not be alarmed. What you heard is lightning striking the hull. Lightning poses no threat to us, but does make quite a clatter. ETA in two minutes. Hang in their folks."

"Still surprises me every time," said Anamara, eyes peering upwards toward the ceiling.

Trent also followed her gaze, as if he was going to actually see the lightning hit. Then it happened again, another ear shattering thud.

"Whoa! I could smell that one!" exclaimed Michael from a few rows ahead. The Kezdari miners seemed to be enjoying the ride, as they chuckled at the comment.

The seatbelts pressed hard against Trent's chest due to the ship's rapid deceleration. He scrutinized the monitor before him, now showing the view from a wide angle camera mounted somewhere underneath the ship, and was relieved to see a compound fade into view through the storm's gray clouds. His mind momentarily flashed back to the visions in his nightmares that bared a similar resemblance, but he shut his eyes for a second or two and purged those visuals.

Ut'ahhziik hovered several hundred meters about the complex and descended painstakingly, occasionally being knocked around by strong wind gusts. The rain fell hard and sheets of it rolled across the view. Lightning lit up the screen periodically, with the sound of thunder following soon after, but at least none had struck the ship again.

Trent inspected the emerging mining facility on his monitor. Two large landing and launch pads sat on the far right side of the screen, one above the other, with the one at top occupied by what appeared to be a sizable cargo ship. Paved taxiways connected each and met up with a gravel or groomed dirt road to their left that led to the rest of the structures in the compound. The modest sized main building rested at least a hundred meters away from the pads, situated just right of center, and to its left were around two dozen long slender buildings, about seven or eight in pairs. Trent guessed these were the cabins for the miners, as well as any visitors to this world. To the left of those, and scattered throughout the bottom area of his view were what looked like supplies needed for the mining operation, a mix of sheds, metal beams, and various mining machines, among other details that couldn't be seen clearly. Surrounding the entire perimeter of the complex, excluding the launch pads, was a formidable wall that seemed several meters high. It was dotted with a few heavy guns and easily kept out the jungle beyond its walls.

After another minute of descent, *Ut'ahhziik* jostled momentarily and rested on the pad. The groan of the engines subsided, and the reduction of noise was a welcome reprieve for everyone. As if on cue, all of the passengers began hooting and hollering, hands clapping in appreciation for the pilot and his expert landing during such conditions. Anamara and Trent joined in, wide grins fixed onto their expressions.

The doors to the bridge slid open and Phil stepped into the open, clasping his hands together in front of his chest. He announced, "Thank you folks, applause not necessary. Just doing my job. Welcome to Circulum. You can now unbuckle your safety harnesses and make your way down to the cargo ramp. The mining facility staff will be waiting just outside to take you to the main facility for further processing, and they'll also take your gear to your assigned cabins. If you require anything from me, please don't hesitate to contact me. Just send me a message through your tablet. I've opted to stay onboard, so I'll be here for the duration of this mission. Thanks folks." Phil gestured with his hands toward the stairwell and everyone slinked out of their seats to exit the ship. But before leaving, all would pass by Phil to shake his hand and thank him personally. He was absolutely beaming.

Trent waited until everyone had their chance and then he approached Phil. "Not bad, sir, not bad. I'm still shaking a little but that's just me."

"Buddy, we made it in one piece. We got a good ship for this trip. I've had worse."

"You'll have to tell me over a drink later."

"You bet. I'll see you later," said Phil as he slapped Trent on the shoulder as he left.

A concern wedged Phil's brow together and he marched back onto the bridge the moment Trent was out of sight. He swung his chair around and leaped into it, spinning it back toward the console. Tapping swiftly on the panel, he called up details during their approach to the planet. The system indicated it had detected an anomaly, but had insufficient data to fully analyze before landing. He punched in a few more commands and the read the display, which indicated the sensors on the ship were unable to function properly during the storm.

"Sheh'geetch. I want you to execute this scan the moment this storm passes, and report the results to me ASAP."

"Understood. Command stored and scheduled."

CHAPTER 12

"Secure connection established," spoke a deep synthesized male voice.

"Yessh," said Koorehg. His booming voice filled the air.

"Our guests have arrived and have settled in," said Maksim.

He stood behind a large arcing console panel on a lavishly sleek bridge, gleaming gunmetal surfaces throughout. Several massive panoramic windows curved halfway around the room, only interrupted by a few reinforcement pillars. Starlight shone down overhead through a flattened dome several meters in diameter, segmented into triangular sections, their points meeting in the middle. The artificial lighting on the bridge was overwhelmed by the warm reflected light cast off the toiling furious clouds of NS-2048a just off to port, a super-Jupiter sized planet orbiting the same star as Circulum, but much farther out. Maksim's battlecruiser, *Hyperion*, orbited over fifty thousand kilometers above the surface of the gas giant, yet the gargantuan planet gave the impression of being a wall next to the ship. Two bridge officers were busily working away to his left and right, and another two manned stations at the rear of the bridge.

"And? Thish ish hardly sschomthing of interessht."

"True. But I want you to take a look at this," Maksim answered as he hit a few icons on his control panel.

A few moments of silence passed by before Koorehg answered. "I sshee. Thish ish unexshpected."

"To say the least. Our informant should have access to secure communications soon enough. I'll keep him apprised of the situation."

"Me ash well." A couple of blips signalled the end of the transmission.

Maksim was hunched over with his hands resting firmly on the console panel, arms outstretched at slight angles away from his body. His head was bowed down, face expressionless, but his eyes peered dead ahead and into the small disc that was NS-2048, the star for this system. If one knew where to look, Circulum would be a mere tiny dot a few degrees to the right of the bright speck.

Rising up, Maksim strode around the perimeter of the impressive console panel and headed toward the large window front and center. He cupped his hands behind his back as he paced, his thumb caressing the large obsidian ring on his right index finger. He stopped a few inches short of the crystal clear viewport and stood there admiring the scene. The mammoth planet loomed to his left, and the gases that permeated the region, remnants of a star that went supernova eons ago, added a spectacular ambiance with their ghostly red and teal trails. A beautiful scene with utterly violent and chaotic origins.

CHAPTER 13

"Welcome to Irradiance Mining Site twenty forty-eight, or more affectionately known as IMS-2048," snickered Fezria Monkash. Trent, and the rest of the team, minus miners and Phil, listened attentively as the late forties Kezdri woman, the head of facility operations, began reviewing the protocols of the mining facility. She stood almost his height, had short swirly dark coffee hair, and tan skin to match. Her muscular physique was apparent even under her light gray work coveralls. A pair of work gloves hung off her belt and sturdy work boots adorned her feet. She continued, "I hope you all had a pleasant trip to our cozy corner of the galaxy. You'll have to excuse the weather. It's been temperamental the last few weeks, but we're expecting it to clear up by tomorrow morning. I'm sure all of you have read the preliminary documentation on our procedures?" Her statement careened into a question as she did a hard take at each team member before her. Everyone responded with some affirmatives and nods.

"Good. Then I'll just emphasize the key points. One of our most important rules is to follow our rules," she smirked. "Seriously. You all know how valuable the heavy element is, and anyone caught trying to take some will be reported. No hard feelings, company policy. You'll always be subject to a scan when entering the mine, where we take note of what you have, and you'll be scanned when leaving, along with a good cleaning. The cleaning is meant to remove even the smallest particulates of the element that are bound to cling to your clothes while you're down in the mines.

"Know where the safe-houses are. This planet is quite seismically active, so it's not unusual to have several tremors a day. The vast majority in this area are relatively weak, as a few small fault lines are about fifty kilometers away to the west. By the way, west is toward the cabins, east toward the launch pads, north faces the star, and that leaves south which is toward the dark side of the planet."

Trent wondered how this would be setup on Circulum. He made a quick mental note of the directions. Fezria continued her key points for another couple of minutes.

"Ok. Any questions?"

Noor raised his right hand to chest height, index finger extended.

"Yes, sir," acknowledged Fezria.

"Are we restricted from entering the mines during any particular hours of the day?"

"No. We operate nonstop. Even as we speak. We're using the few backup machines we have that are manually operated. It's really slowed us down and we're eager get the automated ones back to work. But I guess that's what you're all here to do. Well, except you, Anamara."

Anamara smiled in response.

"I have a question," Trent said.

"Sure."

"You mentioned this area is seismically active. Has the mine ever caved in?" Trent asked nervously.

"I know what you're thinking. I run a good mine and Irradiance thankfully doesn't skimp on safety, so you're in good hands. And yes, we've had a handful of cases where a sector has caved in, but luckily our miners have avoided any serious harm or death. When we place a safe-house, we know exactly where it is from the surface. The mine isn't that deep, so drilling an emergency shaft only takes about half a day. And the safe-houses have air purifiers and enough food and water for up to twenty people for three days. First time in a mine?" Fezria raised an eyebrow.

"Yea. It's going to be a new experience. And thanks, I'm sure you all know what you're doing."

"No worries. With all the lighting and ventilation we've got going, you'll feel like you're at home. Well our floors are bit dustier," chortled Fezria. "But we need to get moving. The good doctor is waiting to get your implants installed. If you have any further questions, don't hesitate to reach out to me. Just give me a few hours to respond, as I might be tied up with my duties." Without a moment to spare, she dashed toward the medical bay with everyone in tow.

Considering Kezdari architects and engineers designed the main building, it was welcoming and functional. A single entry on the south jutted out from the structure and acted as a small and secure lobby to check in visitors. Miners would also enter through the same area, but had a zone they could pass through using their identification cards. Once through the lobby, a long and wide hallway split the innards in two. The southeast quadrant housed a few offices for supervisors and administrative staff, along with a large meeting room that the team had just vacated, whereas a large kitchen that supported the entire workforce at the facility took up the northeast section. The southwest corner of the building housed the onsite medical facility with ten beds, a bay for surgery, as well as a laboratory. Trent thought Anamara would be particularly interested in the northwest block, as it housed a lab to analyze geological samples from the mine or other parts of the planet. As Trent stepped into the hallway, he glanced down to the end of the corridor where two imposing metal doors could be seen, the access to the mine below concealed behind them.

Trent admired the medical bay as he traipsed in behind everyone. It was bright, clean, and looked better than some of the hospitals he'd seen on Earth. Another part of him wondered how many incidents occurred that necessitated such a setup.

"They're all yours, doctor." Fezria grinned and hurried out of the bay.

"Greetings and good day. I am Doctor Malerina Dezdia. I am the head of the medical facility you see before you. To my left are my wonderful and trusted nurses, Trenia Konaw and Miseth Vonalldu." The team nodded and greeted the doctor and the two nurses. Trent found the doctor sympathetic. She looked to him around fifty years of age, almost his height, with chocolate skin lighter than Fezria's. Her figure was well maintained, attractive curves. Her neatly styled short brown hair complimented her gently featured face, with a few wrinkles adding a matured elegance. Her piercing green eyes garnered attention, but had a kind softness to them.

"As you're aware, we'll be preforming a brief medical examination to record your current state of health, as well as to implant a small device that will monitor your vitals and your exposure to various environmental hazards from the mine. The most significant concern is radon gas, but the mine shafts are well ventilated, so you have little to worry about. This process only takes about ten minutes and is painless. And yes, we'll be removing these implants before you leave the planet. Michael, Dvenoor, and Anamara, you're up first. Trent, if you could please take a seat, I'll be with you soon." Malerina gestured toward a row of chairs against the wall by the doorway.

"Sure. Thank you, doctor," Trent responded. He headed over to the seats and sat on the second one in from the entrance. His hands rested on his knees and he watched as the others were shepherded to the examination beds. The doctor and the nurses asked their patients to have a seat on them, but Trent soon lost sight as the privacy curtains concealed the details within a few seconds. The polymer milky sheets unrolled from cylinders attached to the walls and glided around a thin rail secured from the ceiling. Another horizontally mounted cylinder situated on the wall at the height of the rails, spanned the width of the makeshift room, and could also unfurl to seal the top. *Clever. And I really hope this implant thing doesn't hurt.*

After about ten minutes, Trent's restless leg stopped bobbing relentlessly as the curtain around the bed Michael was in partially opened. Michael traipsed out and headed toward Trent with a relaxed expression.

"Your turn, sir," he said with a toothy grin.

"Thanks. Did it hurt?" Trent rose to his feet. He wasn't sure if it was the slightly lower gravity or the upcoming procedure that make his stomach quiver a little.

"Nope. Not one bit. I hope you're not squeamish though. She needs to make a small cut in your arm. Doesn't bleed or anything."

"Great," Trent nodded. As he approached the examination bed, the sheet around the first bed slid open and Anamara stepped out. She veered by Trent.

"It's not bad at all," she said, gently curling up her slender lips.

Trent smiled at her in return. He paused just outside the perimeter of the examination area and peered in. Malerina stood next to the bed, which Trent could now see was more of a luxurious gurney, and she was inputting some details on a medical tablet. After a few quick moments, she calmly turned her head toward him.

"Please come in and have a seat." Malerina released her right hand from the tablet and gestured at the bed.

Trent slinked in and the privacy sheet quickly swooshed around them. He noticed that the chatter from Michael and Anamara had almost completely silenced. With another step, Trent hopped up on the bed. He rubbed his palms against his thighs.

"How are you feeling, Trent?" Malerina asked.

"I'm feeling ok. A bit anxious I guess. It's the first time in a while that I've traveled. First time I'll be in a mine on a strange planet too."

"Ah, I see. New experiences can cause these emotions. Please remove your left arm from your clothing. I'll start by attaching this scanner around your upper arm." Malerina rested her tablet on a table next to the head of the bed and removed a bulky toroid shaped device. She unlatched it and it swung open, waiting for Trent to finish extracting his arm from his shirt. Trent held out his arm to side, giving the doctor enough space to clamp down the device.

"Good. This will only take about a minute as the device records a few measurements like your heartrate, blood pressure and temperature. You'll also feel a small prick as it extracts a few milliliters of your blood for analysis." Malerina's gaze fell to Trent's lower abdomen and ribcage. She reached out and pulled his shirt further up. "How did this bruising happen? Is this medigel?"

Trent grinned sheepishly. "Um. Let's say I live in a tough neighborhood. And yea, that's medigel. My friend gave some to me to help with the bruising."

Malerina palpated Trent's ribs, then moved up to his face where she thumbed his cheeks after noticing some faint remnants of bruising. Her startling green eyes seemed to intensify, looking beyond the physical.

"I see your friendly neighborhood didn't neglect your face either. Any pain?"

"Not really. Unless I really exert myself." *Man. Am I transparent? She can see right through me.*

She locked eyes with Trent and humphed. "There's definitely some heavy bruising on your ribs and possibly some micro fractures, but nothing too serious. Immediately let me know this discomfort does not improve within a few days. I've got something more suitable for this type of injury too. I'll have it sent to your cabin and I'll message you the instructions."

"Thank you, doctor," said Trent.

The device on his arm blipped a few notes. He'd noticed some activity as the scanner performed its tasks, but the conversation with the doctor had mostly put it out of his mind. She expertly removed the device and set it on the table.

"Please lie down," the doctor asked Trent.

Trent took an audible breath and squirmed into position. His brow unconsciously furrowed and he gently bit down on his lower lip.

"You can relax. You will hardly feel this next procedure," reassured Malerina. She took another contraption off the table. This was a bit larger than the one before, with a brushed steel cage that could securely embrace an arm. A complicated looking mechanism jutted from the structure.

"This will implant you with the vitals monitor. Please raise your arm off the bed a little for me… thank you." With some stuttered whirring, the device entangled itself firmly around Trent's upper left arm. Malerina held a thin card-like circuit board in front of Trent's face using thick tweezers. "The machine on your arm will desensitize your nerves, make a razor thin incision a few centimeters long on your arm, and it will insert this module into the opening. This module is powered by your bio-electricity and will automatically position itself between your muscles, releasing micro-strands that will interface with neural pathways. We can communicate with this device to retrieve your vital stats, along with various measurements of the environment around you like the temperature, humidity, composition of the air, and radiation levels."

Trent pursed his lips and blew out some air. "Ok. This'll be a first."

"You will be fine. Please hold still. Initiating the device… now." The doctor tapped at her tablet resting on the table, and the device uttered its tones. The servos kicked in and Trent could feel the device caressing his arm where it was going to make the incision. But not a moment later, his arm felt numb. He instinctively curled the fingers on his right hand more tightly around his thigh in anticipation of the incision, and his eyes bored holes into the ceiling.

Malerina leaned over and carefully inserted the wafer-thin module into a slot on the side of the device. Tiny grippers whizzed out and grabbed the board, slowing to a crawl for a few moments as they precision adjusted it, then paused. An extremely thin ultrasonic blade drove itself into and across

Trent's arm for a few centimeters and withdrew cleanly. Two rubbery pads extended, one on either side of the horizontal cut, and ever so slightly parted the tissue. The actuators then engaged and glided the monitoring device into the incision. Even before the pads released, the thin circuit board began to transform and reposition itself between the muscle fibers, triggered by the bio-electricity in Trent's arm. The rubbery pads came into contact with skin again, but this time to gently close the wound. Another tool oozed a thin layer of transparent goop across the cut, and a bright ultraviolet light flashed momentarily to set the glue. A few uplifting tones later, the device reset and released its grip on Trent's arm.

"And we are done." Malerina took the device by both hands and coaxed it off Trent's arm.

"Ok. That wasn't too bad," said Trent. His right hand rested comfortably next to his leg, forehead void of wrinkles. He turned his head to the left and raised his arm up to inspect the work.

"Be mindful with that. Although the glue is quite strong and will hold firmly for about ten hours, it can be worn off prematurely. But after ten hours, it'll begin to disintegrate and flake away on its own. The restorative accelerant in the glue will decrease the amount of time it takes for your skin heal, so by that time it will feel almost as good as new," informed Malerina. The soft skin from her fingers inspected the machine's work, after which she affixed a gauze patch to better protect the area. Releasing her grip, she continued, "You may sit up and dress. By the way, am I correct that you are the software specialist on this mission?"

"Yes. I am," Trent answered as he delicately slipped his arm back into his clothes. He slid off the side of the gurney and started tucking his shirt back into his pants.

"I don't mean to impose, and I am certain you'll be quite occupied, but might I ask for a favor? Our communications systems have been performing poorly recently, actually at about the same time the mining equipment started failing, and I'm wondering if you might have a chance to take a look at it. I'm afraid paying you any extra is beyond my abilities, but I'm not certain what else to do. I've asked Fezria, but she has shrugged me off and expects me to put up with it."

Trent thought for a moment. Communications affected around the time the bots went down. Well that's odd. Why the hell would these two systems be interconnected? He answered, "You know, I don't mind, doctor. I'm familiar with deep space communication protocols and such, so I'm sure I could spare a few moments."

"That would be greatly appreciated, Trent," she beamed. Her smile was infectious and transformed her personality in an instant, especially after her well-mannered professional conduct. She went on, "Since then I've had to resend several communications due to data corruption, request messages to be resent, and it has been unusually slow too."

"I know I'd definitely be frustrated. Where could I get access to the system?"

"There's a small maintenance building near the cabins. I have to send you some instructions for your treatment, so after I ask the security staff to provide you with access, I'll confirm that I've spoken to them. They'll contact you with the login details."

"Thank you. I'll keep an eye out for the messages, and I'll take a look. Hopefully I can find what's causing this and correct it."

"Great. You're all done here for now. Let me open the curtain." Malerina reached over to her tablet and tapped a couple of icons and the curtain rapidly retreated into its housing.

Trent made some quick last minute clothing adjustments and headed toward Michael and Anamara. They were conversing about something that had to be interesting. Michael seemed quite focused and nodded frequently. As he stepped closer, the two acknowledged him.

"So, big guy. How do you feel?" Michael asked.

"Apparently I'm in decent health, and you were right, it didn't hurt a bit. Little weird knowing there's a device scanning things inside and outside of me, but at least it won't be there forever."

"He's not out yet. I wonder what's taking so long," said Anamara.

Just then, as if on cue, the curtain revealed Noor and Trenia. He appeared to thank the nurse, and in a few moments joined the team.

"Is everything all right, Noor?" asked Michael as he hefted himself off the seat. Anamara wafted up in her usual effortless manner.

"It is. The scanning module had difficulty adapting to my physiology, but the nurse made some adjustments, executed calibration tests, and everything is functional now."

"Great. We were starting get a little worried about you. Excellent then. So here's what we'll do for today. First, let's have a nice meal. I don't know about you folks, but I'm famished." Michael patted his belly and the team members smiled and nodded. "And then, we're turning in for the night. Let's see." Michael looked at his watch and continued, "Yup. It's a few minutes to eight, at least in Earth time. If it wasn't for this storm, the star would be shining down on us. Anyway, set your alarms to five and head into the mine together no later than five thirty."

"Michael," Noor interjected.

"Yes, Noor."

"If it is permissible, I would like to gather my supplies after our evening meal and head into the mine. As I require no rest period, I can get a head start on analyzing and repairing the mining equipment."

"That's right. I forget that you don't need sleep. Well, I have no objections I suppose, so as long as you're comfortable doing that."

"Absolutely. I appreciate that. I am hoping that by the time Trent joins me, he'll be able to begin working with the software aspect."

Michael nodded and raised his eyebrows for a moment. "Good thinking. Irradiance wants us to get this place up and running as quickly as possible, so I'm sure this'll help." Michael peered over to Trent.

"Sounds good to me. More productive than me waiting for Noor to finish while I stare at him," said Trent, nodding away.

"And, Anamara, I'm not ignoring you. Are you good to go in the morning?" Michael shuffled on the spot to face her.

"Yes. I have what I need to complete the survey. According to the schedule, I'll be meeting with a miner who will escort me to the corridor I need to sample," answered Anamara.

"Excellent. Sounds like we're all ready to go. Let's go have some food."

The team filed out of the medical bay and down the hallway to the kitchen.

CHAPTER 14

The hum of the small refrigerator and Trent's deep unsteady breaths quietly filled the cool air of his small cabin. He sat on the edge of the mattress, feet flat on the floor, and arms resting on his knees. His back was hunched, head slumped, with small beads of perspiration dabbed over his face. The time was just past eleven o'clock. He'd hardly been asleep for more than an hour when another nightmare invaded his peace. Each time he'd have his first sleep in a new location, one of these would strike. *What the hell!*

Trent stood and took a couple of steps to place himself before the small kitchen sink. He swung the lever handles toward himself and washed the sweat from his face, drying off with a small washcloth on the counter. The louver shutters on the small window over the sink had a bright gray radiance that crept between the edges of the slats. He reached over and tugged them open. The skies were gray but substantially lighter, and the rain had ceased. It appeared the storm was moving on.

Slipping his bare feet into a pair of sneakers, he stepped outside to get a breath of fresh air. A warm calm breeze wafted into the cabin as he swung the door open, which surprised Trent a little as he expected it to be much cooler. He didn't feel the slightest bit uncomfortable in his sweat shirt and pants. The entrance to his cabin faced south. He could see a couple of security guards patrolling the perimeter of the wall far off in the distance. The clouds overhead blew rapidly toward the southwest, and the gravel between his row of cabins and the one to the south was drying up quickly. Like Earth, the atmosphere had a homey feel to it with the post-rain aroma. Trent slumped back against the wall of the cabin and found an unusual tranquility in this foreign setting.

Anamara's eyes flicked open. She lay on her side facing into the cabin, arm extended off the side of the bed. She propped herself up on her elbow and searched her mind. A tinge of horror, fear, but not her own. Her feet drifted into her slippers and she rose. She extended her arms up, and with palms forced against the low ceiling, she straightened out in a satisfying stretch. After taking a few deep breaths, she let her arms collapse by her side and hang loose for a few moments. Aside from the few appliances softly droning in the cabin, she enjoyed the soothing silence. A few moments passed and she poured a small glass water and took a few sips.

Out of curiosity, she stepped toward the window facing north and angled the louvers open. The sky had brightened up considerably. The planet's star was almost visible through the remnants of the storm's thinning clouds. Amamara's iridescent blue-yellow eyes picked through the scenery; rain water that had almost completely evaporated, activity in a cabin to her far left, and a flock of avian creatures cruising across her perspective. Then a movement caught her eye from the cabin across from her own. *Trent. It was you. Another bad dream?* She watched as he slipped outside and examined the surroundings.

Anamara strode to the door and opened it. The warm air lapped against her skin and tingled her nerves. Trent had noticed her and his smile beamed across the wide gravel expanse between them. She bobbed down the steps and approached him. Her skin hugging crop pants exposed her chins and calves just below her knees, and the matching crop t-shirt revealed a sliver of her pearlescent midriff.

"Trouble sleeping?" she asked, pausing a couple of steps away from Trent.

Trent sighed, "This seems to be a recurring pattern."

Anamara watched as Trent's eyes followed the ebbs and flows of her hair being tossed around by the subtle breeze. She took a moment to wrap some of the loose ends around her ears, and considered him for a second or two.

"Come. I'll make you some tea that should help you rest. Something I have when I need to relax and calm myself."

She stepped to his left and reached out to shut his door. In a graceful twirl, her hand swooped down catching his and she tugged him back to her cabin, feeling no resistance from Trent. Their footsteps crunched against the gravel as they covered the distance.

Anamara entered and led Trent inside. She motioned for him to have a seat at a small two person table, then locked the door.

"Please have a seat. The cabins are actually quite cozy and functional. What do you think?" she asked as she extracted a mug from the cupboard.

"Yea. Not bad actually. I definitely prefer these to those sleeping pods on the ship that's for sure."

"I agree. I like the kitchen. It gives me the chance to make my own meals, although I won't get much time on this trip," Anamara responded as she dispensed hot water into the mug from a small appliance on the counter. She then tenderly packed a tea strainer with leaves from a small wooden case on the counter and set it into the mug. "There. This will be ready in a few minutes."

"Thanks, it's got a nice aroma. And I guess you can also practice your faatausia in here without being rudely interrupted. At least I think you have enough room."

Anamara sat down across form Trent, her posture as perfect as always. She clasped her hands together on the table top. "Not much, but it's acceptable for a few basic routines. Perhaps I can teach you a few more sometime."

Trent chuckled at her comment and he sported a wide grin. He answered, "As long as we take it slowly. I'm not quite as flexible as you."

"Comes with plenty of practice. Are you still anxious about working in the mine?"

Trent brought his hands from beside him up to the table and intertwined his fingers. He gaze lowered to his fidgeting fingers and he sighed, "I don't really think it's the work or the mine. It's just strange to be traveling again. I never thought I do this again, and I kept avoiding it as much as I could. But the more I think about it, the more I come to the conclusion that it was stupid to wait this long." He brought his eyes up to meet Anamara's.

"It takes time to heal and I don't think you had anyone to heal with. That just adds to the challenge. I spent most of my childhood and young adult life on my own. I had a few friends of course, but that lack of family was numbing. For me, the opportunities to travel offered a release. I've made more friends, good friends, in the last few years than growing up." Anamara slipped out of her seat and inspected the steeping tea. "I think this is ready." She used the strainer to gingerly agitate the liquid for a few moments, then removed it and placed it into the sink. She took the mug and carefully placed it before Trent. "Let's see if this helps. Try it."

Trent took the ear of the mug in his right hand, supporting the base with his left, and lifted it closer to his face. He took a deep breath through his nostrils.

"Smells really nice. Reminds me of oregano." Trent took a sip and swallowed, followed by a hefty swig. "Mmm. This is lovely. It's sort of spicy and there's a hint of… quinine, like that flavor you get with tonic water."

Anamara returned to her seat, tilting her head slightly. Her eyes admired Trent. She saw someone unfairly battered by life just as she was. She considered how wonderful it could have been to grow up in a large supportive family. But she didn't envy Trent for this. Rather, she wanted a piece of it. Her thoughts lingered on how having many friends is nice, but the platonic relationships lacked that closeness and intimacy.

"How does your family feel about this excursion?" asked Anamara.

"You know, I'm not sure. I managed to send my parents a quick message that I was headed off world, but it was pretty much at the last minute. Actually, the night before we departed. I'm sure they've replied, but we were already in compression by then. I didn't tell my brother or sister yet."

"I have a sense they will be pleasantly surprised."

"Oh they're probably quite surprised all right. I really wish I would have—" Trent shook his head slightly and looked into the distance through the window next to the table. He took a few gulps of his tea. "I ended up doing more damage to myself, my life, by locking myself away. I should've tried to, to… restart my life sooner."

"No sense in dwelling what you could have done. It's what you're going to do about it now that counts and you've already restarted, as you put it. You have to force yourself out of your comfort zone to change, and that's one of the most difficult first steps to take. You're so lucky to have a family there for you. Lean on them. That's what they're there for, among other things. I'm sure you have friends too. There's Phil. You two seem close."

"I know. My parents were there for me, but I'm the one who ran and hid. Funny. I actually don't have a lot of friends." Trent covered his mouth with his left hand as his mouth stretched into a yawn. "Phil's cool. I've known him for several years but I don't see him that much. He keeps pretty busy flying around."

"Yes, but you've had jobs in the past few years. Haven't you met some people you could talk to or have some fun with?" asked Anamara. She felt the weight of her eyelids.

Trent yawned again and he downed the last of tea. "If you only knew even a tenth of the people I've worked for in the last few years, you wouldn't want them as friends." A sideways grin etched his face and he dropped his gaze to the emptiness of his mug, his shoulders drooped. "I think your tea is working. We've got a crazy day tomorrow. I should really head back to my cabin."

Anamara paused for a splinter of time, then reached out her right hand from across the table and wrapped her fingers into Trent's hand. "It's such a long walk," she said wryly.

She watched Trent's expression mutate from pondering the past to current tranquility. His eyes wandered to her hand and he gently bit down on his lower lip.

"Just for company," she continued, eyes beckoning, lips parted ever so slightly. *Stay with me, Trent.*

Anamara slinked around the table as she rose, remaining close to him and leaning in a touch. She knew he could feel her warm breath on his face. His head turned to follow her movements as she inched to toward the bed.

"Let's get some rest," she cooed. Her body flushed with warmth at the sight of his lips curling gently into a smile.

CHAPTER 15

It was three forty-nine in the morning and the small panel above Phil's head was chiming. Phil stirred in his sleeping pod on the bridge and he quietly moaned as the sound lured him out of his slumber. He scrunched up his face and managed to pry open his left eye. His coordination was still in purgatory, but after the third attempt, he managed to tap the intercom button.

"Yea," he said with a hoarse voice.

"Captain. I have completed the scans and the results are available," said Sheh'geetch.

Phil held his breath for a moment, then popped his eyes wide open. He struck an icon on the panel and the privacy screen slid out of his way. He protested the bright lighting of the bridge for a moment, squinting and grunting, but heaved himself out of the small compartment. Within a few steps, he threw himself into the captain's chair.

"Bring it up. What do we have?" he asked, his voice still groggy.

Sheh'geetch's humanoid digits rapidly taped at the icons on the panel and the holographic projection appeared.

Phil scanned the data surrounding him, eyes squinting, lips screwed up, and brow pressured together like seismic fault. "You've got to be fucken kidding me. What the hell are you doing out there?" His eyes bulged by the time he finished his sentences.

He could barely take his eyes off the projection as he poked a series of icons on the console, and exhaled a large breath of air. Phil paused for a long moment, waiting, eyes flashing up and across the details of the scan. His fingers drummed hastily on the surface of the control panel.

"Where are you, buddy?" he hissed.

He glanced at Sheh'geetch for a second, then his eyes wandered around for a moment. After another moment, he struck nearly the same series of icons again.

The intercom rung in Anamara's cabin. She struggled to force her eyes open as she lay on her side nearly identically to when she had awoken a few hours ago, the difference being that she had an arm wrapped around her waist, along with the ebb and flow of a warm breath on her nape. She freed her right arm from underneath herself and wiggled over a smidge to tap at the comm panel inlayed into the surface of the night table.

"Yes," she murmured.

"Anamara. It's Phil. Hey, I'm sorry to call you this early in the morning, but we have a problem. Is Trent there with you?"

"Yes. He's here," her last word almost transmuted into a question. Her awakening mind wondered how Phil guessed he was with her. She felt Trent rustling to the commotion and voices filling the room.

"Trent. Wake up. Phil wants to tell us something." Anamara tugged repeatedly at Trent's arm that embraced her.

Letting out a moan, Trent began escaping his slumber. He groaned, "What time is it?"

"Sorry, buddy. It's about four. Almost time to wake up anyway. I tried calling your cabin but you didn't answer, I... ah, guessed you might be here. Sorry, Anamara."

"It's all right," she answered, a vague smile caressed her lips. "What's the problem?"

"A big one. There's a massive rogue planet on a collision course with us."

"Man. I'm tired as hell. This is really the wrong time for jo—"

"Trent. Anamara. I'm being dead serious. I really, honestly, truly, wish I was joking."

"System. Lights. Forty percent," instructed Anamara. The lights in the cabin gradually intensified, emitting a warm butterscotch glow throughout the cabin. "Please repeat, Phil." Anamara, still on her side, now had her eyes wide open, staring at the wall on the far end.

"Yup. There's a massive rocky body headed straight at this planet. When we entered this system and prepared for landing, the nav system picked up an anomaly. I was too busy getting us on the ground to pay much attention to it. Plus the storm didn't help. Sensors aren't as affective through electrical interference. So, I had Sheh'geetch look into it as soon as the cloud cover receded and this is what we found."

Trent quickly sat up, bracing himself against his straightened right arm. His jaw hung open, heart pounding. Anamara swiveled around and sat on the edge of the mattress.

"How big is the planet? Velocity?" she asked.

"We still need to run more detailed scans and I'll need the help of the orbiting survey satellite to know more exact numbers, but it's a rocky world, larger than Earth and anything else in the Ty'kape Empire. It's coming at us at about twenty-six kilometers a second."

"Fuck," exhaled Trent. "When's this thing gonna hit us?"

"It's roughly twenty million kilometers out. So about a week. But the sooner we leave the better. I sure as hell wouldn't want to be around 'til the last minute."

Anamara twisted partially toward Trent. "That gives us some time. We could transmit an emergency evacuation request. It would take about three days for a ship to arrive to take the miners and *Ut'ahhziik* has some additional room for a few passengers too."

"*Sahh'lliita*, that cargo ship on the other pad, could transport about twenty. It'd be stuffy, but better than staying here," added Phil.

"Who else knows this?" asked Trent.

"Just you two, but I'm going to inform Michael about this in sec. Then I'll call in for the evac."

Anamara felt a surge of emotions coursing through her mind. Bewilderment. Anger. Fear. *Take it easy, Trent. I'll need to steady him.*

"I want to know how the hell no one saw a giant plant before we got here. Or before they put a fucking mine here." Trent gestured vehemently at the ceiling, his weariness had worn off.

"The Nyomor sector has hardly been studied. Almost no decent surveys have been conducted. Look at this planet. There are only two satellites in orbit. One watches the weather and surveys the ground, and the other's the comm sat. That's it. At least that survey one is useful enough to get a few more readings on the giant coming to get us," said Phil. A few moments of silence slipped by and Phil continued, "As crazy as this sounds, that planet is still quite a distance from us, so we have ample time to leave. Hell, I'd even love to stick around and watch it slam into this ball. I mean it would be a one in a trillion chance of seeing something like that. But whatever, I'll be happy enough watching the video streams from the satellites."

"Yea, I rather not be too close," said Trent.

Anamara tilted her head a smidge, her imaginative curiosity in overdrive. "Would be a spectacular sight though. As far as my knowledge goes, not a single species in our empire has ever seen two planetary sized bodies collide, other than small asteroids and meteorites."

"All right, I'm gonna wake up Michael. I thought I'd let you two know first."

Anamara and Trent thanked Phil. The two sat side by side on the bed staring ahead as if lost in a void. Anamara's empathic senses felt Trent unwind a little.

"I'm starting to think I was right to just stay at home," quipped Trent.

Anamara wound up and backhanded Trent's chest with a fair smack. He fell back with an exaggerated oomph, letting his arms ragdoll. She leapt on him in an instant, straddling her long legs on either side of him, pinning his arms down by the wrists. Her delicate auburn locks cascaded over Trent like a majestic waterfall. She locked eyes on him, with an expression fierce for a Too'ndehrr.

"Don't you dare start thinking like that," she snapped.

Trent eyes danced across her features as a grin matured little by little. He spoke softly, "You're the only one keeping me sane right now."

Anamara felt a hunger surge. Unlike her few male friends of the past with whom she'd found some intimacy, she felt a far more vibrant and intense connection with Trent. His emotions were as clear as crystal to her. And genuine. He had been through so much, yet wasn't tainted by bitterness and hatred. She knew she found someone unique. Someone she needed to save selfishly for herself. She swiftly lowered herself on top of him and pressed her lips against his. Her grip tensed around his wrists. She could feel his warmth, his pulse beating in his chest. Their lips entangled, her hips instinctively ground against his.

She pulled back a few inches, their breaths mingling, eyes admiring. Anamara ran her hands across Trent's arms and chest as she sat up. Her logical senses calmed her passions.

"We should get ready, in case Michael calls a meeting," she said between heavy breaths.

But Trent caught her off guard. He reached behind her with his strong hands and snatched her back down, their lips inches apart again.

"You said there's still some time," breathed Trent.

Anamara met his eyes for a few moments, then steadily shut. The impending doom that awaited in the darkness but a distant spectre.

CHAPTER 16

"Good morning... I think. We're still here I guess." Michael rushed into the meeting room of the main building, tablet in hand, and took a seat at the simple meeting table. His hair was untidy, shirt haphazardly tucked in, and a button was left unsecured above his belly. "So, I'm going to get right to the point. I contacted Irradiance and by now they've started the process to get a ship here to evacuate everyone on the planet. One should arrive in about three or four days. However, they have different plans for us." He looked up at the others to let the last bit sink in.

The rest of the team shot glances at each other, which also included Fezria, Malerina and Phil. Noor had been working in the mine for several hours and recently returned to the surface for the meeting. Trent noticed he looked as alert as always. Phil seemed calm enough. He did have a ship at his command after all, so getting off this world was a non-issue for him. Fezria had bags under her eyes, a frown, and considering everyone had to endure a cleaning cycle upon returning to the surface, her skin lacked a shine. She also had faint damp odour to her clothing. The doctor's expression was harder to determine. Her professional façade was quite thick apparently.

Anamara looked amazing. Not a strand of hair was out of place, and her casual Too'ndehrrehk business wear looked immaculate. Only her slightly off kilter posture indicated that she might not have gotten enough rest during the night. Trent headed back to his cabin after their pre-meeting frolic to shower quickly and change attire. He caressed his day and half old stubble and he also wore satisfied grin that reminded him of the pleasantries of the last hour. But the rogue world that loomed ever nearer, never strayed far from his mind either.

"Phil, how long until this planet gets here?" asked Michael.

"We managed to coax the weather-slash-survey sat to pinpoint the rock, and according to its measurements we're expecting impact in eight days and about nine hours, Earth units. However, we need to get our asses of this world no later than about six days from now. This planet has a diameter around fourteen thousand three hundred kilometers. It's bigger than Earth and any other planet in the Ty'kape Empire. We also have a more accurate velocity. She's incoming at twenty-six point six kilometers per second on a hyperbolic trajectory. That means that this world is interstellar, and it's not sticking around this system either. Based on the simulations, after it grazes Circulum, it'll fling itself around the star and keep on going. But as it gets closer to us, the gravitational tidal forces are going to become more and more apparent. In fact, even without touching this place, Circulum is going to start ripping apart. If you think the tremors are nuisance now, you ain't seen nothing yet," answered Phil.

"Thanks, Phil," said Michael. He took a deep breath and continued, "Irradiance has given us a couple of choices. Option one. We leave as soon as the evacuation vessel comes to pick up the mining staff. Done. That's it. The company will only compensate us for a fraction of the pay, because our contracts won't be fulfilled. Option two. The cargo vessel currently has almost two hundred kilos of processed heavy element on board. There's nearly three hundred kilos that is ready to be processed, but that equipment is sitting idle because of the technical glitches. If we decide to stay a little longer and repair the refinery, and we get that three hundred kilos of the element loaded on the cargo ship, they'll *triple* our pay." The emphasis could be felt on the second option. Michael clearly had his mind made up.

Silence washed over the room. Only the minds of those present were humming. Trent's eyes darted over the surface of the table as if reading an invisible blueprint. He sat slouched down in his chair, left hand clamped onto the side of his seat, right arm extended on the table top, digits fidgeting.

"Could we even get the refinery back up and running in a few days? Even if Noor and I could get the hardware and software going, I sure as fuck don't know how to operate the equipment," said Trent, brows squashed together.

"A few of my moles would stay behind, including myself. We only need six on hand to work the gear in the refinery. The rest is automated," responded Fezria.

"I have full confidence we could complete the task," interjected Noor. "I briefly surveyed the refinery on my way deeper into the mine. The conveyor system and equipment used to analyze the ore require repair. There are some physical aspects I can reinforce using the nanobot kit, and to save time, I can simply swap the processors for some I have on hand. I will need to bridge the existing hardware with what I have, but I could accomplish that in about ten to twelve hours. The ventilation systems, extractors, and recombination units remain operational, as they are isolated from the affected systems. I estimate that it would take Trent and me two to three days to repair this, and based on my knowledge, another thirty-six hours would be required to refine the element. If I had known earlier about the rogue planetary body, I would have begun my work in this area."

"No one could have guessed this was going to happen, Noor," said Michael. He shifted his focus. "Trent, what do you think?"

I want to get off this world now, if you want to know what I'm thinking. But three times the pay! That could really get my life back in order. And Phil could get us out of here quickly, I mean he does have the ship. Or shit could happen and we could all end up being crushed by a planet.

"It'll be tight, but, yea. Yea I think we can pull this off."

"I have a good feeling you two can do this," said Michael.

"What about me?" Anamara asked. "I can't help with the repairs. It's not my expertise."

"Sorry, Anamara. I didn't completely forget about you. If you decide to stay, Irradiance will honor the bonus pay, as long as you can evaluate two sites, one being in this mine and location delta the other. They figure it's worth the effort to return once the planet stabilizes, to start up the operations again or rebuild it. There's still plenty the element on this world."

"Delta is halfway around planet," Anamara responded, glancing over to Phil. "If I decide to stay, would you take me there?"

"Yes. Just give the word and we'll be off, as long as we can get back here before the clock runs out."

Anamara gazed off into a corner of the room for a few moments, then took in a breath. "I accept. I'll visit the two sites."

"Thank you, Anamara. I appreciate the dedication each of you have made. We're in this together. I will assist where I possibly can. Doctor, would you please inform us about your decision?" said Michael.

"Yes. Nurse Trenia and I will stay until the last moment to ensure those who remain have medical support if needed. Miseth will join the majority of miners on the evacuation ship. We'll be here if you need us, but hopefully nothing serious will happen," answered Malerina.

"I'm sure we all appreciate that, doctor," said Michael. Everyone nodded around the table and a few voiced their gratification. Michael continued, "Then it's best that we begin immediately. Noor. Trent. Get that refinery working and let Fezria know how she and her crew can help. Anamara, suit up and head down into the mine to complete the first survey, and call on Phil when you need to access the next site. Doctor Malerina, thank you again and pass on our appreciation to Trenia. I'm going back to my cabin to report in, plus I have paperwork to do. Any questions?"

The members around the table scanned each other and shook their heads. Michael gave a big nod and pushed himself up, then trudged toward the exit. Fezria and Malerina rose to their feet and headed off as well.

"If you gentlemen need me, give me a buzz and I'll get you what you need," said Fezria as she peered behind her shoulder on her way to the mine.

Trent and Noor acknowledged her. Trent felt a soft graze across his shoulder and back. Anamara had gotten up and started back to her cabin.

"Take care, Trent. I'll see you later."

Trent swung his head to face her and he flashed her a warm smile. "You too. Be careful down there."

Anamara returned his smile. Trent regarded her until she turned the corner into the hallway. He returned his focus to Noor.

"Trent, may I ask you for some assistance?"

"Sure, of course. What do you need, Noor?"

"I have several pieces of equipment on one of the levels of the mine. It took me several trips to transfer them there, but I will need to move them up to the refinery. I could do it alone but it would take me much longer. With your assistance, a single trip should be adequate."

"That's no problem at all. The sooner we get this job done, the better."

"Thank you. I agree. I just need a few items from my cabin, and I see you need to change into proper attire. Shall we meet back here in about ten to fifteen minutes?"

"Yea. Sounds good to me. I'll grab some of my stuff too."

With that said, Noor and Trent hurried back to their cabins.

CHAPTER 17

"Reporting in, sir," said a male voice through the intercom.

"*Finally*. Are you aware of the situation?" asked Maksim.

"I am. And my apologies. I did not have the chance earlier to communicate without arousing suspicion. As it is, I must be brief."

Maksim sighed, "Fine. Just give me an update. Where do we stand?" Maksim paced in his windowless quarters. It was a purely functional environment with basic amenities, including a small personal galley and head with standing shower, small desk with a seat, and a double bed. The bulkheads, floor, and ceiling were a mix of gray metals and polymers. Nonetheless, Maksim couldn't help but bring a few paintings from his personal collection and a few pots of greenery, to infuse a more civilized atmosphere into his setting. He took a sip of his freshly brewed gourmet coffee. He couldn't live without that either.

"Yes, sir. Irradiance is sending a vessel to evacuate the mining personnel, which should arrive in about three days. They also provided the crew with a choice to leave with the miners or stay a few days longer to repair the equipment in the heavy element refinery, with triple the pay. Two hundred kilos of it are already on board the cargo vessel, and another three hundred kilos are ready to be treated."

"Please tell me we'll be leaving with five hundred kilos."

"Yes, sir, we will be. The crew decided to stay, as they found the additional payment was worth the risk."

"Not a bad deal. Too bad they won't be able to enjoy it. And lucky for you we've got you covered."

"Yes, sir."

"Good. Keep me informed at least once a day on the progress, and let me know ASAP when you have a precise arrival time for the evac ship. We'll need to take care of that quickly."

"Understood."

Maksim disconnected the transmission. He stood admiring a large oil on canvas painting, *Saturn Devouring His Son*, a 1636 Baroque piece by Rubens. He took a long satisfying sip of his dark nectar and a wide smile crept across his face.

CHAPTER 18

Noor was already patiently waiting by the elevator by the time Trent had crossed through the examination unit. Anamara was also there. She was busily chatting away with Zefisia, a young Kezdari miner who would escort her to the survey location deep in the mines. Noor was holding a medium sized polymer case and wore a Salapernean smile, lips in a straight line with the slightest of curls at each end. Anamara had changed into a more suitable outfit for her first survey, light-blue coveralls and matching footwear. Trent had changed into his work clothes, consisting of a pair of beige denim pants, a durable dark gray collared shirt, hefty work boots and a large black laptop case that was slung over his shoulder. Their only matching attire were their hardhats with built-in headlamps.

"Sorry, I hope I didn't keep you waiting too long," said Trent.

"Not at all. I just arrived a couple of minutes ago," answered Noor.

"Ladies, hello." Trent flashed Anamara and Zefisia a wide grin.

"Hi, Trent. This is Zefisia. She'll be my guide in the mines," said Anamara.

Trent exchanged quick pleasantries with the short and cute miner, who had much gentler features than most women of the species. Her light chocolate skin matched her big brown eyes with long black eyelashes that blinked away at Trent as she smiled in returned. A short bob cut adorned her jet black hair and framed her round face agreeably. She wore the standard issue gray coveralls that did little to hide her ample bust.

The clanging of the wide metal gate jostling to reveal the elevator entry caught everyone's attention. Upon locking out of the way, the elevator's twin sliding doors parted to reveal a large well-lit metal compartment that could comfortably manage at least fifteen individuals. Noor was first to enter and stood close to the wall on the left, followed by Anamara and Zefisia, who took up the area to the right. Trent marched straight in and spun one-eighty to face outward. The two panels from either side sealed shut with a brief hiss, each panel with its own square glass window. Within a moment, the protective outer gate wandered across the restricted view and locked into place. Gravity eased up momentarily as the elevator lurched into action and begun descending.

"Trent. We'll be making a quick stop on the refinery level to drop off what equipment we have before continuing," said Noor.

Trent looked over to Noor and responded, "Ok, sounds good." He returned his gaze to the windows on the door panels. Dim exterior lighting on the elevator illuminated the reinforced concrete lining and occasional framework as they appeared to swoosh by upward at substantial speed. Trent was quite surprised at how steady the journey was. He recalled watching documentaries about some of Earth's mining operations many years ago. The footage denoted how cramped, dark, and rickety those elevators were.

Around twenty seconds after entering, their metal compartment decelerated rapidly, temporarily weighing down the occupants. With a slight jarring, the elevator halted and an identical metal gate began to shudder over. As soon as it did, the twin panels parted ways and revealed the heavy element refinery, situated about a hundred meters underground.

"Good day. You two can drop off your equipment here. Please follow me," said a Kezdari technician.

His outfit, although a similar gray color the miners wore, was much lighter in construction and reminded Trent of something a scientist might wear. And the refinery hardly seemed like what one would expect. This was more like a lab. The floors, walls and ceiling where either painted white or constructed of steel paneling. The substantial open warehouse like structure was well lit and unexpectedly clean. The only area that appeared somewhat filthy was to Trent's far right, where crushed ore was brought up on a shaft and conveyed into a large machine with a hungry opening. Continuing his quick scan of the place, several banks of more complicated looking machinery, the size of those tiny houses, filled the majority of the floor space. To the far left there appeared to be a packaging area and another elevator, which likely hauled the purified heavy element to the surface.

"Your gear will be safe here," said the technician.

Noor and Trent set their belongings down next to the end of one of the machines and thanked the technician who then escorted the two back to the elevator. Just like at the surface, the panels shut, followed by the gate, and then the elevator continued to descend.

"I managed to take a peek at the refinery. It's impressive," said Anamara. "If you and Noor didn't need to venture into the mine, you could have dressed more comfortably."

"I have to admit I was thinking it was going to be this dirty, dusty, oily place and it's more like a cleanroom," replied Trent.

"It has to be clean. There's some expensive and sensitive machinery in there to separate the element from the rocks and stuff. This is one of the few times I've seen it for so long. Miners aren't allowed in there, just the techies," said Zefisia, shrugging her shoulders.

"Do you need special permission to work in the refinery?" asked Trent.

"No. You need to have special training and be certified. It's stupid though. My friend Jabbora works there. He says almost everything is run by the AI, so all they do all day long is just stare at the screens to check that the machines are doing what they're supposed to. Anyone could do that with a little bit of training." Zefisia snickered and shook her head, her hair playing catch-up. "Now look at them. They're just standing around getting paid to do nothing. They're so helpless when something goes wrong."

"Hopefully we can get the systems up and running quickly and we can get off this world soon. How are you and the miners holding up?"

"We're fine. We're a tough bunch. Fezria told us about the crazy planet, but the evac ship is on its way and most of us will be getting out of here well before it hits. I have to hand it to you guys for sticking around though. I hope they're making it worthwhile for you. Irradiance is pretty good with treating their workers right. Cronus sucks. I worked in a mine that had a corridor collapse and it took the bastards over three days to rescue the miners. Three damn days! Even the emergency room wasn't stocked properly, so a bunch of the crew were dehydrated. Idiotic. I'd never work for them again."

"Well that's unfortunate," said Anamara. "I'm glad to see you made it out all right."

"Thanks. Yea. I was lucky to be in a different zone at the time. Shoddy reinforcements too. You'll see how nice ours look."

A quick weight gain overtook the passengers as the elevator came to a stop at about two hundred and thirty meters below the surface.

"My equipment is on this level, Trent. Fezria said she will meet us here and guide us to the location," said Noor.

Trent acknowledged with a quick nod. The doors did the same dance as before and Fezria, true to her word, awaited outside. Noor slinked out first and Trent followed behind, taking a quick turn back as he left the lift.

"A few more levels down for us. I'll see you later, Trent," said Anamara.

Trent beamed, "You bet. Stay safe and take care of yourselves. Nice to meet you, Zefisia." He gave the women a quick wave. Anamara gave her gentle smile and tilted her head.

"Nice to meet you too, Trent," exclaimed Zefisia, her chest swaying rhythmically as she waved back with enthusiasm.

The elevator doors coldly obscured the view of the remaining passengers, and the gate stuttered shut. In a heartbeat, the elevator dropped out of sight. Trent turned on his heels to face Noor and Fezria.

"She's cute," said Fezria.

"Ah, yes. Anamara's a lovely lady."

"I was talking about Zefisia. Not that gangly pasty one," quipped Fezria, letting out a hearty laugh. "C'mon boys, I'll take you to your gear."

As she turned to lead the two deeper into the mine, an eerie vibration grew through the corridor and could be felt before a monstrous roar enveloped the air, drowning out all other sound. The three froze in their tracks, heads turning in all directions. Trent's heart raced and his eyes bulged. Although the ground wasn't outright shaking, the intense vibrations made his knees feel like jelly. The occasional jolt felt like he was being pushed by an invisible hand, and fine dust and small fragments of rock scattered around them. Almost as soon as it came, it went. All Trent could hear was his staccato breath.

"Easy does it. Just a tremor. Like I said, you get used to them after a while. No need to worry about the stability here. The mine's structure, the walls and beams, can withstand a good sized quake. Don't be too surprised if a few more small tremors hit in the next ten to twenty minutes. They tend to come in groups of three to five," explained Fezria, her tone steady as ever.

Noor, not one to be very talkative, gave Trent a good look and said, "Well that was the largest one I've experienced since I've been down here."

"They ebb and flow. About a month ago we had a really good shaker. It actually cracked some of the wall panels. Beams held though," responded Fezria.

Trent pointed back toward the elevator, mouth hanging open. "Are they ok?"

"Oh yea." Fezria waved her hand toward the gate as if it was no big deal at all. "All of our elevators have emergency features. It'll stop, brace itself, and get going once the sensors deem it safe to do so. They'll be all right, just be bumpy for a few seconds."

"Good," nodded Trent, shoulders relaxing. "That's a wild experience. Let's just hope they don't get any bigger than that. At least while we're working below the surface. Hell, I hope another doesn't hit while we're here."

Fezria chuckled to herself and motioned for the two to follow her down the corridor. Trent took up the rear and felt a bit relieved that the mine really didn't feel like one, but more like an underground passageway between skyscrapers or campus buildings. He looked up and to the sides, eyeing the robust beams that supported the rock face above their heads, and to which the sturdy wall panels were anchored to. The main corridor was surprisingly wide, at least six meters he figured, and at least three tall, extending tens of meters into the distance with what appeared to be several rectangular openings to other sections of the mine. The luminescent tubes hanging from above, still swaying gently from the tremor, provided plenty of lighting, even though they were spaced a few meters apart. And completing the industrial décor were large gray ducts that circulated fresh air, droning away with their low pitched white noise, and several conduits that likely carried electrical and communications cabling. Hammering, drilling, and the echoes of voices could be heard resonating in the distance.

"So where are we headed?" asked Trent.

"Just through this first junction to the left. I'll drive you down to the other end where we've parked most of the messed up AI equipment. Noor has his gear there. You guys can load up the cart, I'll drive you back, and then you can unpack the goods into the elevator and return to the refinery," said Fezria.

Having reached the electric utility cart, Fezria hopped into the driver's seat, situated on the right-hand side of the open topped vehicle, Noor took shotgun and Trent sat behind her. The electric motors wailed as the cart took off and down a less attractive and much darker tunnel, its bright headlamps illuminating a few meters of the road ahead, dust sparkling in its beams. Reinforcements were anchored throughout the tunnel at regular intervals.

"Quite a bit darker down this way," said Trent.

"Yea. Shaft stations are prettier. Maintenance and producing levels are functional," responded Fezria.

After a few bumpy minutes, interlaced with a couple of large arcing turns to the left and right, the small group arrived at a large cavern like opening. Massive floodlights shone down on about a dozen mining machines that littered the area, hatches and covers displaced and strewn next to the equipment. A large maintenance shaft could be seen at the far end of the spacious cavity. Fezria stopped the cart short of a large driller.

"All right, we're here. You gentlemen hop on out and grab what you need. I'll swing the cart around so you can pack your stuff in the trunk on the back."

On her command, Noor and Trent egressed the vehicle.

"Trent, I have my equipment by several pieces of equipment. Here, over there, there, and a bit farther over by that small excavator." Noor pointed to the locations.

"Boy, you've been busy." Trent quickly scanned through the locations. "All right, I'll start over at that far end. Anything I need to be careful of?" asked Trent.

"No. Simply unplug any cabling attached to the machinery and close the screens. The systems will automatically enter sleep mode."

"Sounds good." Trent started toward the small pile of Noor's equipment by the excavator, making a quick glance over at Fezria. She had just finished bringing the cart around with its trunk facing them. He looked down at the dimly lit taupe rock beneath his feet as it crunched and faintly sloshed with each step. Trent unconsciously wiped large beads of sweat from his forehead and couldn't help imagine that if he closed his eyes, it would feel like he was meandering through a tropical destination. Even the air was heavy and humid.

Trent examined Noor's equipment as he reached the pile. Several advanced circuit boards lay about and two rugged looking laptops displayed foreign user interfaces with what appeared to be code and some graphs. He stepped over to where one of the many cables was plugged into the excavator and began disconnecting them, after which he squatted down and unhooked them from the computers. Before long he had organized the cables and snatched up the computers to place them into the trunk. He reached the cart shortly before Noor with his stack of items.

"That's one pile. Now onto the next," said Trent.

"This is much more convenient than before. I didn't have the luxury of assistance and this facility lacks a few much needed push carts. Thank you, Trent," replied Noor as he positioned his group of circuit boards and tablets.

"No problem." Trent huffed. He turned to make his next trip to what looked like a drilling unit. It was situated farther away toward the back-middle area of the cavern, near the large maintenance shaft. Having reached the midway point, it happened again. He froze.

"Heads up. Another tremor!" shouted Fezria as she leapt out of the vehicle.

This time the vibrations had a menacing growl to them, which the cavern seemed to aggravate even more. Trent looked above him, shielding his eyes with his hands from streams of dust and fragments of rock, the fine particles clinging onto his face. He teetered on jelly like legs as the vibrations shook him to the bone.

"Trent! Hit the deck! You're going to fall!" yelled Fezria, already on her hands and knees.

Trent managed to twist himself toward her, his teeth bared and clenched tightly, brow crammed together. He caught a glimpse of Noor. He sat with his back to a machine's large wheel, hands over his head, and legs apart and bent at the knees, peering up and around himself. The ground beneath them then lurched back and forth, at first with just hints of motion, and then with renewed vigor. Trent's arms flailed as he tried to keep his balance, but wouldn't need to for much longer. What he felt next turned his soul inside-out.

Ear-splitting thunderous cracks resonated in the cave-like chamber, as the rock under his feet fractured like glass shattering. Trent let out a yell that would put a banshee to shame. His terrified expression leered at his impending demise. *No! This can't be happening! It's a nightmare! It's just another nightmare! Wake up! Wake the fuck up!* Dust seemed to be drawn into the fissures, creating a mesmerizing waterfall effect. The fractured islands below Trent abruptly collapsed about a foot, bringing him down to his rear end. He winced at the impact and let out a wail. Then again the earth gave way again, this time in a disc around him, close to twice his height in diameter.

"Nnoooo!" yelled Fezria. She fell to her stomach as she tried her best to crawl toward Trent, but to no avail. "Hang on! I'll try to get to you!"

With Trent as the centerpiece, a final jolt from the quake sent the fractured bowl of earth into motion, swallowing him up like a hungry beast. A rush of air, dust and jagged little pebbles raced after him, as he vanished into the abyss. A few moments later, a deafening silence shrouded the cavern.

CHAPTER 19

Anamara and Zefisia seized tightly onto the handrail that ran the inside perimeter of elevator. Their eyes searched for answers as the booming reverberations juddered their metal compartment. Both of the women almost lost their footing as the elevator screeched to a sudden halt as the emergency breaks activated. Several ear piercing clangs lashed at their eardrums as stabilizers locked into position. A few hard knocks ragdolled the two against the wall. Anamara tucked her head into her chest to prevent it from hitting any surfaces, and clenched her teeth. Zefisia slipped and collapsed on the floor. She still gripped the rail tightly with both hands, and had a shoulder to the wall. After a few more agonizing seconds, the tremor subsided.

"Are you ok, Zefisia?" asked Anamara, panting hard.

"Yes. I'm ok, I just slipped. You?" Zefisia puffed hard like she had just run a mile.

"I'm all right, thanks. I take it that was a quake?" asked Anamara.

"No, just a minor tremor. Quakes are a lot nastier," responded Zefisia as she pulled herself to her feet. "I've never been in the cage with one of these happening. I'm usually just working on a level when a tremor happens and it doesn't feel as crazy as this." She gestured with her arms to emulate the shaking cabin. "We haven't had one in about a day or two, so don't be too surprised if we get a few more of these in the next couple of hours, like aftershocks."

"Ok, I understand. Are we stuck though?"

"No. The emergency systems kicked in, so in about a minute everything should restart when the sensors decide it's safe."

Anamara nodded in response and took a deep breath. She took off her hardhat, quickly fixed her hair, and replaced the headwear. And just as she finished straightening her clothes, a notification chime sounded and a synthesized voice warned their descent would resume. The stabilizers retracted with a fuss, which gently rocked their metal container, and within a few moments they began sinking deeper into the planet.

The trip to one of the lowest levels of the mine, almost three quarters of a kilometer deep, took nearly two minutes, and Anamara was thankful the rest of the journey was uninterrupted. Upon stepping out of the elevator, she observed the shaft station with its reinforced beams and wall panels. There was a refrigeration unit stocked with water bottles and she decided to take one and clip it onto her belt.

"That's a good idea. I think I'll grab one too," said Zefisia. She hurried over and extracted a bottle that she secured into a sling near her lower back. She continued, "It feels kind of nice here, but once we get to where we're going, the air will be around body temp. The ventilation can only do so much. Well, it could be better but it's usually just the AI machinery running around down here with a few miners to keep tabs on them."

"I see. It seems we will have quite a distance to travel, I believe three and a half kilometers. Will be going on foot?" asked Anamara.

"Nope. We got a ride that we can take almost the whole distance. Though we will need to walk about six or seven hundred meters to get to your survey spot. Those passageways have only been roughed out and the cart can't go there. It's just around this way." Zefisia pointed in the direction they should be heading and led the way. Anamara mused about how quickly the small female Kezdari could move. She liked her. There was a delightful simplicity to this young woman. She was straightforward, and someone who seemed to have no qualms about life.

The two of them walked briskly down to the end of the shaft station, passing by a small break room and one of the safe-houses. Zefisia turned right at a junction and twisted herself partially toward Anamara.

"Sorry, it's a bit of a walk to get to our ride. It'll be the third tunnel on the left," said Zefisia.

"That's all right." Anamara scrutinized the lack of lighting and reduced ductwork. Only a single row of tube lighting hung from the center of the rock face above, with a luminescent bar every three to four meters that cast a shallow diffuse glow on the floor. Their headlamps, when shone on the ground before them, overpowered the light from above. There was also a regular spacing of metal hangers, but they held nothing for the time being. "I'm glad I brought an extra light," she mused aloud to herself.

"I hate to say it, but it gets worse where we're heading. I guess if that planet wasn't about to destroy this place, then your work would decide whether we keep digging down here. If we were to, then they'd install better lights and ducts."

"From what I've been told about the rogue planet, this mine might be reopened once all the calamity has passed. Although I have a feeling it'll be a far different and less hospitable world. It is unfortunate though. Seems like there's plenty of biodiversity here that will likely perish."

"I know what you mean. There are some beautiful birds I've seen with the nicest songs. I wish I could take some home with me," said Zefisia with a hint of sorrow in her voice.

After passing the second tunnel, Anamara couldn't help but pause for a moment. She quickly extracted a device from her satchel, pressed a few buttons, and held it up to a distinct formation on the tunnel wall.

"My apologies, this will only take a few seconds. I've noticed quite a number of these xenoliths. They're unusual though, as I'm certain this area is not igneous rock," said Anamara.

Zefisia pause and replied, "No problem. Yea, the deeper we get, the more of those we see."

"Interesting. Might have something to do with the heavy element concentrations on Circulum. Ok, thanks. Let's proceed." Anamara powered down the scanner and replaced it in her satchel.

A small bright amber electric cart was parked in the middle of the third tunnel. Zefisia jumped into the driver's seat on the right-hand side and Anamara took up the only remaining seat next to her. A shallow open bed with a thin tubular rail that ran its perimeter, sat at the rear of the cart to provide a little extra storage if needed. Zefisia waited until Anamara took her seat and then she floored the pedal. The electric motor whirred to a crescendo after about fifteen seconds, as the utility vehicle hit its maximum speed no faster than a good run.

"It's not that fast. Should take us around ten, maybe fifteen minutes. Gets rough in a few spots."

"That's fine. As long as it gets us there and back." Anamara looked over to Zefisia with a nervous smile and continued, "I'm curious. How long have you been a miner?"

"Oh, let's see. About six and a half Medenza cycles. Most of my adult life."

"You like it?"

Zefisia screwed up her lips for a moment and shrugged. "It's ok. I lived out in a heavily forested region of Medenza. Ehrzadia. Beautiful hilly landscapes as far as the eyes can see. No cities nearby. No noise. Hardly any Kezdaries either. And no other species. Took like thirty minutes to get to school. It was the one school I went to until graduated to premiere status, just before I could head off to advanced education. But we didn't have a lot of credits. Just a simple life. I got tired of it to be honest. But since I didn't really have any good schooling to get me much places, I came across a mining job. It was a Kezdari company, but I've moved around to wherever the jobs are."

"I've been to Medenza on a few surveys. It's a lovely world. Unique in that most of it remains unspoiled. In a way you're lucky to have grown up in such a peaceful setting. But do you intend to keep mining? I just can't see someone like you doing this for their whole lives."

"Oh no. I couldn't do this for much longer. It's kind of neat traveling to different planets, but you don't get to see that much when you're underground. Besides, I already have enough credits to get me through the next two cycles at a nice advanced place, and as soon as I'm done this job, I'm going to apply to a couple of locations. I'd really like to—"

Zefisia hit the brakes on the cart and it reeled to a halt with a metallic whine. The vibrations from the next tremor swelled through the cart, reverberating through Anamara and her guide.

"Here we go again. Just hang on tight," instructed Zefisia.

Anamara clamped onto the handrail that jutted out from the flat dashboard of the small vehicle. But unlike the experience in the elevator, the tremor quickly intensified. Their ride rocked sidewalks, the women lobbing about frantically.

"Damn it! This is a quake! Get out of the cart, it might flip over. Crawl away and back to the tunnel wall," yelled Zefisia, her voice barely audible over the rumble.

Anamara tumbled out of the vehicle as an unexpected jolt caught her off guard. She groaned and scrambled away from and ahead of the rocking cart, her hands, hair, and clothing stained from the damp dingy earth. Out of the corner of her eye she could see Zefisia struggling to crawl on her belly toward the edge of the tunnel. After a few agonizing seconds, her guide squeezed herself against the wall and covered her head. By now, Amamara was in a seated position as well. She managed to brace herself with her right foot against a rock that jutted out of the ground a few inches. Her figure was bent over closely to her knees. and her arms fought to keep her steady.

The rhythmic lashes of the quake were unrelenting. A light a few meters from Anamara's position came loose and flailed wildly. After a few hits to the rock face above, it petered out. Dust filled the air and made it more difficult to breath. Anamara could feel her lungs burn and she sputtered a few coughs. She shut her eyes tight. Tears welled up, irritated by a haze the consistency of powder. Small fragments of rock pelted their bodies from above. Her muscles began to quiver, as she could hardly bare the force needed to keep her somewhat steady, and the vibrations did nothing to help. S*top! Just stop! I can't take any more of this.*

After a few more seconds, the quake ceased. The women stayed in their positions, coughing and panting hard, trying to catch their breaths. Anamara felt like she'd just finished a rigorous faatausia routine. She wiped her hands across her pants and then lightly swept the muck from around her eyes. Her eyelids crept open and she raised herself up a little while running her fingers through her hair to dislodge the miniscule debris caught in the delicate strands. Her eyebrows perked up to the sight of Zefisia already on her feet and approaching her.

"Hey it's over, time to get up. Are you all right." Zefisia leaned down and did a quick look around Anamara. "I think you are, but you'll need a nice hot shower to clear that muck off you." She reached out with her hands, palms up. Anamara, mouth open a bit, smiled widely and reached to take Zefisia's offer. The compact young lady drew Anamara to her feet with ease.

"Thank you," said Anamara, but almost seemed lost for words as she continued, "You appear so… relaxed."

"Ha! I've actually been through worse. Quakes this size happen about two or three times a month here, and this was a fairly short one too. But I get it, if you haven't felt a quake before, especially in a mine, then I can imagine it's a bit scary. I felt pretty much like you did through the first few. Anyway, we should be on our way, we're about halfway there."

"I guess we should continue then." Anamara took her seat and her thoughts shifted to Trent as the cart accelerated and trembled down the tunnel, the newly accumulated debris crunching and popping against the wheels. She hoped he was well and managed to stay calm under the circumstances. Her mind considered if they could remain together after this contract was completed.

"Do you have a life partner, Zefisia?" asked Anamara, turning her head slightly to her.

"I have a handsome man I met a few months before coming here. Not much fun being apart for so long though. Another downside to this job. You?" asked Zefisia, glancing over quickly.

Anamara's thin lips curled up. "Yes. I do."

Almost ten minutes later, Zefisia parked the cart at the mouth of a large hollowed out cavity, which was supported by an array of rocky columns left behind from the excavation. She followed her escort diagonally across the opening, and considered the freshly dislodged fist sized chunks of the half meter wide and seven meter tall monoliths. Powerful floodlights cast eerie shadows of the beams throughout the location. Anamara scrutinized the structure of the compacted sedimentary rock around her and she paused to retrieve the scanner from her satchel.

"We dug out this exploration tunnel about a week ago… and what are you doing here?" asked Zefisia, several meters ahead.

Anamara looked up and inhaled. She was about to query the unusual comment, but upon glancing over, noticed Zefisia approaching a tank treaded drilling machine the size of a small compact passenger car. It was parked at an angle, taking up about two thirds of the width of the passageway. Its amber paintjob was heavily worn, scratched, and pitted. Several sensors dotted the perimeter of the machine with two, one hundred and eighty degree cameras mounted near the front and rear. Two long and powerful hydraulic arms extended from the front left and right sides of the machine, jointed like spider's legs, and had their drills resting on the ground in front of the machine.

Anamara watched as Zefisia paced around the machine and asked, "Something the matter?"

"Yea. We took most of the machines that failed up to the first level so they could be easier to access for Trent and that other guy. But we couldn't locate one. We had no idea where it was and just pretty much ignored it. We figured it would show up sooner than later and here it is. Its AI must've freaked out and it hid here. No wonder we didn't find it. Almost the lowest level and in an exploration tunnel. Crazy."

"Glad we came then. You can let Fezria know. I'm sure she'll be pleased you found it."

"It'll surprise her for sure." Zefisia faced Anamara while speaking with her, but she returned her gaze to the amber drilling machine. She paused near the front of the machine and patted the metal near the fore camera. "You've been a bad boy, we'll have to get you back with your friends."

Just as she finished her sentence, the machine came to life. Its headlamps and positioning indicators illuminated the immediate surroundings, and various internal electrical systems buzzed with activity. Zefisia gasped and jerked her hand back as she retreated a couple of steps.

CHAPTER 20

Trent lay winded on a small pile of loose dirt, rocks, and plenty of dust. Most of the latter covered him. He groaned with almost every breath, coughing every so often. He opened his eyes. Then shut them quickly. Waiting a moment, he quickly opened his eyes again, only to see absolutely nothing. Darkness. Outright darkness. His breathing quickened and his heart received a new jolt of adrenaline. *Am I blind?*

He reached up to his face and his fingertip grazed his right eyeball. Letting out a reflex induced sound of protest as his dirt encrusted digit dabbed the moist tissue, his eyelid slammed shut. Trent pushed down gently on his eyelid and the nerves complained by putting on a lightshow only his mind could see. Tears oozed out of the corners of his eye. *I guess I'm not. Fuck, it's dark. Where's my hardhat? It had a light.*

Trent reached up with his hands and could only feel his soil and muck infused hair. He rubbed his fingers vigorously throughout his scalp to knock out the debris, and shook his head for good measure. The dust and sandy grains of rock susurrated around him as they fell free. He pulled himself into a more comfortable seating position and palpated his arms, legs, and torso for injuries, finding nothing serious other than a few tender spots. Then he just sat for a few moments. *Where am I? How far did I fall? Felt like I was sliding down a tube. Wait…*

It was eerily silent. No drops of water plopped to the ground. No sound of ventilation, machinery, or distant voices. Absolute silence amongst absolute darkness. Except for the slightest movement of air. It seemed to hit him square in the face and was just a tad cooler than the ambient environment around him, which was quite sweltering. He licked his lips and swallowed, realizing that he would be in danger of dehydration if he didn't drink some water soon.

"Hello? Fezria? Noor? Can anyone hear me? Anyone?" shouted Trent.

He waited a few moments for a response, but nothing.

Trent decided he should get up and feel around his new surroundings. At first he tenderly palmed the immediate area around him. Dirt, pebbles, rock fragments. No hardhat. He cautiously rose to his feet, teetering ever so slightly, relying on nothing but the planet's gravity for his sense of balance. Reaching out in from of him, his arms would have resembled the antennae of insects as his arms randomly searched the emptiness before him. He reached to the side with his right arm and his fingertips came in contact with a cool moist surface that flashed briefly with a teal glow. Trent gasped and jerked his arm back. *Did I just imagine that?*

He gingerly reached out again, slight shakiness to his hand, eyes wide open to capture any hint of photons. He grazed the wall again.

"Whoa. That's wild," he muttered to himself after seeing a light blue streak following his fingertips.

Trent slapped the surface a little harder and a larger, roughly circular, area illuminated suddenly and then quickly faded. *It's like that bioluminescent bacteria in the ocean. The texture here feels different though. Maybe it's a fungus? Let's hope it's not toxic.* Trent wound his arm up and released another slap, the hardest thus far. This time, he could momentarily see his surroundings more clearly, an almost perfectly round tunnel of which he was standing nearly in the middle of. The top was just out of his reach and was wider than his outstretched arms. *Is this a mining shaft?*

Using his new found discovery, Trent turned around to face the opposite direction and began repeatedly slapping the tunnel wall hard. He saw a small portion of a circular hole nearly above him and about the same size as the tunnel he was in. However, it was completely blocked by debris. Based on his descent through it, he figured he must have slid about ten to fifteen meters down. The tunnel was also nearly blocked in this direction. With some effort, Trent imagined that he could squeeze through, but doubted it would be worth it as the breeze came from the other direction; perhaps an exit. With a few more good smacks on the wall, he gave up looking for his hardhat. It was likely that it was buried beneath the rubble.

Trent released a big sigh, did an about face and started moving, smacking the wall with the palm of his hand with almost every step. After a few feet, the dust and pebbles thinned out and Trent noticed the organism would light up beneath his boots, negating the need to strike the wall. He was relieved, as his hand was starting to sting from the repetitive impacts. The organism was surprisingly tough, and the nearly smooth surface also made it easier to traipse along.

Pausing for a brief moment, Trent leapt up and slammed his boots down hard. A shockwave of light pulsed through the tunnel for several meters ahead. He did it again for good measure and swore there was a hint of an incline. He figured that was good news, which meant there was an exit to the surface somewhere. Undoing most of the buttons on his shirt to help manage the heat, Trent picked up the pace and strode onward.

Fezria darted to the edge of the sinkhole and yelled, "Trent! Trent! Are you there? Respond!" She waited a few seconds as she eyed the large depression. "Damn it. If he's buried under that much rock, he's done for."

Noor cautiously approached and stopped a couple of feet from the edge. His normally expressionless face now featured sharpened eyes and mouth ajar.

"Can you excavate the area?" he asked.

"We can try, but it'll take time to haul in some of the manually operated equipment. I have no idea how deep he fell. He could be a couple of meters below us, or hell, a lot more. Fezria had been leaning over the edge of the crater and straightened out. Pivoting around, she jogged toward a console station anchored to the rock face. "I'm going to ask the doctor if she can tell me what his condition is. There's a chance his implant is still broadcasting." Fezria jabbed at a few icons and waited.

"This is Doctor Dezdia."

"Mal, we have an emergency. The floor caved in after that last quake and Trent went along with it. Can you see if he's still alive?"

"Oh my. Yes. Give me a moment," responded Malerina. After a few seconds she continued, "Ok, this is what I have. I can see a spike in his heart rate at the time the quake started. That's normal for anyone. Caloric use high, in other words he was physically exerting himself. I see… impacts. I think that's just after the quake ended."

"Yea, the area collapsed just as the quake was ending."

"Ok. So he's getting hit by rocks and by fall, maybe tumbling. Nothing I would call trauma though. Then…"

"Then what?"

"Then, signal loss."

"Shit! He's dead?"

"No. Well not conclusively. I certainly hope not. The data transmission was lost. It's actually intermittent for a few seconds. These implants transmit with very low power. If he's behind a few meters of rock, the sensors throughout the mine wouldn't be able to get a read on him. Best guess, he's still alive. I'll continue to monitor for his signal and I'll have the system alert me the moment I get anything. I'll keep you informed."

"All right. Thank you, doc." Fezria struck an icon to disconnect.

"Is the floor stable here? Is there a chance of further collapse?" asked Noor.

Fezria strode back to the hole and gave it another look through. She squinted and said, "I think we're all right. Look. I think I know what happened. There's a kukat burrow running across here."

Noor leaned in then asked, "Koo kat? What is a Koo kat?"

"*Kukat*. There're these huge subterranean… worm beasts. See how this part sinks in?" Fezria pointed at a cylindrical depression running across the diameter of the crater. "That's at least two meters wide and the ugly things grow over fifteen long. They chew away at the earth creating these massive tunnels. They rarely appear at the surface, but we've found them almost four hundred meters down. Their tunnels often connect to one another. That's my guess to what's happened here. This one was just below the surface and the thin layer of rock couldn't handle the stress of the quake. And if you look at the middle there, there's another depression. There's likely another connection leading down to… hell knows where." Fezria placed her hands on her hips and puffed aloud. "I'm going to get some of the crew together to see what we can do. Assuming we can get some of this cleared up, we can send in our search and rescue drone to look for him. I hope he's all right."

"As am I," responded Noor. "I will quickly collect the rest of my equipment and head to the surface to report to Michael."

Trent didn't have a clue how long he'd been stammering along, but he could feel an ache building in his thighs and his thoughts wandered aimlessly with every step. *How long until the exit? Is there an exit? What made this tunnel? This isn't manufactured. Hey, if I take two steps right after one another, there's this neat light ripple effect. I wonder if there'll be time to finish the job. Stupid planet. I hope Anamara's doing better than me. Anamara…* His mind replayed several moments. The first time he saw her. Their chat in the cargo hold. His first faatausia lesson. This morning. But his mind was quickly brought back to reality.

A low pitched growl resonated throughout the tunnel and the bioluminescent organism that coated its surface began flashing and lighting up, gradually bathing Trent in a bright teal glow. His heart pounded in his chest and throat as he crouched down to brace himself for the incoming quake. His ears rang as the roaring in the passageway overwhelmed his auditory senses. As the seconds fleeted by, the rumbling and vibrations turned into thrusts. Although fear enveloped Trent, he couldn't help but be mystified by the light show. Similar to his accidental double step, ripples surged throughout the strange entity like tossing dozens of pebbles into a pond.

This third quake didn't feel as severe to Trent as the one before. He also noticed how nothing was dropping from the rock face around him. Whatever this creature was, was holding the structure together.

With the inability to move effectively and not much else better to do, Trent waited out the terrestrial storm that seemed to last about two minutes. As the waves concluded, the light show did not. Looking ahead, Trent could easily see the upward slope of the passageway. Taking advantage of the clear view, he shot up, and hurried into a brisk jog. His boots hitting the ground caused the organism to react even more vividly, giving the illusion of leaving a wake behind, like a ship on water.

After what seemed like a couple of minutes of jogging, the organism's activity began to peter out. So did Trent's stamina. The currents and impulses of light relaxed and faded away, leaving only the small luminous splatters beneath his boots. Trent stopped and breathed deeply to catch his breath as he leaned on to the surface to his left. The air was noticeably cooler and crisper. It made him smile for the first time in a while. But his smile was short lived.

The organism began luminescing again. As before, Trent lowered himself, this time sitting up against the curved wall of the tunnel. He waited. Nothing. Just the undulating waves of light. Nowhere near as intense as during the tremors and quake though. His brow furrowed, head turning left and right, eyes seeking answers. The ground wasn't shaking. His ears heard nothing. Or did they? Trent held his breath.

It wasn't much, but a distinct sound came from his right. He rose and faced the way he came, looking along the downward slope of the channel. There it was again, just a tad louder. The blue lighting made it challenging to see and focus. He respired again, but through his mouth as quietly as he could. Slow, even breaths. Trent glanced behind his back for a few moments, now staring at the incline. Everything seemed as normal as it could under the circumstances. The luminescence faded off to darkness this way. He returned to face forward again. The sound was more defined. Pulses. Slightly quicker than a second apart. No. Not just pulses, but ones with a shuffling in between.

Trent blinked his eyes rapidly then squinted into the distance. A dim blue disc with dark features, no more than specks, seemed to throb at the same rate of the pulses. The questionable shape grew in size, taking up the entire diameter of the channel. Trent thought some more and realized it wasn't actually growing, but approaching. His expression grew cold. He took a step back. Then another. Then began backpedaling for a second or two before pulling a U-turn and morphing his steps into an outright run for his life.

A quick look over his shoulder revealed the terrifying details on the massive creature that tore through the tunnel. Trent could make out an undulating beast with several orifices on its mug, each writhing with dozens of teeth in rows one after another, like a shark's mouth but more horrifying. On its extremity by the channel walls were numerous bulky boney hooked extensions that clawed into the rock face and propelled the beast along. As it sped forward, other such appendages gleamed into view momentarily. *What the hellfuck is that thing? This can't be happening! I can't run forever! How the fuck do I get out of this damn tunnel!*

The burrow curved gently left and right as Trent ran up its increasing slope, making it more challenging to keep up the pace. He was already panting hard and sweat soaked his armpits and dotted his face, a flow of drops streaming down his neck. The creature was about twenty meters from his position and closing in rapidly, its unrelenting cadence a constant reminder of its hulking squirming presence.

Trent was becoming winded. The muscles in his legs burned and he felt a cramp invading his abdominal area. He grunted his disapproval of the situation and forced his body to keep going. Regardless of his mental want, his body was succumbing to exhaustion and kept slowing. Then he felt a chill, but not the kind that would attack the bones. The air was unexpectedly becoming considerably cooler. *The end of the tunnel! It must be near!*

This gave Trent the proverbial second wind, and a new burst of energy coursed through him. A quick glance to the rear confirmed the alien entity had closed the distance to around ten meters. Its hideous thick skin excreted some sort of heavy slimy substance that oozed into its many mouths that belched and burbled. The goop also appeared to act as a lubricant between the wall and its gargantuan caterpillar-like body.

Then Trent spotted it. A large opening in the top section of the channel. Even ambient light from the surface made its down and cast a subtle warm glow on the floor. His heart sank. *How in the hell am I supposed to get up there?*

As he approached, he found his answer. He could make out what looked like roots hanging just below the edge of the shaft. But with the behemoth edging ever closer, he had but one attempt to succeed. Even if he could latch on, Trent had no clue if they would hold his weight or be slippery or if he'd even have the strength left to pull himself up and out of the way quickly enough. He had no intentions of dying on this planet. Not from a rogue planet. And definitely not from being crushed or chewed up by a monster exoworm.

Only a few meters away, Trent could clearly make out a series of roots that hung down at least half a meter toward the left side of the shaft. *If I run up the side of the wall, I think I could grab them.* It was now or never. Trent veered left and slammed his steps hard into the steep incline, swinging his arms up to add to his upward momentum. He tensed his fingers and opened them like claws. He reached for the thickest part of the roots he could grab. The flesh of the meaty tubers met the palms of his hands. His fingers wrapped around them as hard as they could. He swung off to the right and hung in midair, but the root held. Trent flexed his arm muscles and pulled himself up so he could shift his grip higher up.

Glancing to his left sent Trent into a panic. A single mouth on this living nightmare could swallow him whole. His body was still hanging just beyond the bottom edge of the shaft. The impact from the creature's head, if one could call it that, could send Trent flying or squash him against the rock wall.

He frantically tried grabbing at the thick root higher up and clenched his stomach muscles to pull him out of the way, but realized quickly he hadn't the strength.

The monster worm's rhythmic cadence lunged its eyeless head forward, but it stopped just short of Trent. Then he saw it. Another chance. Using his last ounce of strength, Trent wiggled to face the beast. He managed to place his left boot just to the side of its nearest mouth. When the creature lurched forward again, Trent used the beast's momentum to propel himself upward and into the shaft. He roared at the top of his lungs and forced his right arm deep into the roots where his hand found solid purchase. Bending his knees up quickly, he managed to keep them from getting caught on the monster's many boney hooks.

Trent glanced down and watched the undulating flesh beneath him push on. He looked back up and continued to climb, grunting with agony as every muscle in this body protested. The entire shaft was packed with roots. Many hung down several meters, while others jutted out from the sides. Trent scrambled toward the side of the shaft, finding two thick roots for his feet, and pulling himself up into a standing position. He quickly wrapped a pair of roots tightly around his arms and let his muscles unwind as she watched the back end of the beast slither out of view.

CHAPTER 21

The drilling machine abruptly reversed about a meter. Its right rear bumper rammed into the tunnel wall with a thud, the polymer material absorbing the impact. It heaved up its two appendages with haste and the drills on each engaged with an electromagnetic yelp.

"Zefisia! Watch out!" yelled Anamara.

"Machine, emergency shutdo—"

The left-hand drill speared Zefisia in chest under her collarbone. The force of the arm crumpled her body against the ground in an instant, slamming the back of her head to the rocky floor. Zefisia grimaced momentarily, then her eyes flared up and her mouth gaped wide open but made no sound. Her small hands wrapped around the section just above the screaming drill bit in hopes of pushing it back, but to no avail. A harpoon in a minnow. Within a second, the bit chewed at the rock beneath her back. Her face was locked in utter agony. Tears formed in the corners of her eyes. She arched her head and neck back, mouth still silently screaming. Her legs flailed and kicked aimlessly. The grip of her left hand had slipped and her right arm was outstretched, hand reaching for help.

Anamara could hardly believe the horror that unfolded before her eyes. "Zefisia! No!" she screamed like never before. She stood posed to fight, her muscles tensed, but understood that the machine could end her just as easily. Her eyes flicked over the machine and spotted a control panel on the side toward the tail end of the body. On it a palm sized red button. *I need to get to it now. Damn this machine!* She dropped the scanner and let the satchel drop from her shoulder.

With a burst of rage and a copious quantity of adrenaline coursing through her veins, Anamara launched into a sprint and bolted toward the control panel. She hardly slowed her pace upon reaching the machine. She slammed the red button with her fist. Then again. Then repeatedly.

"Stop!" she cried with fury.

The machine responded. It slowly extracted the drill bit from Zefisia's chest and sent a whirlwind of crimson droplets through the air. The splattering of her bodily fluid on the side of the machine and on Anamara's clothing was audible over the whine of the dill's motor. Zefisia writhed in utter agony as the fist-sized hole gushed blood over her coverall and hands. Her fingers did more harm than good as they reached and tore into the hideous wound. Her eyes were clamped shut, teeth bared and clenched to breaking point.

The two stereo camera units disjointedly swivelled as if on the hunt and halted abruptly. Anamara jerked her head up to the rear camera and her furious gaze met the machine's. But in an instant her eyebrows raised in epiphany.

The AI machine raised its drills to head height and the treads jolted into action. Anamara thrust her arms out and pushed off its side into a backwards roll. The possessed device narrowly missed her as it turned on the spot. She quickly jumped to her feet and pivoted toward the exit of the exploration tunnel, her long legs putting distance between them quickly. The roar of the treads and powerful howl of the electric motors boomed in the enclosed space as the machine raced after her.

Anamara shot a glace behind her shoulder and let out a cry. Dried bits of muddy goop flew from her hair that stuck to the grime encrusted skin on her face and neck. There was no way she could outrun the rogue vehicle that was closing in fast. She raced back into the hollowed out giant's room with the array of pillars. The large maintenance elevator was to the far right, at least twenty-five to thirty meters away. She could just make out the console panel to the left of the large doorway.

With a rabbit like change in direction, she bolted to the right. Anamara could hear the machine come to a sliding stop and pausing for a moment before changing course. *You might be a machine, but you are inferior.*

Anamara continued her strategy of running zigzags, pausing a few meters to the side of a column, then sprinting diagonally another eight to ten meters. This forced the AI to either go around or back up behind a pillar to continue its pursuit. With her lead having grown by almost ten meters, she rushed up to the panel and struck the call icon. It protested with a few hoarse buzzes indicating a passcode was required. With panic building, she tapped the icon repeatedly. Same result. She then hit the comm icon. It chimed a confirmation. But she could not wait for an answer.

Once again, Anamara darted from her location. The enraged machine stabbed toward her but the right armature nailed the gate and made a hefty dent. At the same time it swung its outstretched left appendage, missing the Too'ndehrr's head by less than half a meter. And rather than immediately racing after her, the fore camera jerked over to the panel. A voice called from it. A drill bit answered.

"Ro'addassh!" Anamara exclaimed a few more expletives in her native language. She hoped that someone would investigate the broken panel, but she knew couldn't wait around for that to happen. By now, she was breathing hard and sweat saturated her clothing in the roasting heat of the mine. Her lungs burned and her throat was as dry as a desert. Although fresh air was being pumped in by the ventilation system, fine dust still permeated the air, causing a spontaneous series of cough attacks.

The width of one of the columns around the midpoint of the cavern easily hid Anamara's slim figure. She had her butt against the rock, knees locked and legs at a slight angle before her, and was bent over wheezing as quietly as she could with her hands clasping her lower thighs, muscles trembling. Her sweaty mucky tangled hair drooped around her head. Drops of sweat patted against the dark brown rock at her feet. *The cart. I need to reach it. Maybe I can outrun this thing. Or block its path. I can do this.*

The roar of the vehicle approaching tore Anamara back to reality. The mining bot was headed directly for her. She wondered how it spotted her, as she thought she had temporarily escaped. As she scanned around herself, she noticed the culprits. Her dark silhouetted figure was projected on the ground by the floodlights and they copied her every move. She clenched her teeth, flexed her muscles and took off running in the direction of the nearest column.

Anamara glanced back to check the progress of her opponent. Still a few meters behind. Then what felt like a bolt of electricity surged through her left foot, as her step was interrupted by a jagged soccer ball sized fragment that had broken off one of the pillars and lay in her way. She let out a yell of pain and frustration as she tumbled toward the ground. Her faatausia training instinctively kicked in, and Anamara managed to roll onto her shoulder, albeit ungracefully. Dirt and small pebbles scattered as she used her hands to push off the ground and propel herself back into action again. She felt a throbbing in her foot and a sensation of heat, but forced herself to ignore it.

The machine had extended its drills directly ahead as if preparing for a joust. The high pitched squeal of the bits loomed far too close for Anamara's comfort. Just as she arrived at another pillar, she reached out with her left hand and clawed at the column to help her round the structure. A large chunk of rock dislodged from corner as the drill bit impacted. If she would have left her hand there a moment longer, it too would've been freed.

Anamara felt exhaustion seeping into every cell of her body. The heat on this level of the mine was manageable if traipsing through, but at this level of physical exertion it was nearly unbearable. She wheezed painfully. Her mind felt clouded. A sticky film had coated her eyes and made her vision blurry. Then the machine took another swipe at the rock, knocking another section of stones loose.

This area. The layers. The deposits are unstable. Crumbling. Anamara's legs quivered from fatigue and her foot felt numb, like it was larger than her boots. "Come get me! Over here you slow piece of trav'tehh!"

Anamara stood on the opposite side of the column from the machine and waved her arms wildly. The mining bot lurched forwarded and tried to approach her, but Anamara kept rounding the pillar to stay on the opposite end. A cat and mouse game ensued. She knew the vehicle could beat her in straight line speed, but this seemed to be a challenging task for the AI. A few chunks of rock flung off the edges of the pillar as the drill bits slammed into them.

"Yes! Come on! Get me!"

The machine froze momentarily. Only its cameras jerked around as if the AI was considering its next move. Its tracks turned the vehicle perpendicular to the column and it began rolling forward slowly. Meanwhile, its drilling arms begun methodically chipping away at the support, dislodging bits the size of fists to the occasional small pillow sized chunks that would crash to the floor. The machine occasionally corrected its course to keep its drilling limbs within reach of the objective.

Anamara kept herself just within view of the rogue driller, taunting and egging it on as they danced in a slow circle. She stayed as close as she dared to the pillar, trying to dodge the occasional shrapnel flung by the drill bits, as well as keeping a close eye on her footing. The rocky litter was building up at a rapid pace. And to combat the heat, she had managed to quickly unzip her coverall to her waist and tie the sleeves together as a makeshift belt. In doing so, Anamara noticed the neck of the water bottle was still clipped on. If only the rest of the bottle with its contents was still there. Nonetheless, her sleeveless shirt, soaked in sweat, let her body release some of the built up heat.

Waiting until the right moment, Anamara rushed over to the next pillar situated closer to the midsection of the cavern. She almost lost her footing during the scramble and could feel her foot pulsating. She grimaced and huffed at the discomfort, and betted the flesh was swollen.

As expected, the machine chased after her and took to ravaging the new beam. From a distance, the previous one looked like a trunk of tree a beaver had taken a liking to. As their dance progressed about three quarters of the way around the column, Anamara noticed that this support was crumbling apart much quicker. Then it happened again.

The cavern reverberated for the third time in a row. Anamara's breathing became frantic as she realized she would hardly be able to stay upright, never mind running away from the machine. At first the vibrations intensified and then the oscillations picked up. Anamara had her back to the last column with the drilling bot on the far side of their current beam. She decided to make a run for it and realized this quake might just save her life. Or end it if she wasn't lucky.

As she imagined, the thrusting jolts knocked her clean off her already weary legs. She fought with every ounce of strength left in her body to clamber across the next few meters. Chunks of the ravaged column gave way as she neared it. Then to add to the escalating terror, Anamara could make out the whir and rumble of the mad machine. At about two thirds of the way to her destination, she twisted her neck to look behind her from her prone position. It appeared the she was not alone in the struggle as the drilling machine teetered violently from side to side. It's apparently high center of gravity made its AI work overtime to keep itself from tipping over and yet still be on course to its target.

Anamara returned to her crawl, occasionally being tossed over onto her back. She screamed, but could barely hear her voice over the rumble. The litter of sharp, pointy rocks cut and jabbed into her skin, the sleeveless shirt offering next to no protection. With great effort Anamara crept closer to the base of a nearby column. She rolled onto her back, eyes glaring at the oncoming bot. The AI had adapted to using its drilling arms like walking sticks, which improved its traction by a small margin. The quake rocked the machine from side to side like a ship in a storm, dust and debris flying out from behind the vehicle as its heavy rubbery treads spun out.

Kicking as hard as she could, Anamara inched further back. She was now about half a meter away from the side of the column with the tottering beast just over five meters away and closing. Then she heard an ear-splitting crack that shuddered the entire chamber. And again. Small boulders plummeted from the rocky ceiling. One was half the size of the cart she and Zefisia rode on, the other twice the vehicle's size. Although they fell several meters away from both her and the mining machine, Anamara could feel the shockwaves of the impacts.

She glanced up. The ceiling was caving in. She scanned the structure of the damaged columns. The one next to her had leaned inwards from its weakened section, and the beam in the distance had appeared to have sunk slightly.

Another wicked series of thrusts jostled the earth and it was enough to set the ceiling in motion. Anamara's blood curdling scream could not be heard, only seen as her mouth gaped open. She kicked violently at the ground and thrashed with her arms as if doing the backstroke, which helped get her nearer to the wall. She then forced her knees up into her chest and locked her left arm around her chins. She clumped up as much of her shirt as she could with her right hand and stuffed it hard against her mouth and nose, her eyes shut tightly.

With a thunderous boom, mammoth slabs of the ceiling fell free. The insane drilling machine powered its treads to the max and lunged forward. But before it could move a fraction of a meter, it vanished almost instantly under a thousand tonnes of rock. The columns weakened by the bot followed suit, with the one nearest the wall toppling into the rock pile first, followed by the support beam further away. A previously undamaged support gave way as well, shattering and collapsing in place. Several of the floodlights flickered out, and the rest of the lighting was heavily obscured by the immense amounts of dust buildup caused by the cave-in and quake. A few seconds after the last of the tremors, an eerie silence was left behind.

Anamara could only guess for how long she had been curled up. Thirty minutes? Forty-five? Coughing fits ravaged her already dehydrated and exhausted lungs. If it wasn't for her last second decision to use her shirt as a makeshift mask, she would have likely suffocated in the sea of dust that flooded the air. She started to slowly unfurl herself and sit up. Her muscles ached and skin burned. The dust susurrated as it slid off her body. She was nearly buried in it. She slowly let her shirt back down and opened her eyes. Darkly shadows etched the rocky surfaces in what dim light was cast by the remaining dust cloaked floodlights. She also listened. The ventilation system still functioned and was hissing more loudly than before. It appeared the system detected the increase in particulates and began working harder to purify the space.

She slowly rose to her feet, the blanket of dust releasing its grip. Her arms hung limp by her side, and fits of coughing set her lungs on fire. Her thought's had almost all but ceased. Her body shuddered as she stood hunched over. She turned her head and shuffled over a feets so she could see across the chamber. Two pinpricks of light shone at the far end from her position where the living nightmare began, along some tube lighting that hung loose. Mustering the energy, she looked up. A yawning shallow cavity above revealed the extent of the collapsed rock. Anamara could just make out a trace of a more stable layer of sediment unaffected by the quake.

With labored steps, feet sinking into an inch or two of dust and fine rubble, Anamara trudged toward the far end of the chamber. She passed the position of the crushed mining bot and noticed one of its drill bits sticking out about a foot between the rocks. She stopped, glowered at the instrument, and spat at it. A desiccated puff of air left her mouth, along with a thin track of sticky saliva that clung to her chin. She returned to her slow trek and evenually reached her destination.

Anamara carefully bent over, fighting off the vertigo, and picked up her hardhat that flew off her head during the first encounter with the machine. She wiped the dust off the lamp and squinted at its bright lit. At least it still worked. Adorning the headwear, she wandered over Zefisia's still body. She collapsed to her knees next to her and sobbed, "You poor dear. You didn't deserve this."

Running her left hand gently across the girl's eyelids, Anamara gently put them to rest. Zefisia's face looked slightly more at peace, but her mouth still hung open, now filled grotesquely with dust. Anamara took the young woman's arms and folded them as neatly as she could across her chest, and noticed that some sort of object was trapped beneath her. She reached under her lower back and discovered her water bottle was still attached and intact. With a spur of renewed strength, Anamara quickly removed it and fiddled with the lid for a few seconds before managing to open it. She paused for a moment.

"Sorry. I know this is yours, but I need it," she whispered, then voraciously consumed the warm water. She sat for a few moments after, savoring the temporary relief the liquid offered.

"We'll come back for you." Anamara's eyes welled up with tears. She started toward the electric cart, ignoring her satchel and scanner as she passed by them.

CHAPTER 22

Trent lay exhausted next to the opening of the unusual vertical shaft he crawled up from. The twisted thick exoplanetary vegetation surrounding him had inadvertently saved his life, their roots entangled in the shaft. The cool atmosphere washed over his discomfort and he starred up at the dark blue sky that peeked through the sparse canopy. Several bright pinpricks in the cloudless sheet above twinkled, and a spectre of the bright nebulae around the star system teased their existence.

After about ten minutes, Trent eased himself up and took a few deep breaths. A quick self-exam revealed nothing too serious, mostly some new bruises, several cuts, and muscle pains from overexertion. His mouth was a bit dry, his stomach grumbled, but that fresh air gave him much needed solace. Trent glanced over at the planet's star, which hugged the horizon and cast a blood orange glow between the trees. He had at most a couple of hours of light left before nightfall and needed to find higher ground to get his bearings to traverse back to the mining facility.

The landscape was hilly and Trent noticed a good sized bump with a clearing about a fifteen minute walk away. Wasting no time, he started slogging through the dense undergrowth that covered the forest floor, listening to the calls and songs of the native avian species. The occasional unfamiliar grunt and burble kept him on his toes, especially after his recent escape from a lifeform the size of a bus.

Reaching the clearing on the hill, Trent could easily spot the mining facility to the east, little to the north, and about four clicks away. The massive security walls with their gun turrets outlined the destination, and within them the near silhouettes of the cabins, storage sheds, and main building were visible. The bright floodlights on the walls and major buildings gave the location a sense of civilisation Trent currently longed for. He raised his eyebrows in surprise of the distance he had covered in the underground race, and took a long deep breath and stretch before starting on his way back.

Trent was not having much luck making good time. Rock outcroppings, a deep stream, and unwieldy geography slowed him down to a crawl in some places, and even made him turn back once. To add to his growing frustration, a cold wind had rushed in from the south and low lying clouds began pouring into through the trees. As Trent stepped over a few large bushes, he did a double take, and froze. He leaned partially against a tree that he gripped tightly with his left hand, right arm drooping by his side. *You've got to be kidding me.*

The gray mist obscured his visibility. He could no longer see past twenty to thirty meters. Trees and rocks at that distance would pose as ominous shadowy figures dancing in the forceful breeze. Strange yelps and growls surrounded him. He couldn't pinpoint their direction as the sound seemed to come from all around him. Leaves whispered and murmured unintelligibly, with the odd rustling from a random place. Trent tried to pick up the pace as best he could, while still keeping in mind where he needed to go.

The leaves rustled somewhere behind him. "Hello?" Trent called out, only his eyes quickly glancing around as he plowed onward. The area he was crossing was covered in a slippery lichen and Trent momentarily lost his footing. He stumbled to his hands and knees, letting out a grunt, and slipped toward more level ground. A series of barks and squeals erupted around him and the activity picked up in the bushes.

"Hey! Who the hell's out there?" Trent leapt to his feet, adrenaline pumping through his bloodstream. *I hate this! I fucking hate this planet!*

Another yap came from somewhere to Trent's left. The cold air chilled his skin and the humid mist clung to his clothing, making it feel worse. He was breathing fast and his throat felt painfully dry. Pattering in the greenery around him accompanied his footsteps.

"Leave me alone!"

Then an eerie yip-yap came from somewhere ahead of Trent.

Yap-Yappie

What? That sounded human. Someone's out there. He was sure it was a voice. Or was it? Branches swiped across his body, some on his face. He tried to run but the terrain and his fatigue held him back. Bouts of shivers rippled through his muscles, knees giving away. It didn't help that the thick covering of bushes in some areas hid depressions that would leave him staggering.

Yappie

"What? Who's there?" Trent's voice was hoarse as he tried to belt out the question. His head swivelled around looking for whoever or whatever was making that sound. The iciness of the air striking his eyes made them tear up. He'd blink and the sticky film on his eyes would make his environment even more mysterious. Still hobbling as fast as he could, he used his palms to rub the muck from his eyes. It hardly improved his vision.

Yap-Yappie

"Where are you? I'm coming for you!" Trent felt nauseous. That high-pitched voice sounded almost human. Maybe it was. He called out again, "I hear you! I'm here for you!" He swore he was running in circles. The trees all looked the same. Did he already pass that one? What about that rock? His mind raced in all directions.

"Ok honey. You two have a nice time. Take some photos while you're out there," said Vivian. She finished arranging her large beach towel on the fine light rose sand that ran for a several kilometer stretch along Bu'onatia Lake. The body of water on Medenza, the Kezdari's second homeworld, was more like a small ocean. Hundreds of tourists dotted the beach and surfers coasted along giant rolling waves. With nary a cloud in the azure sky, Lanamaranda, the Kezdari system's star, shone warmly down in the early afternoon. Vivian adjusted her favorite floral adorned bikini, slipped off her flip flops and made herself comfortable on the towel. Trent admired his wife affectionately, her jet black hair splayed out around her head.

"We sure will. Won't we darling?" replied Trent, as he looked as his daughter.

"Yes! I wanna take the pictures though," said Isla.

"I think we have a budding photographer here. Ok, you can take the pictures, but be careful with daddy's camera. See you soon, sweetheart." Trent handed Isla his camera.

Vivian smiled and waved the two off, "Bye. Be back around five. We have reservations."

About halfway up to a lookout on top of a hill that overlooked the beach, Isla squatted down and took a photo of a grouping of small bright orange flowers by the pathway. The twelve year old flicked a few loose strands of her long golden brown hair out of her face as she leaned in to smell the small blossoms. The large brim of her white woven straw hat curled up at the front as it pushed gently against a bundle of fine branches from a bush nearby.

"They smell so sweet," said Isla.

Trent grinned. "Did you get some nice pictures for mom?"

"I sure did. She'll love them." Isla replaced the lens cap and slung the camera strap over her neck. She hopped to her feet and continued to skip along the path.

Trent watched her lovingly as she trotted along in her pastel t-shirt with a graphic of her favorite cartoon character on the front, and her dark violet shorts with numerous pockets. A pair of colourful sandals fit the young girl's personality.

Trent's mobile sounded off. He retrieved the device from his pocket and answered it. "Hey babe."

"Hey, how are you two doing? Conquered the mighty hills yet?" asked Vivian.

"I think Isla has. She's loving it up here. I think we'll have a few hundred pics to go through though. She's quite trigger happy. Wish you were here. It's actually quite nice in this area. The trees are amazing and it smells so fresh."

"Oh you know me, I'm not one for these hikes. Give me my beach any day. I found a cute bar here and they serve a bunch of drinks from other systems. Lucky for me, they have margaritas and they're nice and cold. It really heated up on the beach but I'm not complaining. I'm buying you a drink when you get back. Lots to choose from."

"I'm looking forward to it. We should be back in a couple hours anyway. Isla will tire out by then."

"Well it sounds like you two are doing fine. I just wanted to check in. Send her my love. Love you hon."

"Love you too, darling." Trent disconnected and stowed his mobile.

"Hey, photobug, that was your mom. She wanted to know how we're doing," said Trent, looking up and along the path, Isla nowhere in sight.

"Isla. Where's my little photographer?" Trent paused. "Isla? Hey. Where are you?" A tinge of worry crossed his face.

Trent started scanning the area, calling Isla's name with increased urgency. He hurried along the worn pathway and looked deeper into the forest that lined it. Although they had passed a few other beings earlier, he hadn't seen anyone for a while. A clearing up ahead presented itself and Trent rushed toward it in hopes of seeing Isla.

Upon entering the small meadow, a high pitched scream came from nearby, somewhere toward his right.

"Isla!"

Trent rushed toward the sound. He heard another scream. It was Isla and she was closer. His feet carried him as fast as they could through the denser vegetation and rougher terrain. To his left, a rocky cliff face covered with moss loomed over him. As he continued along its edge, a commotion could be heard coming from a cavern like opening. Sounds of scuffling, growling, and grunts, along with whimpers and wails could be heard. Then Trent froze in outright horror, eyes bulging out of his head.

A lanky marro, a dog like species native to Medenza, just larger than a Great Dane, straddled over Isla's body. The sickly looking creature's narrow long maw, with numerous tiny razor sharp teeth, trickled with bloody saliva. Its shallow head and short pointed ears gave the ravenous beast a demon like appearance, along with its long bony neck. Its malnourished body prominently featured its ribcage and spinal column, and from it extended long angular legs with large paws, claws like a hawk's. Two short tails whipped at the air as it noticed Trent appear by the entrance of the cave.

Trent roared and sprinted toward the gray mass with dark green stripes randomly streaming along its scaly hairless body. The powerful rugby like tackle launched the monstrosity off Isla and took it by surprise, a yelp escaping from the creature's mouth. They came to a sliding halt along the rocky chasm floor coated in a thin layer of soil. The beast kicked, pawed, and snapped at Trent. His left hand tightened around the animal's neck as the right repeatedly pummelled at its ribs and stomach, while Trent roared at the top of his lungs.

The marro writhed in pain and tossed about, freeing itself from Trent's grip. It righted quickly, hissing and growling, gaping its maw toward him. But a powerful backhanded fist to the side of its head sent the ugliness staggering momentarily. Trent sprung to his feet and missed with a kick that would've sent a football clear out of a stadium. The animal reeled to its hind legs, showing considerable adeptness to balance, and swiped its long fore legs and claws at Trent. It landed a swing that carved a few crimson lines into his right forearm, but Trent felt no pain in his rage mode.

The creature took another swipe with its left foreleg, but Trent managed to grab a hold of it with both hands. He took the beast's momentum and flung it to the ground. The marro's leg extended outward as it landed on its belly, with most of Trent's weight now on its back. With a sound like a bundle of celery being torn in half, a bone in the beast's upper leg snapped. A long hoarse sheik reverberated in the cavern.

Trent scrambled over the wounded animal's body, forcing it down with as much of his weight as he could. His hands clamped around the marro's nape as best they could as it struggled and wriggled to free itself. Trent's furious gaze spotted a large jagged stone within arm's length. He released his right hand from the beast and snatched up the rock. He swung his arm over his head, roaring with pure anger, and propelled his arm down with every ounce of his strength. The first blow grazed the side of the marro's head, but lacerated its tough skin. The creature yelped. Almost before it could do anything else, Trent brought the rock down square on the top of its head. The creature snarled, but with less enthusiasm. Then the rock struck again. The creature hissed and convulsed weakly. Again. Again. Again.

Trent screamed, spit flying from his mouth. He breathed hard, releasing the stone from his hand. He looked at the stillness, thick blood seeping from its cracked skull. He pushed himself off the carcass and quickly located Isla, rushing to her. He dropped to his knees and scooped her up into his arms, calling her name. Her tiny limbs were covered in lacerations and stained with crimson. Her t-shirt with her favorite character had been heavily shredded. Her face was covered in blood and soil. And a gash across her throat throbbed and slowly discharged her life force.

"Dad… daddy…"

On his knees, armed curled into his chest, Trent wailed at the top of lungs. Several small brightly speckled lifeforms, the size of ferrets, rushed together and scurried quickly away. Tears ran down Trent's face as he wept.

After a few moments, Trent regained most of his composure, his face of sorrow. He reached up and massaged his temples with his fingertips. His head pounded and his mouth was bone dry. His eyes slowly took in his surroundings and discovered he was positioned in a clearing. Off to his right was a jungle of trees. And to his left, the *Ut'ahhziik* rested calmly on its landing pad about sixty meters from his position. If he hadn't come back to his senses sooner, he might've gone too far, passing by the mining facility. Trent raised his eyebrows and began to smile. Then chuckle. Ending with him almost doubled over with laughter. He staggered to his feet and stood for a moment.

A bright streak in the sky to his upper left caught his attention. *I should make a wish. I need something better than this shit.*

The streak became more pronounced as the seconds passed by. Trent tilted his head and furrowed his brow as he followed the path of the object. Brighter still. Faster. Larger. Racing... toward him. His mouth hung open as his head tracked the glowing orb speeding toward the ground. In the last fraction of a second, it seemed to tear through the air instantly and plow directly into their way off this planet.

The *Ut'ahhziik* vanished in a spherical inferno of blinding light. Before Trent could even react to or hear the explosion, darkness.

CHAPTER 23

After quickly but cautiously collecting the rest of his equipment from around the disabled mining equipment and buckled floor, Noor was driven back to the main personnel elevator while Fezria stayed behind to provide instructions for the excavation crew. Noor dropped off the tablets, laptops, and circuit boards on the refinery level, then headed over to Michael's cabin to inform him about Trent. After a few minutes of detailing the mishap, Michael leaned back into his seat and shook his head in disbelief.

"When shit rains, it's diarrhea," exclaimed Michael, slapping his tablet down on the small table in his cabin. He sighed and continued, "Seems this planet is cursed. Hell, it's doomed. Shit. I hope he'll be all right. I wouldn't want to die on this planet. Well, Noor, sitting on our asses won't help. There's nothing we can do for Trent at this time and I'm sure Fezria is doing everything she and her miners can. Since we haven't got a clue if he'll show up at all, can you get that damned refinery working?"

"I should be able to replace the hardware as planned. The software might be problematic," Noor responded.

"Can't be that damned tough. I mean you seem to know a lot about the hardware."

"True. Salapernean technology. However, I will conduct some research and attempt to install and test the systems. Perhaps I will be able to restart the refinery."

"It doesn't have to look pretty. It just needs to work. Even if it isn't perfect or as easy to use or whatever. As long as that machinery can function to get some of that element refined, we'll be in good shape. If we've come this far, had gone through this much, it'd be a real shame to leave that much of it behind. Our bonuses depend on it. Otherwise, we've really come for nothing."

Noor listened attentively and nodded. "I understand, sir. I will double my efforts. I am indeed looking forward to leaving this world, as I'm sure everyone else is too. Have they sent the evacuation vessel?"

"Yes they have." Michael picked up his tablet and entered a few commands. "Looks like it'll be here in about two days, twenty-two hours. You're not intending to leave early are you?" He looked up at Noor with a serious mug.

"No, sir. I was just curious."

"Great. Great. Ok, good. Keep me informed of your progress. I'll probably head to the refinery later after I've reported in." Michael shot Noor a quick smile.

Noor shuffled out from under his seat and left Michael's cabin.

The console's incoming communications icon lit up and an auditory signal chimed. Maksim glanced over to the readout eyeing the identification code. He furrowed his brow and tapped the icon.

"You're a bit early."

"Sorry, sir. We have a… another situation," said a male voice.

Maksim sighed and glanced around at the windows on the bridge. The massive gas giant still loomed next to the ship. After a moment he continued, "What do we have now."

"Trent, the software developer. There was an accident, a quake in the mine. The floor collapsed—"

"Get to the point," urged Maksim.

"Yes, sir. We're unsure if he's still alive, so we might not be able to get the refinery restarted."

Maksim stood straight and cupped his hands behind his back, stroking his ring with his thumb. He began pacing around the bridge.

"Sir?" asked the male voice.

"You told me you'd let me know when that evac ship'll arrive."

"Yes, sir." The male voice was accompanied by uneven breaths. "The ship will arrive in two days and twenty-two hours."

Maksim continued pacing. As he traipsed by the windows facing the massive world, he peered up at it, his face lit by the pastel glow of the multitude of colors from the swirling clouds. "Good. Then you have exactly two days and twenty-two hours to get that fucking refinery working. If you don't get that fucking refinery working, then I will personally ensure that the big planet on its way is the last thing you'll see. I'm not leaving this godforsaken shithole of a system without that load of the element. Do I make myself clear?"

A couple of quick nervous breaths could be heard before the male voice answered. "Yes, sir. I will ensure the refinery is operational by the time you arrive."

Maksim forced a smile on his face, even though his operative wouldn't see it. "I was hoping you'd say that." He turned toward one of the crew members behind the sweeping control panel and swiped his extended index finger across his neck. The crew member gave a quick nod and disconnected the transmission.

CHAPTER 24

The elevator's twin panels pulled apart and the security gate shuddered open at the surface. A dishevelled Anamara stood stooped over in the center of the compartment and begun slowly stepping out. Two pairs of cool hands rushed in to offer support on either arm. Malerina's nurses, Trenia and Miseth, guided the frail woman out into the open.

"System. Bypass security protocol on my authorization. Ehn'gezda kii kehrleck," stated Fezria.

"Voice authorization accepted. Security protocol bypass initiated. Opening airlocks and disabling scanning systems," responded a synthesized voice.

"She's dead," whispered Anamara as her eyes shifted to Fezria.

Fezria frowned and swallowed hard. "We know. We're glad you're ok. Mal's going to take good care you."

"I want off this nehm'ormaliish planet," she hissed.

"At this point, we all do."

Malerina appeared at the far end of the cleaning unit, a stunned look on her face. "Oh my! You poor dear. Bring her through. The bed is prepped."

The nurses acknowledge her and helped Anamara though the unit and into the infirmary. Malerina rushed for a drink she prepared a few moments earlier and returned with it, handing it to Anamara. "Drink this water, Anamara. It's infused with electrolytes, which should improve your condition. We'll hook you up to an IV next to get you rehydrated." Anamara took the glass and greedily drank it the fluid.

"Where's Trent?" asked Anamara between a gulp.

Malerina looked her in the eyes and hesitated to speak.

"Where's Trent?" Anamara asked again with emphasis on the two words.

Malerina sighed. "As far as we know he's ok—"

"What happened?" Anamara's voice conveyed her irritation and her eyes glowered.

"The floor caved in and he got sucked down with it," stated Fezria as she walked in to check on her. "That quake, the one after the small tremor you probably felt during your elevator descent, weakened the floor above a kukat burrow. In case you're wondering, kukat's are these huge subterranean worms. And I mean huge. Anyway, Trent was standing in the wrong place at the wrong time and away he went. I have a team that'll clear a path through the debris so we can get a better idea of the situation. But Mal's right. His implant registered some bumps and bruises, but he should be fine. We know some of the worm tunnels head out to the surface, so maybe he got lucky and he'll walk right out of one."

Anamara slunk her shoulders in dismay, then gazed up at Fezria, her thoughts shifting to another individual. "We should get her to the surface."

Fezria answered more softly, "I've already sent a couple of miners from the level above to retrieve her. She'll get a proper farewell ceremony."

Anamara nodded.

"I'll leave Anamara in your capable hands, Mal. I've got a bunch of work left with this evac." Fezria pursed her lips and hustled off.

Laying on the gurney, Anamara felt marginally better as the IV pumped much needed fluids and nutrients into her system, and the pain killers she got eased the burning and throbbing from her cuts and bruises. Several larger gashes had been attended to, but the nurses were busily working away on the rest. A figure appeared enthusiastically by the end of her bed that caught her attention.

"Anamara, I have great news and I thought you should be the first to know. Trent's implant just registered in our system," announced Malerina. She excitedly clutched her medical tablet in front of her chest with both hands.

A look of relief spread across Anamara's face. She lowered her head back onto the pillow. "Thank you, doctor. I needed to hear that. I assume he's well?"

Malerina beamed. "He's stable and moving around. In fact, he's somewhere near the landing pads. His blood sugar is low, that is, he's hungry, and he's dehydrated. So whatever happened to him, wherever he's been, has taken a bit of a toll but nothing serious at least." Malerina's eyes scanned Anamara's arms, now considerably cleaner than when she first saw her. "Nurses, how she coming along?"

Miseth answered, "Coming along nicely. Anamara's a tough a lady. The most severe lacerations, which thankfully weren't that bad, have been stitched up and we've begun tending to the minor cuts. Anamara, how's the pain?"

"Much more manageable," Anamara nodded.

"Thank you, Miseth and Trenia. Once the nurses have finished, you're welcome to have some food. You must hungry," Malerina presumed.

"A little yes. I'd really like a shower too."

"Of course. If you're gentle with the adhesive, a shower is accept—"

Everyone froze, eyes darting around. A muffled yet thunderous roar rocked the facility.

Anamara was still frazzled by her last experience and a dread overcame her expression. She sat up on her elbows and asked, "Another quake?"

By the time she finished her question, the noise subsided.

Malerina looked toward the doorway of the infirmary, eyes squinting. "I don't think so. That sounded more like an explosion."

CHAPTER 25

"Commander. We have returned to normal space. Deceleration initiated. Time to destination, fourteen kunors," announced First Pilot Ekor in their native Vadokor language.

"Scan the surface for hostile structures," ordered Command Ubikor of the warship *Keetovor*.

First Security Officer Atikor diligently manipulated the three dimensional holo-controls that surrounded the majority of his station.

"Located. There are seven plasma cannons built into the perimeter wall of the mining complex. No immediate threat. Recommend landing party disable the weaponry using the shuttle. There are also two vessels occupying the only two landing pads on site. One is a small passenger transport, the other is partially loaded with purified heavy element. Both vessels are Too'ndehrrehk origin."

"Destroy the passenger craft. Leave the other."

"Acknowledged. Firing."

Atikor swiped his alien digits over a symbol floating in midair and watched the holographic display animate the flightpath of the projectile. A simulated flash triggered him to report. "Target destroyed."

"Is the intel on the satellites current?" asked Ubikor.

"Affirmative. Two in orbit. A communications and geological survey satellite," reported Atikor.

Ubikor lifted his large hand like appendage and a holo-projection of various symbols appeared in midair. He flicked at one of them and spoke, "Recovery team assemble as planned." He rose out of his large commander's seat and headed off the bridge.

Within a minute, Ubikor reached one of the hanger bays on the ship. A stealthy angular vessel, shades of dark metallic alloys, about twenty meters long, eight wide, and about the same at its tallest point, awaited him and five other Vadokors. Around a dozen thruster like vents, with vertical grates blazing in a fluorescent orange-yellow, strategically dotted the shuttle's exterior. Several small winglets, two to three meters in length, jutted out from the fore, middle and aft sections. The thick hatch door at the aft, parted in the middle with a zigzag like cut, hung wide open.

Ubikor motioned with his head for the team to follow him into the ship. Once they were in, the hatch doors rapidly sealed shut and the shuttle's lower thrusters thundered to life, the glow from the vents intensifying. The craft launched off its six stubby landing feet that tucked away the moment they cleared the floor with enough room. The hanger bay doors, similar in appearance to the ones on the shuttle but supersized and horizontally oriented, flipped open to reveal the dark vastness of space. The rear thrusters boomed and shone brightly as they accelerated the ship out of the bay. A green plasmic glow rippled around the contour of the shuttle as it passed through the force field that kept the atmosphere within the mothership. After safely clearing the hanger doors by a fair margin, the two large panels closed in on each other.

"Dememek," Ubikor spoke over the pilot's shoulder, "you have been sent coordinates for the plasma canons situated along the perimeter wall of the mining complex. Display them."

Dememek tossed a few items to the side in her holo-display and located the schematic of the mining facility.

Ubikor pointed to the west-most wall. "Bring us through this end. Destroy the three plasma cannons nearest to this location. Drop us off here. Continue on and eliminate the remaining plasma cannons, then return to *Keetovor*."

"Understood," acknowledged the shuttle pilot as she entered the flight path.

Ubikor pushed through his team to the front of the line by the rear hatch, and clamped onto a handrail suspended overhead. He, along with his troop, wore their Romanesque style helmets, made of dark gray metals and polymers. The angular design protected the back and sides of their heads, with a portion that swooped down across their foreheads. A functional beam jutted down between their large black eyes, no noticeable pupils or irises, just three eyelids, two inner membranes and one outer for protection. With no noses or even nostrils, only their thin long mouths completed their faces. The edges of their lips connected to a shallow depression that angled down slightly and across the jaw line. When speaking, a membrane would stretch between the top and bottom sections, making their jaw look puppet like.

Their chests were proportional to those of an extreme body builder's, substantially bulky shoulders and large thighs. Flexible armor plated their torsos, from which extended their long and powerful arms and legs, also shielded by protective gear. Their lower arms were wrapped in modern gauntlets with deadly surprises concealed. But unlike most species, the Vadokor had four equally sized and highly dextrous digits that extended from their palms, similar to how a crab's legs spread out from their undersides; their immense size and strength could crush a human skull with little effort. A gap along the sides of the armor around their upper arms allowed a spiny edge to protrude that the creatures could flare out or retract. Large feet, somewhat similar in design to their version of hands, were encased in durable boots. These beings had tough exoskeletons, shades of dark caramel and celadon, and all of this stood in a package over eight feet tall.

The agile shuttlecraft veered toward the planet's atmosphere and a fiery glow encompassed its exterior. Holographic projections displayed the view and the pilot watched attentively, correcting for the minor turbulence. The weather in the vicinity of the mining complex was breezy, cloudless, and the sun had just set. Grazing the treetops, the pilot saw the security wall approaching quickly, the holo-projection highlighting the location first three guns.

"Commander. Firing on initial targets. Deployment in twelve kunors," said the pilot.

"Team at the ready," stated Ubikor, and the team grunted in unison to acknowledge him.

The high velocity kinetic weapons could be heard firing. Two shots for each plasma cannon. The holo-projection conveyed the destruction. The projectiles obliterated the cannons and sections of the wall, large chunks plunging into the compound.

"Targets destroyed. Deployment in six kumors."

The craft lurched over the wall and extended its six landing feet. Within a few seconds the pilot set the ship down and the rear hatch flew open. Ubikor and his team rushed out of the aft section and onto the soil of the compound, dust from the explosions adding cover. The commander strode several meters away and crouched on his right knee. The other team members formed a circle relative to his position and faced outward. The hatch doors shut with a heavy metal clang and the shuttle lifted into the air. As the craft continued its mission, the twin shots could be heard ringing out, along with their respective explosions instants later. Within no time at all, the shuttle's engines roared with a crescendo and it disappeared briskly into the starry night sky.

"Secure the facility. Move out." Ubikor got up, spun around and sprang into a run, his long powerful legs moving him at unimaginable speed with ease. Two of the Vadokors headed toward the northern side of the facility, and another two toward the south. The remaining fighter took Ubikor's six and hung back a few meters.

By now, alarms wailed throughout the mining facility, and stunned guards on the grounds could be seen scrambling to figure out what happened.

Several others were exiting the security quarters, weapons drawn. In all, almost two dozen were prepared to defend the area.

Six of the guards rushed the area between the cabins and spotted the two giants galloping toward them. One of them took aim and fired off a few rounds from his pistol. Several shots found purchase, but the bullets simply ricocheted off their armor. Worst of all, the creatures didn't even flinch. The Vadokor nearest him charged. A few more shots rang out that struck the chest plates, but the small firearm soon clicked its absence of ammunition. At full sprint with his massive left arm and four digits extended, the alien fighter wrapped its hand around the face of the guard. The momentum lifted the Kezdari's body off the ground and the back of his head slammed into the exterior of a cabin with a crack. Several of the other guard retched at the sight of their colleague's head being crushed nearly halfway in, blood, brain matter, and fragments of skull trailing the lifeless body as it slid down the side of the cabin wall.

The Vadokor's teammate follow up the carnage by extending his matt black foot long blades from his gauntlets and ramming one through the chest of a human guard. A sudden gasp of air burst from him as his face crumpled in pain. The giant let the body slip from the blade as he took a swing at another who managed to block the attack by grabbing onto the Vadokor's arm. But the massive creature's heft hurdled the human guard to the ground with a thud. The giant beast swiftly brought up his knee, took aim with the sole of his foot, and unleashed it like lightning bolt from cloud to ground. The thunderous impact left the man's head viciously deformed. Pieces of shattered skull, dislodged brains, and blood soaked the area like a bomb blast.

The remaining three guards screamed and wailed at the top of their lungs as they scrambled away from the fruitless battle. The two Vadokor fighters stood side by side, each raising their gauntlets and firing multiple rounds. The energy weapons pinged with a hollow metallic sound and the projectiles ripped through the clothing and flesh of their victims.

On the south end, the next pair of Vadokors rushed their prey amongst a setting of scattered supply sheds, racks of reinforcement beams, and a few pieces of machinery. The two beasts stormed their way across and chose to mirror each other with blades extended, darting in between the objects dotting the field. The Irradiance guards took cover behind the various items and shot indiscriminately at the intruders. Most missed, but some shots met their targets, only to be ricocheted off the durable alien armor.

As the two titans encroached on the guards, one eyed the other and indicated with a quick glance toward three huddled behind a stack of heavy iron beams. With a grunt to acknowledge the tactic, the two began flanking the trio, pinning them down against a large supply shed. One guard, a heavyset Kezdari, whipped his gun at the Vadokor approaching from the left, striking the tough padding on its right arm. The guard's mouth and eyes gaped open in terror, his arms outstretched with legs bracing for a hit, did nothing to keep the invader from spearing him through his mouth. The razor sharp edges sliced easily through the back of his throat, destroying a vertebra in his neck. With a sudden jerk to the right, the beast freed his blade through the side of the guard's face and head.

Meanwhile, the Vadokor on the right dealt with a human guard who wielded a large baton and flung it around frantically. The giant towered over its tiny human opponent, and although nearly expressionless, seemed to find the situation amusing. With a swift motion, the predator caught the guard's left wrist and with his other hand clasped onto his shoulder. A horrid crunch came from bones within the human's arms, as the beast jerked his hands together. Blood rapidly soaked the sleeve of the guard's uniform, his arm bent in a terribly unnatural angle. The shrieks of pain didn't deter the Vadokor from shoving his victim back a few feet, then explosively kicking him in the gut. The guard doubled over, lifting a couple of feet off the ground, while expelling the contents of his stomach with haste. Sprawled out on the ground with his face embedded in the fine sandy gravel, the Vadokor used the energy weapon in his gauntlet to blow a fist size hole in the back of the man's neck.

The third guard, now the attention of the two invaders, threw his firearm on the ground before him and dropped to his knees, bawling almost incoherently for his life, repeating his surrender. His hands were clasped, fingers intertwined tightly, tears running down his face. A few shots rang out from the right, bullets grazing the Vadokor fighter nearest to the shooters. He glowered over at those guards and bolted for them, his teammate implicitly getting the honor to impale the pleading Kezdari through the top of his skull with his gauntlet blade, several inches of it jutting out from under his chin. His appeals for life fell silent as the beast retracted his weapon and took off after his comrade. The guard's carcass froze in place for a beat or two, toppling over a few moments later.

Heading up the fairway between the cabins and the supply zone, Ubikor and his teammate cleared the area with gruesome efficiency. A female Kezdari guard's body lay right-side up and splayed out on the ground with her head wrenched around a hundred eighty degrees and embedded in the moist mud. The skin around her neck had torn in several places. The upper torso of another guard was separated by over a foot from the lower half of his body, entrails spread across the divide. Several other corpses dotted the field. An arm severed here, a leg over there, and a chunk of face missing off another.

Ubikor and his teammate were closing in on the main building, now about thirty meters from their position, when his shoulder pad was met with a substantial impact. A loud crack echoed a second later as the sound caught up to the action. He released a grunt as the hit jolted him slightly.

"Sniper. He's mine," Ubikor stated. His fighter escort relayed the details to the rest of the team.

Ubikor lunged ahead and spotted the sniper standing with a heavy rifle by a shed near a collapsed section of the perimeter wall, beyond which would have been *Ut'ahhziik*. Another shot struck his arm, the large caliber projectile sending it flailing back momentarily. Regaining his pace and extending his right arm, he took quick aim of the guard who had shot him twice. Ubikor realized he'd need to take down his adversary quickly, as a well-placed shot to his head could end him. But before the guard could pull the trigger again, the gauntlet's energy weapon hurled a small bright orb at immense speed toward the Irradiance employee.

The power of the blow shredded a football sized hole in the guard's abdomen on the left side. The human staggered backward, thudding against the side of a shed. He struggled for air, but the tremendous pain had a relentless stranglehold over him. The exterior of the small building held him up for a few seconds, after which the man, blinking feverishly and beginning to tremble, slid downwards, rifle dropping to the ground next to him.

His legs skidded outwards, right leg remaining outstretched, left buckling underneath his weight. Minuscule whimpers escaped his throat as his lungs reflexively fought for a fresh breath. His head and eyes drooped to examine his wound, but reeled back upon the realization this would be the end of him. Tears welled up in his blue eyes, then caressed his cheeks. He wanted to raise his hands to wipe his eyes and face, but with his life nearly drained and lacking the strength to do so, his hands merely dropped limply into his lap. An eerie peace washed over his face as his mouth gently feigned his last few breaths.

"Report," ordered Ubikor as he scanned the area for further hostiles.

"Zone one clear."

"Zone two clear."

He growled to himself as a twinge of pain dashed into his right shoulder. The sniper's shot had chipped a piece of his armor and sliced into his exoskeleton. He peered toward his injury and palpated it with one of his digits. Content that no serious harm was done, he let his arm drop back to his side and headed toward the entrance of the main building. His purposeful march thumped against the earth and his combat boots left sizable footprints in his wake. "Regroup. Set the charges. Secure the facility as planned," he ordered.

CHAPTER 26

Trent's eyes fluttered open about halfway, and after a few seconds of focusing he could make out the stars floating over the canopy of several nearby trees gently swaying in the cool breeze. A wet sensation on his left ear, along with a sloshing sound, made him turn his head slowly to investigate the oddity. It took him a beat to realize that a small fuzzy rabbit like face with a large tongue hanging out was staring him in the face. He let out a howl that startled the creature and sent it veering off into the bushes on its stubby furry legs.

Trent tried to sit up quickly but a jack hammer in his head put an end to that, and it didn't help that the landscape and trees started tossing back and forth in his vision. He shut his eyes tightly, grimaced, and moaned loudly at the myriad of sensations. In his stillness, his mind started to piece together the fragments of the last few moments of time. *Ut'ahhziik* on the landing pad. The streak in the sky. The bright flash. *The ship! What happened to it?*

Rising warily to his feet and fighting off bouts of nausea, Trent reached up and placed a palm on either side of his head to hold it together in case it fell apart. He lifted his gaze slowly and noticed that he was just within the grasp of the forest. His last position should have been in the clearing right ahead. He raised his eyes further up and let his arms drop slowly. In the distance he saw *Sahh'lliita*, the cargo vessel, but no *Ut'ahhziik*.

Easing himself ahead and through the clearing toward the landing pad, his eyelids opened wide apart. There was no ship. Just a crater in its place. Trent stood for several seconds as he investigated the calamity, a hint of charred metal and polymers wafting in the air. *Phil. Please no. Someone tell me Phil wasn't here when this happened… whatever the hell might have happened.*

Trent, with a frown etched on his face, turned his head to the left and noticed large swaths of the wall had crumbled. He fought his excruciating headache and trudged forward more quickly near the pathway that connected the landing pad with the entrance to the mining facility, a new surge of adrenaline helping him along. The pillars upon which the heavy guns were situated were no more.

Trent felt quite lightheaded and remembered how thirsty he was. He thought about the doctor. She could help him get better and perhaps give an explanation as to what happened, as well as the others. His mind flashed to Anamara. It was almost like a hallucination. He felt like reaching out to put his fingers through her hair, then across her face to caress her silky skin. It was almost like she wanted to say something, her mouth parting momentarily. Then the image of her vanished as suddenly as it appeared, replaced by the marred scenery of the mining facility. *I'm coming for you, Anamara. I'm here.*

Looking around as he arrived at a collapsed section of the wall, he noticed that not a single guard was around. "H-hel—" Trent's voice failed him as he tried to call out to anyone who would listen. Instead, he was met with a coughing fit that agitated his pounding head. After a few seconds of deeply inhaling and exhaling, Trent decided to climb over the rubble and into the compound. The jaunt over the concrete remains was relatively uneventful, as the material had packed in tightly when it fell.

There was a shed nearby and Trent noticed what appeared to be an outstretched leg just around the corner of it. Traipsing carefully toward the appendage, Trent rounded the corner and gasped, lunging back a few steps so quickly that he almost lost his balance.

The guard sat slumped against the wall of the shed. His dulled eyes stared aimlessly at the ground, hands palm up in his lap. His left leg was bent at the knee and lying on its side, his right leg straight out. A yawning hole in his left side revealed what was left of his lower ribcage, along with hints of various internal organs. A hoard of small winged insects buzzed and crawled along the coagulated blood encrusted surfaces. *What the fuck! Damn it! What the hell happened here?*

Trent felt squeamish as he eyed the cadaver. He wanted to look away but the dim lighting around the top edge of the shed glinted off a metallic surface that caught his eye. Next to the fallen guard, a heavy rifle lay near him. His eyes locked onto it. He felt a strange need to retrieve it. He winced at the thought. It lay so close to the open wound on the body. The voracious activity of the alien bugs didn't help either.

Taking a few unsteady deep breaths, Trent held the last one and approached the body. He respectfully walked around the guard and sidestepped toward the firearm, trying to keep his back toward him. The buzzing from the feeding insects seemed to drown out the rustling of the wind and ambience of the alien landscape. He held his clenched right fist near his chest, while his left hand jerked at the sensation of a bug or two landing on it. Swatting a few times, Trent slowly squatted down and wrapped a few fingers around the muzzle.

Rising up, Trent didn't anticipate the weapon was going to weigh as much, and it promptly slipped out of his grasp with a clatter, sending the alien insect activity surging. His lungs couldn't hold it any longer either, and the next gasp for air left him dry heaving, as the stench of the guard's innards invaded his olfactory senses. Trent frantically reached down, brow tightly squeezed together, lips about to eject what little he had inside him out. He palmed the accessory rail near the middle of the barrel and clamped onto it as tightly as his current state would allow. Dragging himself and the rifle away, he discovered that the strap had snagged on the fallen guard. He howled hoarsely at the body toppling over and onto the butt end of the rifle, alien bugs now buzzing all around him.

With a final huff, Trent managed to pull the weapon free and staggered away as quickly as he could, dropping to his knees a few meters away to catch his breath and let the pounding in his brain settle down. *I. Hate. This. Fucking. Planet.*

Using the rifle to help himself up, Trent started toward the main building. He gazed into the stockyard and noticed several other lifeless figures lying about, with gory stains pooled around the victims. Some appeared to have died while taking cover, whereas others looked like they put up a fight. Trent couldn't help pausing for a moment to take in the carnage. His mind searched for clues as to what could inflict such vicious harm. After a subtle shake of his head in disbelief, he moved on.

As he approached the entrance, he noticed the doorway had been torn apart, most likely by an explosion or two. Trent's boots crunched on the debris littered entryway. His pulse throbbed hard, sweat beaded down his forehead and face, and he breathed nervously through his mouth. Moving at a snail's pace, his bloodshot exhausted eyes scanned the environment for who knows what. Trent's fingers were becoming white at the knuckles, and his new found firearm clattered quietly as his arms trembled.

Having past the reception area, Trent inched down the wide hallway that split the building in two. To his left, the doors to the medical bay were wide open, whereas the administrative area ones were locked. Trent backed himself against the outer wall of the medical bay, rifle pulled tightly to his chest, and crept along it until reaching the edge of the entrance. After a quick pause and a few blinks and breaths, Trent rounded the edge of the doorway and burst in. He pointed his rifle around the room like a B movie action, eyes bulging and hunting for any foe. But nothing.

Trent took a few moments to cool off and backed out of the bay and into the large corridor. A shuffle from the kitchen startled him and he quickly turned to face down the hall. He readied the rifle, staring down its barrel. His head throbbed with every beat of his heart, but he gradually mustered up the courage to keep placing one foot after the other. As he neared the doorway to the kitchen, Trent slinked next to the opposite wall and slid himself along it. Arriving at the edge, he clenched his teeth, and shut his eyes tightly, mentally prepping himself for a fight.

He popped his eyes wide open. Sucked in a large breath. Then hurled himself into the middle of the entryway. A mortified expression possessed his face, as the sight before him was almost unbelievable. Several colossal creatures in lustrous dark amour towered over him, even though they were a few meters away, some holding their arms outstretched toward him. The tables were haphazardly rearranged, and sitting in a group were familiar faces. The doctor and her nurses huddled together with Fezria toward the right end of the table. Heading inward to the left, Michael and Noor sat next to each other, while Phil, his left arm heavily bandaged up, sat almost at the end of the table. He managed a hint of a smile as his eyes met Trent's, pain etched into his features. Three of the alien beings stood behind and loomed over them.

But it was the sight dead ahead that worried Trent the most. One of the mammoth creatures stood with his left hand and thick digits wrapped completely around Anamara's neck. An eerie déjà vu shot through his subconscious. She stood stiffly upright. Or was she being held up by that thing? Her hair was a mess, and her clothes and skin were filthy. "Anamara..." Trent's mouth barely moved as he uttered her name. Her eyes were lit with fear, but also relief that Trent was in her presence.

"You must be Trent," boomed Commander Ubikor. "We've been expecting you. If you'd be so kind to discard your weapon, we would appreciate it. We have a few items to discuss."

Trent almost leapt on the spot. The alien's perfect English and chest ramming throaty voice caught him by surprise. "Who are you? What are you? What the fuck is going on? Anamara? Are you ok?" The rifle swung aimlessly at a few of the creatures, trembling heavily in his grip now. The foreign species remained calm, unnerved by Trent's demeanor.

Ubikor tightened his grip around Anamara's throat. She began to struggle for air, but held her composure as best she could under the circumstances. "Now, now. There's no need for any hostility. I'm Commander Ubikor, and I'm aware that you are the software developer tasked to bring the heavy element refinery back online. To get straight to the point, as your species puts it, once you complete your task, we will release your friends and the remaining workforce of this facility. We know that an evacuation vessel is on approach and will arrive within the next two days. If you fail to cooperate with us, then we will execute each and every miner, along with your friends here. I will personally leave you until the end and I will strip you of your precious life myself. However, I'm hoping you are a reasonable human and will take the best option."

Trent stood for several seconds, still processing the chaos. He finally spoke. "How do I know you won't kill us after I get everything working?

You… you things slaughtered the guards. They didn't deserve to die."

"Unfortunate casualties. Our methods might seem harsh, but they are quite effective. And to address your question, you don't know. However, you have our word for what it might be worth to you. Our species, whether you believe it or not, holds true to our words. For example, I've chosen to negotiate, even though it's less efficient. I could've ordered a soldier to simply apprehend you, beat you into submission, and force you to work on the systems. That does have its downsides though. You'd be physically injured, psychologically traumatised, and perhaps even left in a dysfunctional state. We have the means to reconstruct this facility, but it will take you a much shorter period of time to repair the equipment using the existing technology. As soon as the facility is operational, you, your friends, and the miners will be released."

After his answer, Ubikor tightened his grip around Anamara's neck and raised her up several inches. Anamara reached up and tugged at the commander's substantial digits to no avail. Her toes dangled in midair.

"I do have a limited amount of patience though. As I suspected, and our interrogations have inferred, you and this Too'ndehrr appear to have a personal connection. I consider her disposable to this mission. She lacks the necessary technical expertise to be of any use. On the other hand, you have something to lose."

Trent gasped, eyes and nostrils flaring. A familiar voice caught his attention.

"Buddy. Might as well give'em a chance. You know, man, if we have the slightest chance of getting off this rock, I think we should take it," urged Phil, his eyes glancing over to Anamara.

Trent shot his gaze back to Anamara. Her eyes fluttered at the lack of oxygen and her arms started to fall limp. Trent let out a long hoarse roar and chucked the rifle toward a pair of the huge aliens to his left.

"Damn you to hell if you lied to me, you fucking monsters!"

"Such an amusing species," responded Ubikor as he released his grip on Anamara. Her limp body crashed to the smooth white floor. She gasped for air laboriously, her face flat against the synthetic surface, eyes still lost.

Trent met eyes with Ubikor. Strangely, his large black orbs seemed to allow Trent to rush to Anamara, which he did with only a moment of hesitation. He dropped to his knees and scooped her up into his arms, her head resting on his left bicep. Caressing her face with his right hand, Anamara began breathing more steadily. Her eyes soaked in his weary features, and her emotions soon spilled over as she began sobbing, tears escaping from the corners of her eyes. Trent leaned in and kissed her forehead.

As he pulled back up, a bout of light-headedness struck him, causing him to waver.

"Trent?" Anamara huffed. With a few winces, she brought her legs into a more stable position and now held Trent steady.

Ubikor, looming over the two, reached up with his massive hands and arms and pulled off his helmet, cradling it under his right arm. He looked up with his large bald cranium and locked his sights on Malerina. "Doctor, I believe Trent requires your medical expertise. You have no more than four hours to assist him. And, Trent. We are not monsters. Or things. We are Vadokor."

CHAPTER 27

"How long has it been?" asked Maksim as he paced slowly across the starboard side of the bridge on the battlecruiser *Hyperion*, eyeing the stars and wispy nebulae remnants through the large panoramic windows. Pastel colors from the gas giant seeped through the port side, gently reflecting off the lustrous metallic and polymer panels. A gargantuan swirling teal cyclone facing the ship added a ghostly cool tint to the otherwise warm glow.

"Fifty-two hours, sir," responded a bridge officer.

Maksim fidgeted with his ring, his thumb caressing the large obsidian stone. "That's two updates missed. The fuck is going on down there?"

"Shomthing that washn't planned," said Koorehg, his voice reverberating on the metallic panelling throughout the bridge. He continued, "I shuhggessht you move in and invesshtigate the manner. We've waited long enough."

"Agreed. Too damn long."

"If you meet resshisshtansh on the shurfash, kill thossh non-critical to the misshion. It will might alsho sherve ash a motivator for thosh uncooperative."

"I might finish off a few myself. I need to blow off a little steam. Helm. We jump at the top of the hour." Maksim turned on his heels and marched quickly off the bridge.

After Trent's introduction to the Vadokors almost two days ago, Malerina and the nurses tended to his dehydration and minor bumps and bruises. He was physically exhausted after his psychedelic-like trip through the kukat hole, and his return journey back to the mining facility took its toll on him mentally. Although he was relegated to sleep on a gurney, a sedative allowed him to squeeze in almost three hours of sleep before starting his first shift at the heavy element refinery. After a quick much needed meal, Ubikor and two others from his team escorted Trent and Noor to the refinery, where they worked under the menacing gaze of their new supervisors. The doctor and both nurses would also join them, to remain within arm's length of their new alien hosts. They would pass most of their time by chatting quietly amongst each other or reading various materials they had permission to access.

The other half of the Vadokor team watched over Michael, Phil, Fezria, and Anamara, who were all squeezed into a single larger cabin. As for the miners, Ubikor instructed Fezria to order them to stay in the underground safe-houses until the refinery was operational, and they would be free to leave when it was time.

"Try firing it up now," requested Trent. He squinted at his tablet screen as tiny text scrolled by, a multitude of colored code reflecting against the skin of his face.

Trent had now worked two complete shifts lasting about eighteen hours a piece, and had recently started the third. The Vadokors were kind enough to allow him and Noor a few washroom and meal breaks, but unlike his teammate, Trent was feeling the strain from a substantial lack of sleep. Less than five hours was not nearly enough for him, especially under these circumstances.

"Understood," responded Noor. After a few pokes at the control panel before him, he continued, "The last sub-processor of this station is functioning within normal operating parameters," answered Noor.

Trent lowered his head and released a gaping yawn that he had been holding back. He straightened up as best he could and placed his tablet on the edge of a machine's maintenance cover, then rubbed the stickiness out of his eyes.

"Well done. At this pace, you'll be free to go even sooner than I thought," announced Ubikor. "I believe you're both due for a brief meal. Ushtor." Ubikor turned his head toward one of his fighters and gave a quick nod. Ushtor was seated on a conveyor belt but quickly rose to his feet upon hearing his name. He extended one of his large digits on his left hand toward Trenia, then swiped it in the direction of the elevator. Trenia knew the drill. She would be accompanied by the Vadokor to the kitchen where she'd quickly assemble a few meals, then be escorted back to deliver them.

"I wish it was time for a nap," said Trent to himself. He started gathering up his gear to move it to the next system.

"I'm sure you'll manage, Trent. You'll have plenty of time to nap onboard the evacuation vessel," stated Ubikor. He finished speaking as a minor tremor lasting over ten seconds shuddered the refinery, then continued, "Besides, I doubt taking a nap would be the best course of action currently. These tremors will soon become quakes, and I doubt any of us would want to be here longer than needed."

"I will agree with that," nervously spoke Noor as he pressed himself tightly against the side of some paneling. He eyed the ceiling for several seconds to ensure nothing would come crashing down.

"Yea. I'm definitely not a fan of this place. Can't really say I ever was." Trent had paused for a few moments after the tremor but quickly continued to the next refinery system. After laying out his equipment, he turned to Ubikor and shook his head slightly. "I can't figure you guys out."

Ubikor pondered Trent's statement, blinking with his three eyelids a few times. "Not quite certain I understand what you mean."

Trent quickly inhaled and exhaled a long breath of air before responding. "You guys obviously came to this planet to get this heavy element shit. You have advanced tech. I guess you're intelligent." Trent shrugged and looked away for a beat. "But you come down with this savage violence, when you could've just scared everyone in to surrendering. And yet…" Trent bit down on his lip before continuing. "Here we are chatting. We're not being forced to work till we drop dead. If you aren't bullshitting us, then we'll actually be released. Why? I just don't get it."

"Humans." An air of amusement wafted over Ubikor. "From what I know of your species, your kind rarely expresses what you really think. You apply a façade to your words. Most wouldn't dare approach a superior and express dissatisfaction with their plans or methods of administration in fear of retaliation, even though there might very well be a logical reason for doing so. When a truth is spoken outright, your kind often becomes offended or emotionally hurt. This, again, being regardless that there might very well be some merit in the act. Humans also act terribly strange when one is fond of another. Your species plays a long drawn out, and often financially costly, game of sorts to entice the other.

"If something is known to be harmful to the welfare of others or even to one's self, such as the use of toxic chemicals, the majority of your kind will turn a blind eye to it if it suits them personally or monetarily. I believe your planet's food, water, and even air is still tainted with micro-polymers. And my personal favorite is how the vast majority of your kind refuses to think and learn. If your worldwide network system transmits a piece of information, it's generally accepted by the populace without any verification of facts or determination if the source is reliable and unbiased. I wonder little, how in the hands of a few, the many are nothing more than pawns and peasants. It's as if humanity was designed to be stupid."

Trent's mouth gaped open in utter surprise at the commander's knowledge and view of the human race. Malerina and Miseth couldn't help but grin at the situation.

Ubikor turned his head toward them. "Not that the rest of the beloved Ty'kape Empire is much different or better." He turned his attention back to Trent. "But I suppose it's not all negative. Your species does have a resiliency.

Somehow you've managed not to wipe yourselves out completely. At least not yet. With all the destruction your progress and ideologies leave in its wake, humans have managed to repair some of the damage and move forward." Ubikor stomped over to a series of cabinets and sat on top of them, making them groan beneath his weight.

Trent's lips formed a sideways smile. "I take it you see us as the monsters."

Ubikor produced a low guttural sound that was likely their version of a laugh. "Perhaps that would be a bit harsh. I'd be more inclined to call the Hynalfol that. But I believe you're beginning to see that what you know and understand will change based on your perspective."

The outer gates to the elevator made a ruckus as they shifted open. A few seconds later, Trenia pushed out a cart loaded with various food items, and her massive Vadokor escort followed closely behind.

"Come. Get your meals, then continue on your tasks," announced Ubikor. As he finished speaking, it appeared as if something had caught his attention, and his team responded in a similar fashion.

"I really hope these piiskoksh things don't kill us. I mean, how the hell can you trust anyone who comes in here, blows half the place up, and murders every single guard? Damn it! They killed them like animals," vented Fezria.

"We should probably keep our voices down. They might hear us and—"

"And what? I don't trust these aliens one damn bit! I don't give a shit if they know that or not," said Fezria, interrupting Michael.

"Fezria, please." Anamara flicked her head up and locked her gaze with Fezria. She continued in her soft but stern voice, "We all realize what they've done and what they're capable of, but they could have easily killed us all if they wanted to, and yet they haven't." She huffed and her eyes darted around for a moment. "A part of me hates to say this, but I feel they say what they mean. They're just after the element and want to get it out of here before that rogue planet arrives."

Fezria paused a moment, dropped her shoulders, and let out a big sigh. She lowered her eyes to her fidgeting fingers on the table top the four of them sat around. "Sorry. Bit on edge. I knew those people, a few of them closely." Her voice drifted off.

Anamara reached up with her right hand and cupped her fingers over Fezria's hands in sympathy. As she did, a mild tremor began shuddering the cabin.

"Not again. Not another tremor." Michael grasped the edge of the table as if his life depended on it. He didn't let go until the shuddering ceased.

"Easy, Michael. Remember, these aren't typical quakes. There're the gravitational tidal forces from the rogue planet. The closer that rock gets, the more frequently we'll get to enjoy these. And they'll get bigger and bigger," said Phil. "At least for another day or two they'll just rumble on by, but shit, I sure don't want to be here more than a another couple of days." Phil winced from a bolt of pane that surged through his left side and arm.

"How's your arm?" asked Anamara.

"It's fine. I'm due for my meds soon. How's the neck?"

"Almost back to normal," answered Anamara, her eyes seemed distant.

"I'm sure Trent is fine."

Anamara tilted her to the side a little, squinting momentarily. "Yes. He seems calmer than usual. The work might be progressing well." She turned her head and stared out the window, reminiscing about the last time she saw Trent.

Anamara stood by the elevator as two of the Vadokor fighters escorted Trent from the kitchen after he had finished his first meal. She recalled his face, alert but glazed with exhaustion; three hours of sleep hardly enough after what he'd gone through. His facial hair was curiously attractive to her, especially since Too'ndehrrehk men had none. Trent's hair was disheveled. The invaders saw no importance in allowing him to groom himself. Even his clothes were the same soiled ones he'd worn throughout the last day.

She remembered Trent's expression as he saw her waiting by the lift. His eyes lit up and a smile widened across his face, posture straightening up as if a new found source of energy had been injected into his system. He walked briskly up to her and stopped about a foot away, glancing up at Ubikor. The commander motioned subtly with his head and Trent took the cue. His eyes leapt back to hers as he reached up with his hands and slid them back across Anamara's face. His fingers passed through her delicately soft hair, warm palms against her jawline. Anamara's lips parted, hungrily awaiting his. He pulled her in and their lips met. Anamara snaked her right hand under Trent's arm, running it up and across his chest, and finally resting it on his cheeks. She relished the feeling his facial hair, gently prickling her finger tips and palm. Trent slid his left hand to the nape of her neck and squeezed it gently, sending a tingle down her spine.

But their embrace was much too short lived, as one of the Vadokor fighters latched onto Anamara and dragged her off to the side, while another pried Trent off her and shoved him into the elevator. Trent spun around to face outward and examined the scene. One of the beasts held her by the shoulders, a look of despair washing over her face.

Ubikor locked his dark gaze onto Trent catching his attention and spoke, "Just a courtesy. But mostly to remind you of what you're working toward." Trent soaked in his words in for a moment, then gave the commander a subtle nod.

Within a beat, his eyes were drawn back to Anamara. She watched Trent for a moment, then moved her lips silently, "I love you." His eyebrows rose almost imperceptibly, and he silently reciprocated, "Me too." The elevator doors mercilessly slid shut, with the safety gate crashing across soon after, a pleasant look of surprise remaining etched on his face.

Tears glistened in the corners of Anamara eyes, but she simply continued to stare aimlessly out of the window of their cabin. Her consciousness grappled with how her life, and those of everyone on this excursion, had their lives so cruelly altered in such a short period of time.

"That must be incredible how you can actually feel him. I couldn't even imagine what that's like. At least it sounds like good news," Fezria chimed in.

Anamara thought to herself that feeling others wasn't always as incredible as people assumed. Even now, the peaceful calm she felt from Trent reminded her of the distance between them. She turned her head back toward the table, but suddenly peered out the window again, a quizzical expression on her face.

"What is it?" asked Phil. He sat on the opposite side of the table next to Michael, away from the window and couldn't see the activity.

Anamara took a moment to reply. "I don't know. The guards stationed outside to watch us are running toward the main building."

CHAPTER 28

Hyperion lunged out of compression almost a million kilometers from Circulum and began decelerating. The icy cold face of the planet grew rapidly in size as the ship careened toward it, its lush atmosphere backlit by the system's star.

"Sir. Scans are picking up an unidentified vessel off to starboard," announced the tactical officer.

"What? Who are they?" asked Maksim. The look of surprise came over him as he briskly turned toward the officer. "Well?"

"Details are just coming in, sir." The office shot a worried glance at Maksim. The computer finally signalled and the officer read off the details, dread imprinted on his voice. "The system identified the vessel as an unknown Vadokor battlecruiser. Multiple armaments detected, unknown class. The ship has scanned us."

"Engage shielding. Battle stations," ordered Maksim. The officers on the bridge jumped into action as the bridge was bathed in a crimson tone and alarms dinned. Massive metallic alloy sheets descended from outside of the large panoramic windows, and holographic projections activated, providing detailed tactical information. *Keetovor* could be seen increasing in size as *Hyperion* was coming within four hundred thousand kilometers of Circulum.

"Sir, the other vessel is hailing us," notified the comms officer.

"Let's hear what they have to say." Maksim gestured with his hand to put the other ship on.

The speakers reverberated in the room, "This is sub-commander Detromor of the *Keetovor*. We have claimed this system as our own and you are trespassing. We will provide you with a single opportunity to vacate this system, or we will take immediate action to remove you."

Maksim stared at the projection of the sleek alien ship for a few moments. *Hyperion* had fallen into a similar orbit and the two ships were within a few thousand kilometers and closing.

"Well," started Maksim, clasping his hands together in front of himself. "I think they sound like a race we could reason with. So let's reason with them. Blow those motherfuckers out of *our* space."

"Yes sir," responded the tactical officer. With a serious but worried look in his eyes, he quickly jabbed at his console and announced, "Torpedoes launched."

Four muted thuds could be heard on the bridge as the torpedoes fired. The holo-projection simulated their trajectories as they raced toward the Vadokor battlecruiser.

"Impact in six seconds," said the tactical officer.

With only a few seconds left before the armaments would tear into ship, *Keetovor's* massive thrusters blasted to life, pitching the ship in an upward direction and swinging it to face *Hyperion*. A series of plasma streams lit up from various spots around the ship's sleek hull and took aim at the projectiles. Two of the torpedoes were hit and exploded in bright balls of light, sending out a spherical shockwave that was too far from the Vadokor ship to do any harm. The remaining pair of torpedoes detonated several tens of meters away from its hull and managed to rattle the battlecruiser.

"No direct hits. There appears to be minimal damage. Sir... look!" reported the tactical officer with his eyes widening, mouth hanging open.

Keetovor continued its maneuver, swinging up and around *Hyperion* in an arc, always facing it. The Vadokor battlecruiser's profile from the front was miniscule compared to its length, but it's what the ship did next that caught the tactical officer's attention. Numerous armatures rotated, extended, and locked together, giving the windowless vessel a new aggressive star-like appearance with the segments jutting outward into space.

"Helm, evasive maneuvers. Hit them with everything we've got! End them!" yelled Maksim, pointing with his right hand at the holo-projection of their target, left hand balled up into a tight fist. His rage had him clench his teeth, baring them like a rabid dog.

"Yes sir! Using high yield torpedoes. Firing sequence delta," acknowledged the tactical officer with a slight tremor in his voice and beads of sweat running down his forehead. But before he could finish entering the commands, *Hyperion*, now with its top and port side facing *Keetovor*, was struck several times. The entire ship rattled violently against the five direct hits. Maksim steadied himself against the shuddering by widening his stance, and flinging his arms about. As soon as the vibrations ceased, he strode with purpose over to the captain's chair and sprang into it.

"What the hell did they hit us with? Helm, move the damn ship already! And keep it in motion." urged Maksim.

"Yes sir," responded the helmsman. The engine noise revved and reverberating throughout the bridge, and the view began to change on the holo-projections.

The tactical officer frantically hit a few symbols on his console and announced, "Firing." Five distinct thuds sounded off amongst the backdrop of several alarms. He continued, "Impact in five seconds."

Maksim watched the panoramic holo-projection without blinking. The five torpedoes barrelled toward *Keetovor* in a *V* formation. Like before, the alien battlecruiser lit up, taking aim at the incoming projectiles. The torpedo at the head of the pack was first to be hit, then the far starboard one, and lastly, the one just to the port side of center disintegrated. The far port side armament swung itself into the starboard side of *Keetovor*, causing the large battlecruiser to roll suddenly. The last torpedo exploded just off to its port, but still caused the Vadokor ship to shudder hard.

"Three down, one direct hit. Power levels of their shields appears to have dropped," exclaimed the tactical officer.

"What damage did we take?" asked Maksim, white-knuckling his armrests. His eyes continued to focus on the reeling ship displayed by the holo-projection.

"Whatever they hit us with shot right through our hull. Automated sealing systems have engaged in three sections, and a team has been dispatched to manually deal with a location. Sir, it's like the weapon they used almost instantly hit us as soon as they fired it."

Maksim pushed himself back into the captain's seat, elbows on the armrests, and had his outstretched fingers in a steeple near his face. "That's the only way we're gonna beat them," he uttered to himself. "Helm. Thrusters, full ahead. Tactical. When we're within two seconds of them, fire a spread of torpedoes, and helm, as soon as those torpedoes are loose, dip us under the ship and put as much distance between us and them as you can. Engage now before they regain control," ordered Maksim, fire in his eyes. The helmsman worrisomely acknowledged the order.

"Sir," the tactical officer started with an uneven tone, "the shockwaves from the explosions are going to impact us too at that range."

"True. But it's not going to kill us. We'll deal with the damage later. But if those fucks hit us again, we're done," responded Maksim.

"Understood, sir." The tactical officer quickly input the firing pattern and started a timer.

Hyperion's aft thrusters fired at maximum power, and their crescendo could be heard resonating throughout the hull. The Hynafol built battlecruiser lurched forward and began picking up speed. *Keetovor's* underbelly became more pronounced as the ship was still rolling over from the torpedo strike.

"Seven seconds to firing position," stated the tactical officer. "Four... three... two... one. Launching torpedoes."

Maksim's eyes widened and he breathed harder. He quickly reached down to a small console panel on the right armrest and tapped a few buttons. "All hands, brace for impact." He forced himself into the chair and clutched the armrests again.

Four heavy beats pounded off in quick succession. *Keetovor* halted its roll, but its vulnerable underside was heavily exposed. The bridge officers and Maksim watched the panoramic holo-projection update as *Hyperion's* nose dipped hard, the rumble of the thrusters atop of the ship washing over them. A section of the holo-projection front and center kept focus on the Vadokor battlecruiser, and not a moment later, four flashes gleamed across the belly of the wounded ship. Just over a second later, *Hyperion* took a violent pummelling from the torpedoes' shockwaves. The crew held on tightly to the consoles, the science officer losing his footing and slipping to his knees. Maksim bared his teeth, set his legs wide, and managed to weather the brief but powerful quake through the vessel.

Keetovor was less fortunate. The impacts hurled hundreds of small blazing fragments off its hull, sending them tumbling aimlessly through the silence and darkness of space. Several of the ship's thrusters failed, leaving voids where there was once a bright orange fury. Plasma streams blew out in several locations in hues of greens and purples, as the ship's internal organs bled out. One gape in particular provided a view into a corridor. Circulum's gravity now had a solid grasp on the fading battlecruiser, pulling it slowly down toward its icy dark side. The sleek ship rolled gently, like a beached whale being coaxed by ocean waves.

"That'll teach those motherfuckers to fuck with us," spit Maksim. "Finish'em off," he continued with a malevolent grin.

"I can't comply, sir. Several systems are offline, including weapons. Damage reports are still coming in but five maneuvering thrusters are down, two of the sealed sections have breached again, and there's a fire in section twelve, near the section of the hull being manually sealed," stated the security officer, then taking in a long breath. "We've also lost a crewmember, sir."

Maksim's grin receded as he took in the news. He continued to stare ahead, watching the Vadokor ship gradually descending toward the planet. After several seconds, his breathing began to relax, along with his muscles. He shifted himself to a more comfortable position and began to speak, "Fuck'em. Let them burn. It'll be a more painful death than what I was going to offer them." He started fidgeting with his obsidian ring. "Helm. Get us into a stable orbit over that fucking mine. Tactical. Assemble the teams. Time to take back what's ours."

"It appears that you have some friends," spoke Ubikor in an accusatory manner.

Trent was hunched over his equipment but straightened up at the sound of the commander's thunderous voice. He eyed him for a moment quizzically, letting out a tired sigh.

"I'm sorry?" Trent squeezed his eyebrows together. His posture spoke of a lack of sleep.

Ubikor shifted his gaze to Noor. "Well, you're awfully quiet."

"I do not know what you are referring to," answered Noor, a slight worry in his voice.

"What's going on?" shrugged Trent, letting his hands fall hard against his thighs.

"What indeed. My vessel has just been attacked by a ship that arrived not a few moments ago," replied Ubikor.

Trent blinked the exhaustion out of his eyes and his heart decided to pick up the pace as his mind considered what he just heard.

"I don't get it. Why would the evacuation ship attack yours? And how come they're here so soon?"

"Oh, that's no evacuation vessel, Trent. Their limited armaments would hardly be a threat to *Keetovor*. Seems this vessel has been designed to fight. And it's also quite likely they've been here since you've arrived. Somewhere nearby at the very least."

Trent shot a glance over to Noor, and after a beat, Noor nervously turned his head toward him. "You know anything about this?"

For an alien that hardly showed any signs of emotions, Noor appeared outright upset about the question. "No. No, of course not. What would I have to do anything about some ship that just materializes out of nowhere?" he asked, searching for the right words.

Ubikor glanced over to the doctor and her nurses, and asked, "Ladies. I don't suspect you might have any knowledge of this? Perhaps one of you managed to hail them."

"You're kidding us?" Malerina huffed. The nurses both shook their heads in unison.

Trent's mind triggered at the sound of the doctor's voice. His eyes flicked around the refinery, searching. After a few seconds, Trent murmured to himself, "The communications systems…"

"What?" Ubikor's head snapped to Trent, and the tone of his voice meant he wouldn't ask again.

"The doctor. When I got here, she asked me to look into the communications systems as they were acting up. Their comm problems started around the time the mining equipment went haywire. That was what? About a week or two before we got here," answered Trent, slightly surprised at the enthusiasm in his voice.

"Yes. That's sounds about right," responded Malerina.

"I never got a chance to look into it with everything that happened. Maybe someone was communicating with that ship you're telling us about. I could check it out. I know how to work with these communications systems."

Ubikor just stared at Trent for a moment, then spoke, "Perhaps it would be a worthwhile undertaking. What do you require to access these systems?"

Trent squinted at Malerina, "You said there's a small building next to the cabins right?"

"Yes, just to the north of them. You should have access. Security should have sent you a message."

"Right. I almost forgot about that." Trent grabbed his tablet, and with a few swipes and strokes, pulled up the access info. "Got it, it's right here."

"Of what importance is this? We need to finish getting the refinery operational," exclaimed Noor.

Ubikor's nearly expressionless face showed signs of suspicion, but didn't respond to Noor. With a quick glance at one of his fighters, Ubikor started moving toward the elevator. "Trent. Come. Bring what you need."

On their way to the maintenance building, Trent couldn't help but glance over to the cabin where the others were held, noting the absence of the three Vadokor guards that should have been positioned there. He hoped Phil's arm was healing up. The last time he saw him was over two days ago, and he had been in quite some pain. But in particular, he was curious how Anamara was doing. He wanted to hold her again, to feel her soft skin in his hands, to run his fingers through her hair, to kiss her. *Anamara, I'm here. I miss you. I love you.*

Anamara stood by the small galley countertop preparing a snack for herself and the others. She was making small talk while arranging the food stuffs, but suddenly stopped in her tracks. Her gaze snapped up and out through the window. She squinted ever so slightly.

"Hey? You ok?" asked Phil, his expression one of concern.

"Trent... how..." whispered Anamara.

"Anamara?"

Anamara snapped back to reality, half-peering over her shoulder. "I'm fine. Everything's ok. I'm almost done." She begun fussing with the snacks again, her eyes glancing out the window for a moment. A hint of a smile curled up the side of her lips.

Within a few minutes, Trent, Ubikor, and a member of his team had reached the small building. Trent input his assigned access code and the lock unhinged with a clack. Swinging the door open, he stepped inside. Ubikor slumped down and slipped his head through the doorway, his right arm flat up against the outside wall around the doorway. He examined the innards of the small structure. He noted that the ceiling wasn't far above Trent's head, and the room could likely hold no more than about three human sized beings.

"With haste, Trent. Ensure you send no communications. Your goal is to find evidence of possible tampering," said Ubikor.

Trent looked over toward the doorway. His mind suddenly reminisced about horror movies. He felt like a character cornered and just out of reach of some beast. "Yea, I understand," he responded, nodding his head. Looking back at his laptop, he continued, "I'll walk you through what I'm doing."

Trent hooked up a couple of his devices to ports on the communications hardware and launched a few applications on his laptop to help him access the systems.

"Ok. I'm hooked up. I'm going to start by pulling up the access logs. Let me see," said Trent as his eyes twitched through the hundreds of lines in the access log. "Kind of what I thought," he uttered to himself.

"And what did you think?" asked Ubikor.

"Nothing really stands out. Just regular activity. If I was a hacker then this is what I'd want. It doesn't arouse any suspicions. So what I'll do next is pull up the hardware log. This will allow me to cross reference the power output of the antenna to the access logs. If all is well, the power should only spike when the messages were sent. Assuming the hacker overlooked this aspect, then there might be evidence of someone messing around with this system."

Ubikor grunted, "Carry on."

A few tens of seconds passed by and Trent slowly pulled back from his laptop screen. "There it is." He shot a quick glance to the doorway. "I'm seeing the power output increase to transmission levels, but there's nothing in the personal access logs during those times. If I could remember where the fuck I was during some of these periods, we could probably pinpoint who was sending these. They're almost all after we arrived on this planet. Ok. I'm going to fish around the program. I've worked with this kind of system before. I'll verify some checksums and see if there's any malicious code embedded."

Trent launched a few more applications and began verifying the program code on the system. Without taking his attention off his equipment, he noticed Ubikor pull himself out of the shed and speak a few words to his teammate in their native language. Trent's face changed hues as the colorful output of the applications flashed by on his screen, along with the ambience from the surrounding equipment. The diminutive shed offered function above all else. The servers and electronics it was chocked full of hummed away, and the cooling systems dinned dominantly throughout the space. The lighting was enough that one could find their seat, a lowly chair with four casters, a low backrest, no armrests, and a cushion too firm to be of any comfort. Trent adjusted himself several times, searching for any elusive sweet spots, but found none.

"What the…" Trent began to say.

Ubikor sqatted down on a knee. "I presume you found something."

Trent's eyebrows were scrunched and his mouth hung open slightly. He turned his head slowly to face the commander. "Yea. There are malicious subroutines that can be called to bypass some of the systems, like the access logs, to change frequencies, and add encryption. The code is definitely Hynafol. I can also see where the last access point was. It came fr—"

A grumbling vibrated the walls of the small building. Trent quickly grabbed the edge of the console in front of him, a worry spreading across his face. "Shit, another tremor?"

Ubikor rose to his feet, his waistline barely visible through the doorway. His booming voice could easily be heard despite his head being out of view. "Not this time. We have incoming."

CHAPTER 29

Trent leapt out of his chair and bolted toward the door using his right hand to snag the frame to control his deceleration. He briefly peered at the Vadokors next to him to determine the direction of their gaze and then turned his head to match them. Only a smattering of small cumulous clouds dotted the morning sky, and between them in a clearing were three dark shapes flying in formation, growing in size every second.

"Remain inside," ordered Ubikor as he placed his giant left hard across Trent's chest and pushed him back inside the shed. With another swift move, the commander shut the door.

Trent barely managed to keep his balance and made a mental note of how easily the alien tossed him aside. Still very curious, he hurried over to one of the two narrow horizontally oriented windows. Beneath each was a table with various electronics equipment and spare tablets strew about. With a swift brush of his arms, he cleared the mess off the table with a clatter so he could kneel up on top and peek through the viewports. Trent found it awkward but managed to glimpse the incoming crafts. After a few moments, the trio broke formation. One of them dipped out of view to the west end of the complex on the far side of the cabins, whereas another passed by and descended toward the east end. The third craft continued on its course and rocketed out of view.

Ubikor and his officer took cover behind the shed. They could hear the thrusters of the two crafts idling after they landed. After a few seconds, the ship to the west fired up its engines, with the one to the east following shortly after, and both crafts could be seen tearing off high into the atmosphere. The third vessel could be heard somewhere in the distance.

"Troops. Take out as many as possible from the west. I will take the east," said Ubikor. The fighter responded with a brief grunt as he engaged his gauntlet's weapon that turned on with a growl.

Ubikor's fighter moved to the opposite end of the building and watched a small hoard of what appeared to be mercenaries, sweeping the area and taking cover.

"Commander. At least ten inbound from this direction. These are trained forces based on their strategy and movement. Heightened caution suggested," reported the fighter.

"Agreed. Approximately the same number advancing from the east," responded Ubikor.

The commander took note that the advancing soldiers from the east took extreme caution around the main building, as if they knew something was awry, but his view was limited by both distance and obstructions in the way, such as the other cabins. Noises could be heard from the south, sheet metal being pried and ripped at.

"They are methodically combing the cabins for hostiles," Ubikor announced.

"What shall we do with the four we are holding?" asked the fighter.

Ubikor considered the question for a moment, then answered, "Our most valuable asset currently is Trent, for he is able to bring the refinery back online. However, if this army eliminates either Anamara or Phil, Trent might not cooperate any further. If we can defeat these invaders, then there might be a chance to salvage this mission. We will move together to the nearest row of cabins and take to the roof. Continue to focus on the west and I will target forces on the east. Be quick as this will place us in the open."

"Understood."

"Move out," ordered Ubikor.

The two Vadokor rounded their respective corners of the maintenance shed and stormed toward the nearest row of cabins, leaping to the roofs with relative ease. Ubikor's fighter, with his right arm outstretched, swept across the horizon, spotting several soldiers. Without hesitation, he quickly took aim and fired several times. Four of the armed personnel dropped to the ground, sending several scrambling for cover. Ubikor did the same on his end and picked off three, heavily wounding one by severing the soldier's leg near the ankle. The two giants vaulted off the roofs and kept up their forward pace.

"The same. Our captives are in this row. We will keep pushing to force them back," instructed Ubikor, and the fighter grunted in acknowledgement.

The two once again scrambled to the roof top of the next row of cabins, but this time were met with heavy fire. Both managed to take a few aimless shots as cover fire, which provided a few moments of relief.

Pings could be heard as projectiles ricocheted off the Vadokors' armor.

"Fall back. We are much too exposed here," ordered Ubikor, taking several shots again as cover fire.

The two backed off quickly and began to traverse over the last row of cabins. As they were mounting the rooftop, Ubikor's fighter let out a roar. A shot from one of the soldiers found its way between the armored plating at the back of his right knee, leaving a small entry wound and splintering the exoskeleton around the area.

"Are you able to continue?" asked Ubikor.

"Yes. I can still bend my knee, so it is not a major impact. The suit should be administering the analgesic," replied the fighter, struggling a little to clamber on top of the roof. Once atop, he rolled across the sheet metal roofing material and cautiously lowered himself on the ground, placing more weight on his left leg.

Now back to where they started, they could hear the armed forces shouting commands louder, urging the team to coalesce and push hard against their targets. Several projectiles struck the small maintenance shed, echoes of their impacts reverberating against the remaining security wall and row of cabins.

"They might kill Trent with their reckless aim. Adjust for wide dispersal," ordered Ubikor, sliding his fingers deftly on the back of his gauntlet, his teammate doing the same.

Ubikor swiftly leaned out enough so he could extend his arm and fire. Instead of a grapefruit sized ball of energy hurtling out from the weapon, over half a dozen grape sized orbs spread out as they were fired. Both warriors needed to wait several seconds before their gauntlets recharged and could fire again, but their tactic of alternating the timing of their shots was holding the advancing troop back, along with landing several kills.

"Release'em!" shouted one of the soldiers.

The two Vadokors shot a glance at each other, both looking for an answer as to what was being released.

Ubikor's fighter leaned out briefly beyond the edge of the maintenance building. "I don't see anything. They have taken cover."

"Wait. Listen," responded Ubikor. He closed his mouth and took on the persona of a statue, with his fighter following suit. After a few seconds, he spoke, "Aerial assault. Drones."

Both of the Vadokors started scanning the skies that had begun to cloud over, a brisk wind picking up. The high pitched whirr of the drones could be heard, but neither were visible to the giants.

"I cannot see them. There is at least two," said the fighter, looking around frantically.

Taking them by surprise, two drones tore around the corners of the shed, one on each side. Ubikor hurled his huge long arm upward and fired off a shot, his gauntlet releasing a flurry of glowing orbs toward the airborne device that twirled around in the air, jostled by the breezy conditions. The shot was a loss though, as the orbs spread out too quickly and left the drone plenty of room. On the opposite side of the small building, the fighter also took aim and fired. As with his commander's shot, the orbs gave the whizzing craft ample room to continue its mission.

"Is this just for reconnaissance?" asked the fighter. "It hasn't returned fire."

"Irrelevant. Take it down. Adjust weapon to rapid fire mode," commanded Ubikor.

Ubikor poked as his gauntlet and released a stream of gleaming streaks toward the unsteadily hovering craft on his side, positioned about twelve meters away. As if reacting to the incoming danger, the drones lunged forward in unison heading straight at their respective Vadokor target, pitching from side to side and dipping and rising as if dancing to some disjointed beats. The fighter's gauntlet had been adjusted and recharged, and he let the weapon fire continuously, drawing a swirling banded track in the air.

"They are too unpredictable," said the fighter with a degree of urgency, shooting a glance over at his commander in case he was withholding a secret strategy to defeat these elusive devices.

"Keep firing. We are bound to strike them eventu—"

As suddenly as they had sprung into action, the two drones halted almost instantly about two meters away from Ubikor and his fighter, each unleashing a set of almost a dozen barb tipped microwires. A few of each had embedded in the sandy gravel around the Vadokors, but most latched onto their armor and exposed exoskeletons. In a bright flash later, electrical bolts coursed through the wires and arcs of brilliant blue energy slithered their way over the bodies of the giants. Ubikor and his fighter tensed up hard, their sizable digits curling unto themselves, eyelids fluttering, jaws clenched, and limbs tremoring uncontrollably against the onslaught of pure power. After several endless seconds of agony, the artificial lightning ceased, and the drones plummeted straight to the ground with a sandy thunk.

Ubikor's eyelids unravelled themselves erratically, until after a few moments his large glossy black orbs were fully visible and staring off to his left and at the sandy gravel. His jaw slowly opened and a lengthy groan escaped. He tried to move but couldn't. His head turned slowly, muscles tender, and noticed that his legs were outstretched in front of him and bound tightly with heavy duty polymer straps. After a moment of continuing to struggle, Ubikor came to the conclusion that his arms were bound behind his back in a similar fashion. He could hear the sound of a ship's engine winding down nearby.

Looking up, about a dozen guards stood around him. A few of the soldiers stood at ease, while others had their weapons trained on him. A few seemed to aim in a slightly different direction. He looked to his right and saw his fighter seated against the maintenance building wall, bound just like him but still unconscious. Returning his gaze to the new invaders, he noticed four captives standing behind most of the men, hands bound behind their backs, flanked by a guard on each side. Sounds of encroaching footsteps caught Ubikor's attention.

"Good. *Good*." Maksim emphasized the second iteration of his words as he walked past his team of trained mercenaries. "It looks like I'm just in time for a chat. Throw some water on the other one to wake him up."

A soldier near to the Vadokor fighter took a canteen from his belt and started unscrewing the cap as he walked toward the alien. He turned the container upside down and water splashed on the Vadokor's head and on his body. After a few seconds, the fighter's eyes fluttered open and took in his surroundings.

"Excellent. Now that you're both awake, I'd like t—"

A clatter of sounds coming from within the shed silenced Maksim, and every soldier in sight readied their arms.

Maksim looked around at his team of mercenaries, expelling a sigh of frustration. "Let me get this straight. We started our wonderful day," he raised his hands palms up toward the sky, "with thirty of you. All fucking armed to the teeth with your guns, grenades, and drones. Then you meet these two. You have a bit of fun getting to know each other. And now there are," Maksim paused for a moment as he casually took a headcount of his remaining force, then continued, "fucking sixteen of you left! And not only that, but you don't even bother to check if that one tiny building is clear, like you've been told to do. Secure the site. Clear the fucking structures." Maksim shook his head and his eyes shot to the sky momentarily.

"You, and you," he pointed at two soldiers nearest to the entry of the maintenance shed. "Get whoever, or whatever, is in that shithole out here."

The two guards shot worrying glances at each other and after a few awkward hand signals, readied their weapons and began approaching the door. But a subtle click stopped them in their tracks. One mercenary dropped to his knee and took aim at the center of the door, while the other held his position. The door slowly began creaking open.

"Wait! Fuck! Wait! I'm not armed! Shit! I'll come out. Just don't shoot! Don't shoot me!" cried Trent.

Maksim's serious expression evaporated and a smile replaced his previously straight lips. "Easy, gentlemen. Easy." He gestured to the soldiers to relax. "It's all right. If you don't try anything stupid, you won't get hurt. Come on out. Slowly."

A few seconds later, Trent cautiously traipsed out of the small building, hands held at head height, trembling. "I'm coming out. Please don't shoot."

Trent already knew what to expect upon exiting the shed. He had been watching the action through the scrawny windows until he accidentally knocked some loose computer equipment off a rickety shelf. He turned to face Maksim, briefly taking a few glances at Ubikor and his fighter. His emotions skipped a beat as he eyed the restrained giants. Almost all of their armor was removed, leaving them with a thick polymer cloth like material that left most of their exoskeleton exposed. Strangely, the massive creatures looked helpless in this state, and nowhere near as menacing as before.

Trent focused back to the people ahead of him, in particular, Anamara and Phil. It appeared to him they weren't hurt, but the emotional wear and tear could easily be seen on their faces, along with a hint of confusion and wonder as to what was happening now. Michael and Fezria were in the same state also.

"Well. Who do we have here? Why let me guess. You must be Trent," said Maksim with a large grim, pointing his right index finger at him, his obsidian ring glinting brightly. "We found our beloved software guy. Wonderful."

Trent could see the looks on the faces of Anamara, Phil, and the others, and he had an answer for them, "Don't be too surprised. They've been here since we arrived. That fucking Salapernean was in on this. He'd been communicating with these… these… who the fuck are you people? Are you here for the element?"

"I'm sorry. I really should have introduced myself. My name is none of your business, Trent. But let me reassure you, there's nothing to be concerned about either. However, you are correct about our purpose. Indeed, we're most interested in the element. In fact, we'll be having a discussion about that in a moment. But first, I have some business to take care of with these two. So which one of you is the commander?"

"I am," spoke Ubikor's fighter.

Trent looked over to the fighter and cocked his head slightly, squinting ever so slightly. Maksim's eyes had caught his nearly imperceptible reaction, and a satisfied smile cross his lips again.

"Wonderful. Shoot him." Maksim pointed a finger at a soldier who adorned a heavier garb than the others, then at the Vadokor fighter.

"Sir?" asked the soldier.

"You heard me."

"Yes sir." As soon as the soldier finished his acknowledgment, he lifted his rifle and fired three shots into the fighter's head, splattering the insides of his cranium on the wall of the shed. The Vadokor's head dropped forward, revealing the aftermath of the heavy caliber projectiles.

"Ahh! What the fuck?" Trent yelled as he took several steps away from the chaos. A guard near him grabbed his arms from behind and held him tightly. Anamara and the others let our various gasps and screams, turning their heads away from the carnage.

"Human. I will personally execute you for what you have done to my crew and my ship," Ubikor said calmly and with a particular edge to his voice.

"Oh. Oh my. I'm so sorry." Maksim couldn't help a laugh finish his sentence. "And how are you going to execute me? You're the only one left alive on the surface. We found and eliminated the rest of your kind in the building over there. I'm betting there's a few more of you fuckers in the refinery. I'm not sure how many, but I doubt you'll tell me. Nonetheless, when we find them, they're going to die too. As for you, well, I'm going to enjoy seeing the results of all the experiments we're going to put you through. What makes you tick? What makes you feel pain? How can we control your kind? It'll come in handy when we advance into what is currently your part of space, and we start to do more important things with it." Maksim had paced slowly over to the Vadokor's feet, but even with Ubikor seated against the wall, he barely had to lower his head to look him in the eyes.

Ubikor jerked himself and grunted loudly, making Maksim instinctively reel back.

Maksim snickered. "Good. We have a feisty one here."

"What is wrong with you people? You going kill us too? You expect me to help you get that damn refinery working again?" asked Trent.

Maksim looked over at Trent, lowering his eyes for a moment and shaking his head gently, then returning his steely gaze. "Trent. I guarantee you won't be harmed. In fact, I'm aware that an evacuation vessel is on route. We'll keep that ship around until you've finished your job and then you can go home."

Trent couldn't help flash his eyes to Anamara and the others. "And them? And the doctor, nurses, and miners? What about them?"

"Of course. Them too." Maksim circled his hands and arms in front of himself in visual reference to mean everyone. "Like I said, I only care about the element."

"How can I trust you? How can we? You've got a bigger army than they had." Trent gestured with his head toward Ubikor and his fallen fighter. You didn't hesitate to kill them."

"Trent. Look at me. I'm human. What makes you think you could have trusted these aliens? You do know this race is known to take over worlds and kill everything in sight?"

Ubikor interjected, "That is false. We are not—"

"Silence you filthy manipulative creature. We know your tactics well," interrupted Maksim.

Trent shot his eyes to Anamara. She gave a faint shake of her head.

"I don't know who to believe." Trent breathed heavily and beads of perspiration formed on his skin. He looked over to Anamara, Phil, and the others. "Let them go. They didn't do anything. They're no harm. Yet you've got them tied up. Even they didn't tie them up." Trent jutted his chin toward Ubikor.

"Calm down, Trent. I'll let them go. I just needed to be sure who I'm dealing with. I'm sure you can appreciate that. You're a smart man. Here, a show of good faith. Bring her over here." Maksim nodded to the soldier nearest Anamara.

The guard took her by the arm and led her through the other soldiers, their footwear munching against the small sandy pebbles. Anamara looked unusually concerned for someone to be released from their shackles. Just before they arrived next to Maksim, with only a few meters left to go, vibrations started rattled the earth around the group. The tremor swelled to a decent strength, making it challenging for everyone to stand, but almost as soon as the seismic event started, it subsided.

Maksim waved at the guard to proceed, pointed at the restraints around her wrists, and said, "Remove them." The guard hopped into action, and after a few seconds detached the cuffs.

Anamara painfully brought her arms forward, wincing at the discomfort. She massaged her wrists and stretched her long fingers.

Maksim turned toward her and smiled, "I bet that feels a lot better. Doesn't it?" Anamara met his gaze and nodded quickly, then looked at Trent and managed a brief smile. "And the others, with of course the exception here. We'll leave that one as is." Maksim jutted his chin toward Ubikor and his smile straightened to a line. His tone of voice took a serious shift and his steely gaze bore through Trent before continuing. "Trent, there's an obvious urgency here." Maksim gestured his hands around as he spoke. "So here's what going to happen. Your lady friend here... I suspect you're close, and your friends over there, will be taken aboard my ship where they'll get some comfortable quarters. You, on the other hand, will be taken down to the refinery to continue your work. Once you finish, you and your friends, and even the miners, can all pack up and head home on that evacuation vessel."

Trent considered his words for a moment and then steeled himself to match Maksim's attitude as best he could. "All right. But if I find out that you're hurting them, or you kill anyone, there's not a chance in hell that I'll get that fucking refinery working."

Maksim's grin doubled in size. "I like you, Trent. You have balls. Big ones!" He laughed. "That's good." He looked around the area, his eyes skipping from Anamara to the others, and then back to Trent again. His thumb impatiently caressed his ring. With his composure regained, Maksim continued, "Time to get to work, Trent."

CHAPTER 30

"Excellent work, Trent! Bravo!" said Maksim as he stood with his chin held up high, clapping his hands together. He wore a sharp midnight blue tracksuit with gold accents, more appropriate for a run on a calm autumn day versus a strut around a mine on a planet about to be crushed by giant rogue world. Even his high fashion sneakers matched his outfit, likely costing an average person a few weeks' pay.

He also accessorized. A comfortable polymer shoulder holster embraced a Hynafol standard issue incendiary pistol, which sat prominently near his left arm. And completing the ensemble was a seven inch nano-serrated edged dagger, surreptitiously tucked away in a calf holster on his right leg under his loose track pants. If only one could see that the blade's exquisite handle was made from the wood of a species of tree nearly extinct on Hynafol.

Trent was outright exhausted. He hadn't bothered shaving for days and his hair was unkempt. His attire began to have an unruly odour to it, and was stained from his activities in the refinery. He had been working for almost two full days with little rest in order to complete the work on the software and equipment. In fact, it was done about a day ago, but a few bugs needed to be cleared, along with some hardware issues that the specialist miners managed to handle. At this point, the equipment around Trent, Noor, and Maksim, plus some of his entourage, churned away as it separated the heavy element from the ore.

After Maksim and Trent had met, Maksim made a deal with Ubikor that he would leave his remaining fighters alive and unharmed if they would exit the refinery peacefully and without causing any damage to the machinery. Ubikor reluctantly agreed after Maksim gave him several reassurances that his show of violence was only to solidify his dominance, essentially a tactical maneuver. However, the moment the mercenaries escorted the remaining Vadokor fighers out into the open, they were all executed. The Vadokor commander, along with Anamara and the others, were then taken aboard *Hyperion*.

"Great," answered Trent, void of any emotion. Maksim had kept him working in a similar style as Ubikor had, with plenty of work and few breaks in between, along with just as little sleep. Before he could begin speaking again, another tremor rippled through the refinery.

"And with the ball of joy hurtling toward us, now less than three days away if I'm correct," begun Maksim, pointing upward with his finger, obsidian ring in full view, "it's a good thing you've quashed those bugs. This gives us enough time to extract at least four hundred kilos. Even more than we'd hoped for. I've sent for a shuttle to come pick us up and take us back to my ship. I think you'll be relieved to see your friends, take a nice warm shower, and have a decent meal. How does that sound, Trent?"

Trent gave a few tired nods and said, "Yea. Sounds good. Is the evac vessel here yet?"

Maksim smiled gently and answered, "I'm afraid not yet. But I have my people monitoring the situation. They'll let me know the moment it appears, and I'll be sure to have you and your friends transferred over to it."

"What if they don't show? What happens to us then? And the miners?"

Maksim paused for a beat, his lower lip almost imperceptibly quivering briefly. He took a long breath before answering, "Lucky for you, I have a big ship. There's plenty of room if we need it. Of course, I'll be dropping everyone off at the next nearest sparsely inhabited planet, I'm sure you understand why, but since you've been such good service to us, I'll have my comms send a distress signal for someone from the Empire to retrieve you all." Maksim mated his outstretched fingertips in front of himself as he stopped speaking.

"Thanks," answered Trent, nodding a few more times, his facial features still muted. He tried his best to hide his disbelief in Maksim's words. He didn't trust him at all. His mind recalled the image of Anamara shaking her head during his first conversation with Maksim outside the maintenance building. *If this asshole kills us, I just hope I get to see Anamara at least once more.*

"Sir. The shuttle has arrived," spoke an officer.

"Wonderful. Trent, shall we?" Maksim gestured toward the elevator and flashed a quick glance to at least include Noor too.

Stepping outside into Circulum's atmosphere provided Trent with a blissful feeling. He took in several deep breaths of the fresh air, humid and cool from a storm that had passed no less than fifteen minutes ago, then couldn't help but look up into the sky he hadn't seen for a couple of days.

"Fuck me," breathed Trent, in stunned marvel at the sight before him and stopping dead in his tracks. The massive rogue planet could be easily seen looming over the hilly southern horizon, even with Circulum's star set low in the opposite direction. Although still a mere fraction of the size the full moon would be as seen from Earth, the bright disc dominated the sky. Even after what could have been tens or even hundreds of millions of years travelling through the void of space, a thick atmospheric aura glowed around its surface. Trent swore he could make out the faintest traces of what were likely to be significant geological structures like mountain ranges, vast plateaus, and what could be great oceans frozen solid. He also wondered if amongst those details were towns and cities of a once thriving civilization.

Maksim and Noor paused, both turning back to see Trent staring into the sky.

"Quite the sight, isn't it?" said Maksim, glancing up at the foreign body. "Can you even imagine what is hiding on that world? There could be technology that supersedes anything we can imagine. And think of the resources. Hell, if there was any kind of life on that world, you wouldn't even need to mine for them. There could be stockpiles of metals and materials ready to be loaded up and taken away. And I'm sure there's still plenty to mine for. Maybe there's more heavy element there than what's on this miniscule rock." He took a deep breath. "But alas, it simply wouldn't be feasible to chase it down and transport the goods off it. It's forever heading off into the depths of space. Too damn bad really. Well, let's keep moving."

Maksim emphasized his final words loudly, snapping Trent out of his stupor. He picked up the pace, but his eyes kept snapping up toward the strange world, even as another strong tremor tore through the landscape.

The trio stepped into the shuttle that awaited them, its engines idly rumbling, thrusters tossing up a whirlwind of dust and dirt now and again. Trent sat down at the back and strapped himself in, while Maksim and Noor took seats in the front row, just behind the pilot and co-pilot. He caught Makism's eyes for a moment as he scanned the innards of the shuttle. The man in the tracksuit flashed him a quick grin, then turned away and spoke a few words with the pilot. Trent couldn't be certain but he felt a strange malice behind the friendly façade. He shrugged it off and continued to explore the craft as the rear hatch pulled up and locked into place. Nothing prominently stood out in the vessel. There were no distinct markings. Everything appeared functional. Trent did consider that this shuttle, and perhaps its mothership, were built by the Hynafol, based on his findings in the malicious communications code. Yet something was off.

He wished Phil were here. The guy knew almost everything about ships. Trent made a mental note to ask him what he thought when they would meet. He missed bantering with him and the laughs they'd have together. Phil always knew what to say to cheer him up or put him on track. Anamara's face then materialized in his mind. He just hoped he'd be able to put her hands on her cheeks. To feel the warmth of her skin and her breath.

The shuttle jostled and Trent clutched his armrests. Regardless of their situation, he still loathed flying. The inertial forces of the shuttle could be felt as it rose into the atmosphere and picked up speed. He couldn't see where they were headed though, as protective metal shutters were extended over the few windows, and Trent couldn't see the holographic projections by the pilots that much from his position at the back. *I really should start sitting up front.*

"*Tethys* to *Hyperion*, we are on approach. Requesting access. Over," announced the co-pilot.

"*Hyperion*. That's your ship?" asked Trent.

"Indeed it is," answered Maksim with a single nod, performing a quick half-glance back toward Trent.

Trent could feel the inertial forces nudging him around as the shuttle veered into position to enter the mothership's bay. The sudden clatter of the metal window shields retracting caught him by surprise, but at least he could now get a glimpse of them entering *Hyperion*. There wasn't much to see at this point, but he could guess by the width of the bay doors that *Hyperion* was significant in size. The other shuttles he'd seen a few days ago was off to port as their own glided into the starboard most side of the bay. Within a few moments, the shuttle touched down with a minor knocking, and the thrusters began to wind down.

Peering out the window near him, Trent could see amber warning lights pulsating slowly, and the ambient light in the large bay changing hues to match the artificial internal lighting as the bay doors slowly closed up, sealing away the darkness of space. After another twenty to thirty seconds, the amber lights ceased their caution.

"It is now safe to disembark, sir. Lowering access ramp," informed the pilot.

"Good. Thank you," acknowledged Maksim.

He begun to undo his seat harness along with Noor, and Trent took the cue to do the same. About the time he finished placing the belts aside, the ramp thudded against the bay floor and relieved itself with a loud hiss.

"Come now, Trent," Maksim said as he strode by him and walked down the ramp and into the bay.

Trent pulled himself off the seat and followed a few steps behind Noor.

"Welcome aboard *Hyperion*. Little do you know that you are standing on one of the most advanced battlecruisers ever constructed in the Empire. I have to admit," Maksim paused for a moment, crossing his left arm over his chest and thoughtfully grasping his chin with his right hand, "I wish circumstances were different. You know, I could use a talented software developer like yourself. Considering the events that took place, all that you've been through, I must say you've held up remarkably well. All that stress and, sure, you could use a shower and a shave, but you haven't lost it one bit. Look at Dvenoor here. I know he's a Salapernean of few words, but look at him. He's not himself. In fact, Dvenoor, get over to the infirmary and have yourself checked out, then get some rest."

Trent's eyes jumped to Noor. Considering he wasn't terribly communicative and lacked some level of emotional response compared to a human, he looked strangely perplexed. Nonetheless, the diminutive blue alien didn't question Maksim.

"Yes, sir. Wise words. I shall visit the infirmary immediately. Thank you." And with that, Noor turned on his heels and began wandering toward the exit of the bay, his gaze locking on Trent for several steps before returning to face in the direction he headed.

Maksim stood quietly until the doors to the bay locked behind Noor. "Follow me, Trent." Maksim began pacing toward the exit, arms still in the same position, but with his posture straighter. "Have a strange feeling that a man like you actually craves this sort of lifestyle. Most people might see you as a dull office dwelling clone, sitting on his computer system all day long, typing up endless lines of code. But I must admit, I just don't get that impression from you."

Trent followed a step or two to the left and behind Maksim, eyes exploring his new surroundings and occasionally flicking back to his captor. He figured he'd just listen to Maksim's ramblings for now before speaking up in anyway. He certainly didn't agree with his assessment, as this was not what he signed up for. Trent accepted this contract to get away from the Chief, his goons, the shady work, and start a better life. But at this point, if he could do things all over again, he'd just suck it up and stick it out with them. Although, he probably wouldn't have had the chance to meet Anamara. *I miss Anamara so much. I wish this asshole would stop talking and just take me to her already.*

The doors to the bay slid open with haste and revealed a lackluster corridor. As the two of them entered the passageway, two guards began following a few steps behind. Trent ignored them and examined the metallic and polymer infused walls and floors. Even with his experience he could tell this was no ordinary ship. But some details still felt off. He considered how the few other vessels he'd flown on had insignia throughout and various safety measures that weren't present here. Or at least not that he was aware of.

"Impressive isn't it. And you've only had a tiny glimpse of this ship," said Maksim as he took notice of Trent's curiosity. He gestured with his left hand for Trent to keep following, then dropped his arms by his side. Picking up the pace, Maksim continued, "Our operations are vast, far reaching. We have clientele from all over the Empire. Humans. Hyhafol. Too'ndehrrehk. Even Salaperneans."

The small group arrived at an elevator, and within a few seconds the doors slid apart. Maksim entered first and stood just off center, and the two guards flanked them, one on either side of the cozy compartment. Maksim reached over to a small console panel on the right side of the door and poked a few times at it. A muffled hum sounded as soon as the doors slid shut, and the elevator lurched into motion.

"The investments people and businesses make to accomplish their goals can be... astronomical," snickered Maksim.

"I have to admit I find it hard to believe that this is *your* ship. There are only a handful of celebrities and politicians who could afford their own private spacecraft, and then it wouldn't exactly be a battleship," speculated Trent, keeping his head and body mostly forward, only his eyes peering to the side toward Maksim.

Maksim snickered again. "Indeed, Trent. It would be quite something to pull off the construction of such a vessel by a single individual. But with some adequate funding from a corporation large enough to hardly bat an eye at the design and development of a new '*research vessel*'," he air quoted the two words using his fingers, "and with a little help from an interested third party, it's quite amazing what one can accomplish. And none the wiser. Just make sure you send in your reports on time." A mischievous grim etched its way across Maksim's lips.

The elevator halted sharply and its doors parted. Maksim marched out, and after a quick breath, Trent followed with the guards in tow.

"If only circumstances were different..." ruminated Maksim, mostly to himself. He flashed Trent a quick glance as he continued down another corridor. This hallway looked almost identical to the last, but a myriad of gouges, scorch marks on the metallic plating, and melted polymer paneling could tell an interesting story from a few days ago.

"Please excuse the mess. Not often we run into such vicious hostiles. The moment we came out of compression, they attacked us. Hardly a fair fight, but we prevailed in the end."

Trent mulled about Maksim's comment regarding different circumstances. He was about to ask for clarification but Maksim came to a sudden stop by a sealed doorway. One of the guards remained just behind Trent, whereas the other stepped over to the left side of the door.

"Well this is our stop, Trent. Welcome to your quarters." Maksim jutted his chin toward a guard and the large man jabbed several times at the console panel on the left side of the door. A moment later, the panels slid apart and the guard behind Trent shoved him through the entrance.

Trent took a moment to take in the sight. His eyes widened, mouth hanging open. "What the...?"

CHAPTER 31

"Hey! Wait!" protested Trent, trying to wiggle his way out of the grasp of the guard who shoved him into the brig. But at this point it was hopeless, as the guard had pinned his right arm behind his back and had a firm grip on his left wrist. Trent quickly glanced around the brig, revealing eight holding cells, four to his left and four to his right. Looking to his left at the cell nearest the entry, Fezria pursed her lips together in an awkward smile as she saw him. Across and to the right sat Michael. He raised himself to his feet and gave a slight nod, looking weary and withdrawn.

"Glad you could finally join us," said Phil, gesturing with his good arm in the cell next to Fezria. Trent couldn't help huff out a shallow grin. Malerina, across from Phil, stood with her arms crossed across her chest. She raised her fingers in a lazy wave and gave him a wide smile, her eyes drained. The nurses, Miseth and Trenia, were neighbors to the doctor. Both curved their lips up upon seeing him.

Quickly turning his head to the left, he saw her.

"Anamara. It's so good to see you. I missed you," said Trent, struggling against the guard as hard as he could to slow him down. He winced at the pain in his shoulder as the muscle behind him forced his arm higher.

"It's great to see you too, Trent. I've missed you also," she replied, her voice cracking. She looked well. Her eyes were wide and glossy from the tears building up. Her hair was a bit slovenly, but still managed to elegantly caress her gentle facial features. With her fingers extended, she held her hands out as if to reach for Trent, but carefully stopped short of a wraith like force field that almost undetectably shimmered and rippled sporadically.

"Are you ok? Did they hurt you?" asked Trent, staggering against the guard.

"I'm ok. They've kept us here since I last saw you."

The guard heaved Trent forward with a grunt and thrust him hard into his cell. Trent managed to get his right arm in front of him just in time to keep himself from slamming into the far corner of the small room. He growled aloud at the pain in his arm as he swung himself around, only to see the guard punch at the console panel. The force field squealed with an electronic hum, then suddenly snapped into place. He moved forward only to be stopped by a familiar sonorous voice.

"Don't touch the force field," warned Ubikor. His large dark pupils were focused on Trent as the giant sat awkwardly at the far end of his cell. His back was propped against the wall, knees bent, with his forearms resting on each peak. He continued, "It will burn your skin and supply an electric shock strong enough to knock you down."

"For once, the alien speaks the truth," said Maksim as he traipsed into view, then stood facing Trent's cell a couple of feet away from the force field.

"You son of a bitch. You kept everyone here like prisoners. You lied to us."

Maksim sported a wide grin. He stood with his feet slightly apart, hands cupped behind his back. He eyed Trent for a few moments, then continued, "Now, now. If it's any consolation, as they say, it's just business. Nothing personal. You're a nice guy, Trent. But from day one you've tried to pull one over me. Where is that evac ship? Where is it indeed? I suppose you didn't suspect us to be monitoring *all* communications in and out of this system. After all, there's only one lonely little comm satellite in orbit. Would you not think we'd not notice it transmitting a message?"

"I knew you would."

"Is that so?" A hint of confusion wafted briefly across Maksim's face.

"Yes. I take it you didn't get the message though."

Maksim humphed, his expression steeling.

Trent nodded a few times, "I see." He stepped closer to the force field to face Maksim. "In about a day, you won't be the only ship in this system. In fact, I have a feeling there will dozens of ships. All kinds."

Maksim's grin reappeared. "You think the almighty Empire will send a fleet of their finest military vessels to this far off world to come and save you and your friends here? They wouldn't believe a distress call from you," he snickered and gestured with his hands toward the other cells.

"Oh I know. I mean, by now they've probably gotten the message too. But see, you're mistaken. I didn't send out a distress call. Instead, I sent out the coordinates for this facility, along with details about the heavy element like where it can be found on Circulum, how much of it there is, etcetera, etcetera. I also mentioned how this planet is going to be hit by the rogue world in a few days, so that should put some urgency into the message. And of course, I included info about hostiles on this planet, which would be you and your friendly mercenaries here, so hopefully anyone who does come won't be too surprised. I mentioned that your ship is fair game. I mean, even if half a dozen ships manage to get their hands on even a few kilograms of heavy element, they'll be set for… forever. That's quite the motivation for some. I'm betting you're not the only pirates flying about. As for the evac vessel, they got some special instructions, and since they're not here, I'm pretty sure they got that message." Trent's eyes bored into Maksim's and didn't relent for a second. He felt a strange new energy coursing through this essence. Something felt good about this to Trent. Maybe Maksim had a point about him after all.

Maksim's face twitched ever so slightly, his façade cracking and alluding to one of seething infuriation. It took him a few moments to respond, his arms now by his side, thumb rhythmically flicking at his ring as if following the beat of a war drum. "Inconsequential. If anyone does show up, if what you're actually telling me is the truth, we'll have no problems taking out a few small freighters. My well trained team can handle it."

"You mean what's left of them?"

Ubikor made some low frequency gurgling sounds of Vadokor laughter. Maksim shifted his eyes away from Trent and to the right, his head turning a smidge in response to the giant.

Maksim forced his gaze to return forward, and through his clenched teeth said, "You've played a dangerous game, Trent. This will not end well for you and your friends."

"You were going to kill us all from the start, so it's not like it matters. At the least you'll have a few problems to deal with. And I'm still hoping there's even the slightest chance you won't even get to take a gram of the element off that planet."

"We'll see about that." Maksim turned abruptly and marched toward the exit, locking his eyes on Anamara on his way out. "Your deaths are going to be painful in more ways that you can imagine." The doors snapped open before him and he took a sharp right, followed closely by his guards. A few seconds later, the panels sealed shut.

"Well you know how to piss people off, buddy. Where did that come from? Is that really you, Trent?" jabbed Phil.

"I've fucking had it. This was supposed to be a fairly simple, no frills job. Ever since we got here, everything's gone wrong. That rogue planet, the quakes. I've almost been eaten alive by a house sized worm, then these giants," Trent flicked his hand toward Ubikor, "and now these assholes." He struck the wall next to him with the base of his fist.

"Trent, please" Anamara's soft voice slipped around the wall of their adjacent cells.

"Anamara… I'm sorry. I guess not everything went wrong." Trent took a couple of steps toward the wall between then, reached up with his right hand and laid it flat against the wall. He couldn't see her, but Anamara reached up with her left hand and lay it against the wall on her side at exactly the same spot. Miseth and Trenia both raised their eyebrows at the mysterious sight.

"And yet we are still here. We are all still alive. Not one of us here has been without something unfortunate happening," spoke Anamara, her eyes focused somewhere beyond the floor plates.

"How are you?" asked Trent.

"I'm ok. Better now that I know you're alive and here with me. I missed you."

"I thought about you often. It helped keep me going."

"I know. I could feel it."

After a brief pause, Fezria's voice projected from her cell at the other end of the brig, "Sorry to interrupt the moment, but you said something about the evac ship. You mind letting us in on what you did?"

"Yea, but I'd rather not say. There's a good chance whoever that guy is, is listening to us or one of his people are. I'll tell you this much though. Assuming my idea works, there's still going to be a chance that that ship can rescue the miners. Who knows, maybe even us. I'm really banking on other ships showing up here to cause chaos. We might be on some sort of warship, but judging by the damage I saw along the way here, they're not invincible. There still seemed to be a lot of activity too, so it's likely there's ongoing issues. Looks like Ubikor's ship did plenty of damage before it went down."

"Let's hope you're right," acknowledged Fezria.

"So how about the rest of you? How have you been treated? What have I missed?" Trent slowly removed his hand from the wall and turned around to examine his cell. A cantilevered single sized bed jutted coldly out from the shared wall between his cell and Anamara's. The bed floated about a foot off the ground, its thin gray mattress covered by an equally lean olive drab blanket, topped off with a diminutive white pillow. A tiny room at the back of the cell behind the bed housed the toilet, and a metal sink protruded from the back wall with a single spout and towel hanging off the front. A small bar of soap sat on its left side, a metal cup on the right, and a mirror the size of a tablet hung a tad lower than eye level. The remaining three foot wide area of the cell was bare of any further amenities. He turned back to face outwards and noticed the nurses pursing their lips and shrugging at their situation. Malerina's attention was focused on the cell across from her.

"They pretty much brought us straight here as soon as the shuttle docked, and we've been here ever since. We got to shower once. They feed us," started Phil.

"The food basic but seems palatable. Not quite enough, but better than nothing," added Malerina, glancing over to Trent's block.

"Yup," agreed Phil. "Toilets flush too. View's nice in the morning."

Trent could see smiles appear on the doctor and nurses faces, and Trenia turned a darker shade. At least Phil still had his charm and sense of humor.

He asked him, "How's the arm?"

"Meh. It still hurts. Bastards didn't give me anything for it, but it's getting better slowly. I'll live. For a while anyway it seems," chucked Phil.

"That's good. Michael. You're awfully quiet. You ok?"

"Yes. I'm as good as I'll be in these circumstances. I couldn't have ever imagined this was going to turn out like this. I just want to get out of here and see my wife and kids again. Guess that's just not gonna happen." His voice cracked. "I want to hold my children."

"Stay positive, Michael. We don't know how things will turn out. Maybe you will get to see your family again, and you can cradle your loved ones in your arms soon enough. I've been through some unfortunate events in my past, although not as severe I admit, but I never gave up. And I'm still not going to. So don't give up, Michael. If it means anything, you're surrounded by people who care about you. You are not alone," replied Anamara, with voices of encouragement around, Ubikor remaining quiet.

"Thank you," Michael said solemnly.

"Fezria, how are you holding up?" asked Trent, standing as close as he dared to the force field humming a few inches away from his face.

"I'm fine. I just can't believe that over fifty good people are going to die. I can't imagine being in those shelters for that long. I'm hoping they can move around a little to salvage what supplies they need. It's just not fair. They have a tough enough life as it is. Damn this rotten place."

Trent heard her plop down hard on the firm mattress. "I'm hoping that if turns out the way I think it will, that evac ship will do its job."

"Thanks, Trent. I hope so."

Trent looked across from his cell. "And you?"

Ubikor raised his head a smidge. "Interesting that you would ask."

"Your kind treated us better than these morons. You look all right I suppose," shrugged Trent. "Although, that's really got to be uncomfortable."

Ubikor turned his head around a tad as he scrutinised his cell. "I have no choice at this point. I have been left relatively unharmed for the time being."

Trent nodded. "I take it there isn't much of a chance of getting out? Anyone tried shorting out their fields? Like throwing a blanket at it?"

"I wouldn't recommend it. Mine's missing a chunk out of the corner. And it takes a while for the ventilation to get rid of the smoke," said Phil, sharing his experiences. "I've looked, but there's not a lot that can be done with these rooms. It's pretty solid as far as any brig goes."

"That's great. Hey, you said you were allowed showers. Where are they?" asked Trent, swinging around and inspecting his cell again in case he missed something.

"See that door by your end. There's a small room in there with a couple of showers. It's as secure as these rooms too."

"Nice." Trent released a long sigh, sat down on his bed, and let his back rest against the cold metallic wall. The mattress might have well have been made out of concrete, for it wasn't a whole lot softer. Nonetheless, he tried to get comfortable and shut his eyes.

"You know, if it wasn't for your big mouth, Trent, they would have fed us by now," announced Phil.

It had been quiet for at least two or three hours since Trent filled everyone in on his progress in the refinery and spent time chatting with everyone in general. Ubikor being the exception, as he stayed almost completely silent throughout. The passage of time was difficult to keep track of, as no time keeping devices were visible in the cells or what could be seen in the area just outside of them. Trent tried to take a nap, but nothing felt comfortable, and his consciousness kept reminiscing about the last few weeks.

"Yea, sorry about that. I owe everyone a nice dinner if we get out of here," answered Trent.

"I recommend we stay hydrated. Drink a cup of water. It'll help quell the hunger a little," informed Malerina, getting to her feet and taking a few steps to the sink. Water gurgling into her cup could be heard throughout the small spaces.

"Not a bad idea, doctor," said Trent. He swung his feet off the mattress, rose up into a stretch, and let out a big yawn. He turned toward the sink and traipsed over to it, placed a hand on either side, and leaned down to look himself in the mirror. After a few seconds, he grabbed his cup, filled it with water, and took a few gulps of the cool liquid. Although it wasn't hot food, Trent took some solace in the act. He looked down into his cup, about half full, and started to raise it up to his mouth. But before the edge of the metal container reached his lips, an intense rumble and shudder made him release the object.

Everyone in the brig let out various unintelligible expressions in their surprise, other than Ubikor who remained quiet but braced himself easily against the walls of his cell, his long arms barely outstretched.

"Anamara! You ok? Everyone?" Trent yelled.

Trent helped himself along the wall opposite of his bed and scurried quickly to look out into the brig. He eyed Ubikor, but couldn't make out if he was concerned or not. *Man it's tough to read these guys.* He then peered over to the nurse's cell and saw Miseth helping Trenia off the floor. Since they had to share their bunk, it appeared Trenia was resting and got knocked to the ground. Malerina, almost out of view, looked as though she was crouched down and grabbing onto her mattress for support.

"I'm ok. What was that?" responded Anamara.

"Wow! That was a hell of a hit!" exclaimed Fezria.

"You ok, Fezria?" asked Michael.

"Yea, I think so."

"Whoa! Looks like your friends have arrived, man." As soon as Phil finished his sentence, the ambient lighting turned crimson and a wail of alarms pervaded the airspace.

CHAPTER 32

The ship rocked hard again, sending everyone reeling. Thunderous sounds boomed through the brig, shuddering the metal plating and temporarily destabilizing the force fields, which cracked, popped, and hummed much louder than before.

"A few more of those and these shields are gonna fail," yelled Phil over the ruckus.

"Let's hope so. There might some escape pods we could use to get out of here," replied Trent.

Hyperion's engines and thrusters could be heard reverberating throughout the deck, and a small amount of inertial force affected the captives.

"The ship's moving. Likely evasive maneuvers," said Phil.

Anamara spoke after several moments of relative calmness, "I can still hear the thrusters, but nothing else."

"Damn. I was hoping we'd get hit again and these fields would come down," said Trent.

"I hope we don't get hit again," said Michael, worry heavy in his voice.

"I second that," agreed Fezria.

"Trenia, Miseth, are you ok?" asked Malerina.

The two nurses looked at each other, nodding subconsciously. Trenia answered, "Yes, we're all right. I fell off the bunk but no harm done."

"Good, glad to hear you two are ok."

Trent stood braced against the wall opposite from his bunk so he could get a slightly better view of the rest of the cells, when a light from the entrance to the brig streamed in as the two paneled doorway slid apart. A shadowy figure stood centered and grew in size as it stammered into the brig. Trent squinted and shifted his position to get a clearer view, but to no avail. The angle didn't help him and nor did the force field that blurred the scene.

"What are *you* doing here?" asked Fezria.

"Who's that? Who's here?" asked Trent.

"It's Noor," answered Anamara, "He's standing by Fezria's cell doing something, but I can't see exactly what."

"He's waving his wrist around the console panel. What are you doing, Noor?" asked Phil.

"Wait a moment," said Noor, his voice unsteady as he focused hard on the task at hand.

A few seconds later, the force fields on Fezria and Phil's cells collapsed with an electric thud.

"I never knew about this. I would have never partaken in such a mission if I would have known this would be the outcome. Maksim lied to us all," said Noor, now working to take down Michael and Malerina's force fields.

"Maksim? Is he the captain of this ship?" asked Phil. He stood just outside of his cell and glanced momentarily at Fezria, stepping over to her to give her a reassuring hug. She reciprocated, closing her eyes, moist with a buildup of tears.

"Hardly a captain. He is the exoplanetary research director for the Cronos Corporation. However, the company is not completely aware of his actions, although they are not entirely against them either. They tend to be ignorant of his methods if it improves their profits. Most of his power comes from his involvement with a powerful Hynafol criminal syndicate. They are the ones who upgraded this ship for him, which was originally designed to be a long-term deep space exploration and research vessel. It is now far better equipped as a battlecruiser. These are done." The fields to Michael and Malerina's blocks deactivated and Noor rushed over to the next console panel between the nurses and Ubikor's cells.

Michael plodded a few steps beyond the edge of his cell and just stood there in a bewildered state. Malerina approached him and placed her left hand on his nearest shoulder, cupping his hand with her right. "It's going to be all right, Michael," she reassured. Michael turned his head to face her and managed a half-smile, squeezing her hand gently in return.

Trent waited eagerly and hoped Noor would get to Anamara and his cells soon. He listened as Noor kept talking and hovering his wrist over the panel with subtle undulating motions.

"This mission has gone too far. I am usually stationed in some sort of corporate office. The assignments I am entrusted with require me to monitor and retrieve information."

"You mean steal," interjected Phil.

Noor looked away from the console for a moment. "Yes. I essentially operate as a spy, gathering intelligence for Maksim's purposes." The force field for the nurse's cell dropped and Noor whipped himself around, heading toward Trent and Anamara's control panel to begin working on it. Trent looked across to Ubikor. The field for his cell was still active. The nurses leapt out of their cramp compartment, relief spread across their faces. Upon seeing them, Malerina pulled away from Michael and the three hugged.

"But I cannot continue this. My life has been in put in considerable danger with this expedition. I have never worked in such hazardous environments in my career. And when I overheard Maksim speaking to his officers about executions and leaving the miners," Noor paused, struggling to complete his sentence, "I could not tolerate it any longer. I do not wish to partake in executions and assassinations."

Another blast rippled through the ship, although this one wasn't as powerful as the last. It still made everyone, other than Ubikor, wince and duck slightly from the roar and sudden jolt.

Trent asked, "Do you know who's attacking us?"

"Yes. The Vadokor ship has returned. Apparently it survived the battle when Maksim ordered it to be attacked. *Hyperion* was heavily damaged during the skirmish, and is unlikely to survive this one. Many systems have not been fully repaired, including the extensive damage to the hull. Finally, this one is done."

The force fields for Trent and Anamara's cells shut down. Trent stepped out of his cell and his gaze fell upon Anamara, whose eyes locked with his. They rushed to each other and embraced for a moment.

"We need to go," started Noor, "The soldiers are occupied with emergency repairs and fighting. The ship's three shuttles are docked in the bay where you were brought on board. We should be able to commandeer one." Noor shifted toward the exit.

"Wait!" shouted Trent. "What about him?" He pointed to Ubikor.

"We can't leave him here," Anamara agreed.

Noor looked perplexed. "What do you mean? They are attacking us?"

"Sure, their ship, because they probably don't know we're on board and might think Ubikor has been killed. We are not leaving him."

"If I release him, he is likely to kill us."

Trent shot over to Ubikor's cell, "Ubikor. Things didn't turn out as they would've under your plan, but I know," Trent beat on his chest with his palm, fingers extended, "that you wouldn't have killed us. You would've left the evac ship to pick us up. You promised you'd release us. You probably won't get the element at this point with all the shit happening, but you could be a lot of help to us. You're a hell of a lot stronger. You definitely know how to fight. Help us get out of here. We'll help each other. And when we get free, we'll go our separate ways. At least you'll still manage to keep your end of the deal to let us go… please."

Ubikor sat calmly in his cell, or at least that was what his nearly expressionless face conveyed. After a few moments that seemed like minutes had passed, he answered, "You are different than the rest of your species, Trent. Agreed."

Trent felt like a boulder had been lifted off his back. "Thank you." He looked over to Noor. "Get him out of there, he's not going to hurt us. We can trust him more than we can trust Maksim's guys."

Noor looked unconvinced, but nodded hesitantly and moved quickly to the panel. He began waving his left wrist in front of the panel as before. "Just a few moments."

"What exactly are you doing?" asked Trent.

"Most Salaperneans are augmented. We have various embedded systems for communications and scanning our environments. I'm disrupting the electrical components controlling the force field."

"How do you control which system you need access to?" asked Anamara.

"I have a display over my cornea and various sensors in my brain. With some practice, one can become quite adapt at manipulating these devices."

The force field for Ubikor's cell couldn't have disengaged sooner. Another two significant impacts rocked the vessel, sending everyone staggering, even Ubikor had to find support as he crawled out of his block. A new alarm frantically bellowed shortly after the hit.

"Fusion core critical. Retention field failure imminent. All hands abandon ship," announced a synthetic female voice with urgency.

"We need to leave now. I know the way to the shuttle bay. Follow me." Noor hurried to the brig doorway and it parted before his arrival. The corridor reverberated with the call of the alarm, and the emergency lighting shone through thick wisps of smoke that hung in the air as if one was in a shady bar.

Michael, already close to the exit, ushered Malerina and her nurses ahead of himself and urged Fezria to follow suit. With a quick nod she started after Miseth, but latched on tightly to Michael's arm and dragged him along with herself. Phil jogged after them, supporting his arm, but hesitated for a moment as he flicked a glance back. Seeing Trent and Anamara tagging closely behind, he smiled and picked up the pace.

"C'mon slow pokes!" hollered Phil. "I call shotgun!"

"You can have it, I just wanna be in a shuttle and off this ship," replied Trent.

Anamara looked over her shoulder and cried out, "Hurry, Ubikor!"

The large commander couldn't quite straighten up in the corridor, but still moved with a particular grace and efficiency. He nodded in response to Anamara.

"This way. To the end and down the stairwell. The elevators are down," shouted Noor.

Before they could cross a junction, two soldiers appeared from the right and stopped in their tracks as they saw the group rushing toward them.

"Hey? Where are you going? Aren't those the prisoners?" called out one of the guards.

"Where do you think we are going? We are getting off this ship!" answered Noor.

"With them? I don't think you've got clearance for that."

By now the group came to a stop, except for Ubikor who firmly but carefully nudged his way quickly through to the front. The guards' eyes flew open upon seeing the giant careen toward them. They both started to reach for their sidearm but it was too late. Ubikor's mammoth right hand enveloped the face of the guard to the right, and his left elbow swung with such force against the other soldier that he flew off his feet and against the wall of the passage way. A spine-chilling bone crushing sound cracked as he smashed the head of the man he'd grabbed, after which he tossed the guard's corpse hard against the metal plated floor. With another step, Ubikor's large left foot crashed onto the back of the second guard, pinning him down as if he was nothing more than an insect. The man howled briefly in pain but it ceased swiftly, as Ubikor's large digits wrapped around his head and twisted it nearly a hundred and eighty degrees around. The sound of bone and cartilage snapping and tearing was enough to make Michael dry heave a few times.

"Ugh! Did you need to do that?" coughed Michael. He was doubled over with Fezria holding him by the shoulders.

"Would you prefer I try negotiation next time?" replied Ubikor, he deep voice rumbling through the hallway. "Grab their weapons. You'll need them."

Trent moved up, taking a deep breath before he bent over to retrieve first dead guards pistol. Although this wasn't his first time seeing a dead body, he was careful to keep his eyes focused on the weapon. Once he got it, Trent descended on the second soldier and picked up his gun.

"Phil, here." Trent held out the pistol for Phil.

"Give it to Anamara. She's more able than I am right now," said Phil, motioning with his head toward her.

Trent nodded and held out the firearm by the muzzle for Anamara to take by the grip. "Ok. You know to use these?"

Anamara took the gun and responded, "What? You think because I'm a lady I don't know how to use a pistol?"

"No, no. I just didn't know if you've use—"

"I'm kidding, Trent," she said flashing him a quick smile. "Yes. I know how to use these."

Trent relaxed his shoulders and managed a quick chuckle.

The ship's innards squealed in pain, catching everyone's attention.

"Down two flights, then left," instructed Noor as he took off for the stairs.

Trent and Anamara quickly hustled after Noor, with everyone else sandwiched in between them and Ubikor taking up the rear again. With no resistance down the stairs, the group made their way down to the shuttle bay deck with relative ease.

As they headed down the corridor, the group came to a sudden halt. Trent and Anamara held out their firearms and took aim at the oncoming trio of *Hyperion* personnel, who slid to an abrupt stop and held up their arms.

"Don't shoot! We're not armed! We're just maintenance!" cried the slim young man in the lead. The others nodded their heads frantically and gestured to their bodies that they had nothing on them.

"They speak the truth," said Noor. "Where are you headed?"

"Escape pods. A deck down. The others on this level are damaged."

"Go." Noor waved them on with his hands.

"Don't try anything you'll regret," warned Trent as he and Anamara lowered their weapons.

"Thanks," nodded the worker and they took off running, their heads synchronously locked on Ubikor as they passed by him.

"One look at you and no one would try anything they'd regret," snickered Phil, looking up at Ubikor. The giant nodded a few times in response.

A few muffled explosions on other decks rattled the paneling around the group as they rushed toward the bay, now only a few meters away.

"Through here," informed Noor.

Trent found familiarity with the area and watched as Noor performed his magic trick with his wrist to unlock the large bay access door. But he couldn't help but sense a niggling feeling in the back of his mind. Like they've missed something, or?

"Trent? Are you ok?" Anamara asked softly, turning her back to the others not to alarm them.

Trent snapped out of his trance. "Yea. I... I think so. It's nothing. I guess. Just feels strange. Probably just hungry." He managed an awkward smile.

"That was strange. I had this feeling you—"

The hefty panes slid apart, providing a view into the ship's hangar.

"Let's take the nearest shuttle," said Noor, rushing into the bay.

"No. Wait!" Trent reached out with his hand, but not because he necessarily wanted to. It's as if something made him do it. However, no one waited.

CHAPTER 33

Almost the whole group dashed after Noor, and Trent couldn't help but run in after them. Anamara flashed Ubikor and Phil a look, and as if reading her mind, they followed her in cautiously.

Trent passed Michael and the ladies and caught up to Noor who had just stepped into the open area beyond a few sets of large supply bundles. Trent whipped his attention down the length of the bay and his mouth fell open.

"Get to cover! Now!" yelled Trent, as several shots rang out from the other end of the bay.

The doctor and her nurses let out shrieks of fear and hurtled themselves toward another large supply package sitting about seven meters from the aft end of *Tethys*, the shuttle Trent was transported on. The three ladies huddled together behind the stacks of polymer crates with their backs to it, shielding their heads with their arms against the onslaught of bullets.

Noor, Michael, and Fezria, on the other hand, sprinted toward a pair of control panels a few meters ahead, along the port side of the shuttle. Noor dove behind the one farthest from their starting position, giving Michael and Fezria the chance to take the one closer. But just before Michael reached it, a bullet tore through his left thigh, sending a spray of blood and muscle tissue across the light gray floor panelling. Michael wailed in pain as he fell and dragged himself behind the cabinet styled control panel an arm's length away. Fezria, only a step or two behind slid down next to him.

"Get closer, this thing doesn't give us enough cover," said Michael, gritting his teeth as he grabbed Fezria and essentially rolled her into his lap. Within a second or two, she was huddled with her back to his chest, knees pulled up tightly.

"Damn it! You're bleeding heavily. Shit!" exclaimed Fezria. She clawed at her left arm sleeve and began tearing it off. "I'm going to wrap this around your leg to try and stop the bleeding."

Trent backpedaled promptly. He took cover, crouching down with his back against the corner of the first set of supply creates. Anamara followed suit getting next to him and Phil joined but remained standing, stooping over to keep his head below the line of sight. Ubikor took shelter behind an adjacent bundle, down on a knee to hide his large stature as best he could.

After a few moments, the firing stopped. Subdued roars and rumbles could be heard emanating from various parts of the ship, with the occasional tremor rippling through the floor plates that reminded Trent of the ones on Circulum.

"Well, well, well," started a familiar voice in the distance. "Looks like we have some uninvited guests. Noor? Is that you? Did you set our captives free? Because I think you did. Which means, you're no longer a guest on my ship anymore."

"I do not care. You deceived me. And these people. No one was supposed to die," responded Noor, his voice surprisingly loud for his petite size.

Trent cautiously peered around the corner of the crates and pulled back quickly.

"Trent. Peek-a-boo! I saw you. I'm glad you could join your friends. I suppose at least you won't die alone. I will try to kill your girlfriend first, just to add to the unpleasantness of your death," snickered Maksim.

Trent fumed for a moment but quickly let it go, turning toward Anamara and Ubikor. "There's about half a dozen guards, look like the heavies on the surface, and this prick. A few are taking cover behind the third shuttle at the far end, and the rest are hiding behind the crates. I don't see any by the ship in the middle." Trent ejected his magazine and checked it. "Looks full. Twenty-five rounds. Probably the same for you," he said, jutting his chin at the gun Anamara was holding. She nodded in agreement.

"At this range you don't stand much of a chance against their rifles," breathed Ubikor quietly. "It also appears the ramp to enter the shuttle is locked. Perhaps the Salapernean can access it."

Trent turned toward Noor, who was around eight to ten meters away. "Noor. Noor," he called out in a loud whisper.

Noor sat forward a little from underneath the console he hid under and responded, "I can hear you. What it is?"

Trent thought to himself that his hearing was likely augmented like the rest of him. He continued, "Can you get us into the shuttle?"

"I can. I need to either access this panel or the one at the back of the shuttle. But obviously not under these circumstances." Noor hissed aloud from his position, mouthing the words prominently.

Trent nodded and took a big breath. "We'll think of a way to cover you."

"Activity. At least one soldier has advanced. He's taken a position by the fore section of the second shuttle," informed Ubikor.

"Shit." Trent carefully leaned out again and spotted a sliver of the soldier behind nose of the craft. He quickly extended his arm and fired off a couple of rounds, striking the shuttle on the side near the soldier, hardly leaving any scratches. The fighter jerked himself completely behind the shuttle's nose.

"Aww. That's cute. You've got a little toy gun. My men could just walk up to you and take you out. Those rounds won't even leave a dent in their armor," jabbed Maksim.

A jarring bang and the shrapnel off the edge of a polymer crate not far above Trent's head caught him and everyone else by surprise. Flames erupted on the edge of the case, as well as the shrapnel which it incinerated.

"The hell?" exclaimed Trent.

"Incendiary round. I believe the Hynafol use these types of weapons," informed Ubikor. "Not a pleasant way to die."

Anamara flashed Ubikor a stern look. He shrugged and motioned with his hand to indicate an, "it's true," gesture.

"Any ideas? Because he's right. There's no way in hell we can fight them like this," said Phil, his voice void of hope. He looked over to Michael and Fezria. "How is he?"

"The makeshift bandage has slowed the bleeding, but that bullet mushroomed right through his muscle," responded Fezria.

"I'll be fine," winced Michael, waving off the issue.

Trent could tell from his position that Michael looked paler, and appeared to be sweating hard. Something had to change quickly or else he'd bleed out.

"They're moving up. If I had my gauntlet, I alone could remove this threat. But since I cannot operate your weapons," Ubikor spread out his large digits, "and I no longer have my armor, I stand about as much chance against them as you do."

Anamara slumped closer to Trent and rested her head against his shoulder. Trent dropped his right arm to the floor, the gun making a clack against the metal plating. He was just about to say something, when the entire ship rolled hard in their favor, with the structure of the vessel moaning in pain. Trent felt his back press against the crates. In fact, he was sure that the whole supply bundle skidded a foot across the floor. He also heard screams coming from the doctor and the nurses.

Trent could hear a commotion building at the other end of the bay. He rolled over and poked his head out to take a look, noticing several of the heavies lying on their backs, along with Maksim who was struggling to get his bearings. Trent slithered up the side of the crate and took aim at Maksim, firing off three rounds. He then changed his target and shot at a few of the mercenaries, hitting one in the chest. Noticing that Maksim had raised his weapon, Trent quickly rolled back behind the crate.

Several shots rang out from the far end, bullets riddling the crates and crashing into the wall before them, leaving smoldering pits behind in the process. The ship lurched again, this time toward the hanger doors.

Anamara's weight pushed against Trent as the muscles in his left arm tensed up, grasping tightly against the rigging on the crate. His legs started to swing outward and he could no longer keep himself behind the crate. That is until Ubikor lent a big hand and pulled Trent back, also helping to replace Anamara in the process.

"Thank you," said Trent.

"Me too," said Phil. Ubikor's right arm was extended in the other direction to help keep him in place.

Ubikor grunted in acknowledgment, then said, "The inertial suppression system is failing. The rotational forces of this ship and gravitational forces of Circulum and the rogue planet are beginning to affect us. We need to get on that shuttle immediately."

"Noor! You have to try and open the shuttle or we won't get another chance at this no matter what! We'll cover you!" yelled Trent.

The ship began to slowly recover and Noor peered out from under the control panel. Fezria had squeezed in tightly next to Michael, and the open space underneath their console kept them relatively secure.

"Any help? I don't think we can hold on any longer if that happens again," called out Malerina.

"Noor's going to see if he can open the shuttle," Trent shouted back, peering around the corner, "Just hold on a little longer".

He noticed the doctor on the right side of the crates, with Miseth in the middle and Trenia on the left. They looked absolutely exhausted and scared to the bone. He swore he could see tears running down Trenia's face. He also eyed the activity in the back and noticed the shuttle farthest from them had its ramp extended, and Maksim's henchmen were almost done pushing a small crate into its innards. Maksim looked flustered, and Trent figured he was giving his men instructions based on his gestures and mouth flapping about.

"Noor's doing his thing," observed Phil.

"Trent, he's going to get shot. The rear of the shuttle doesn't give enough protection, they can still shoot him from an angle. We need to provide him with cover fire." Anamara slinked over Trent and poked her head around the corner of the crate stack, examining the situation.

"Hey! Scrunch together!" Anamara hissed loudly at the medical staff as he gestured her palms together repeatedly. "They get it. Let's go."

"Oh boy. Ok!" Trent waited a split second for Anamara to leap to her feet and start sprinting before he did the same. The quick run wasn't as easy as it looked, as the ship shuddered and vibrated almost continually.

The doctor had stood up and had her back to the crate, her arms wrapped tightly around the shoulders of her nurses, who were huddled closely into her body. Both Miseth and Trenia had one of their hands clenching madly onto netting around the supply bundle, desperately trying to keep them steady.

"Noor is working on getting the shuttle open. Just keep holding on a little longer," said Anamara as she took position on the right side of the bundle.

Trent arrived a few moments behind her and took the left side, giving the frightened ladies a look of reassurance. He glanced over to Anamara to see her lean out, fire a few shots, and quickly retreat behind the edge. A flurry of bullets tore at the crates, sending bits of plastic shrapnel around them.

"Hurry, Noor!" shouted Phil. He crept closer to the edge of the bundle to see the action better. "I wish I could help them somehow," he said, shaking his head in disbelief at Ubikor.

Ubikor grunted, "I hope I'm not going to regret this." He grabbed Phil by his good arm and pulled him over to the supply bundle he used as cover. "These aren't that heavy."

The giant stepped into position so he could push the bundle deeper into the bay, grabbed it with his large spread out digits, and lunged into the cube of goods. To his surprise, it slid along the floor with relative ease. Now with more room to spare, Ubikor spread his arms out and essentially hugged the packages, putting his shoulder into it. With a mighty roar, the Vadokor commander took one step after another, each growing in gait and picking up speed in the process.

"Trent. Look," exclaimed Anamara, motioning with her face where to look.

Trent couldn't help a smile escape. He looked at Anamara. "Hey. I have an idea. Follow my lead."

Anamara furrowed her brows, uncertain of what Trent had in mind. She watched him step around the doctor and nurses and stop near her to keep out of sight of the soldiers.

"He's almost here," said Trent, eyeing the commander as he approached, pushing the crate with one of its corners facing forward. "There's enough room on either side of him. I'll take his right."

"I get it," Anamara responded, clutching her pistol with both hands.

Ubikor scooted by at a good pace, like a human jogging. Trent rushed around him as he passed by the bundle at the rear of *Tethys*, and Anamara followed suit.

"Wait until we get closer to shot," instructed Trent.

"Yes," answered Anamara.

"Try to fire at their lower legs, throats, and faces. They lack sufficient protection in those areas. A few well-placed hits should disable them," informed Ubikor.

Within a few moments, the trio had passed by the aft section of the second shuttle and were advancing quickly on Maksim's position. Bullets tore at their polymer crate bundle, but it provided enough defence against their assault.

"Ana. Look. We can each take a position behind those other bundles," said Trent. Anamara nodded in agreement.

"I have a plan. Leave me room. Go now!" roared Ubikor.

Trent and Anamara fired a few shots and darted for their respective package sets. As for Ubikor, he stopped thrusting the bundle forward and tore away at the straps holding the netting over the crates. He then snatched the netting off and begun swinging it around his head, the material whipping through the air. After a few rotations to get the momentum going, Ubikor raised to his full height and unleashed his payload at a pair of guards nearly ten meters away. The mass of webbing opened up as it hurled toward the two soldiers, and their reactions were too slow to dodge it. The barrels of their rifles became entangled with the limp square openings, along with their arms and anything else that protruded from their bodies. Their opposing motions brought both of the mercenaries down in an embarrassing heap.

Maksim stood halfway up the shuttle's loading ramp and took a few messy shots at Ubikor as he sidestepped up the incline. But by then, the commander had hunched safely behind the loose crates and started to dislodge one. Anamara swung out from her position and fired several shots at the heavies flopping around in the net, most hitting their legs. The soldiers howled in pain, letting go of their rifles in the process. Trent used this opportunity to take aim at a lone gunner whose attention was focused on the netted heavies. He fired three shots directed at the guy's neck, of which two hit the mark, sending him crumpling to the floor.

After removing the polymer container, Ubikor noticed three armed mercenaries at the top of the ramp. With relative easy, the commander repositioned the large luggage sized item in his grip, spun around in place twice, and sent the container whipping across the air. The guard furthest up the ramp managed to stop in time, but his buddies were nailed across their chests, collapsing them to the ramp and sending their rifles flying. The guard still standing began laying down fire, causing Ubikor to duck behind the remaining bundle of polymer crates.

"Ramp!" Trent called out.

Without hesitation, Anamara turned toward the ramp and began returning fire, along with Trent.

"Get us out of here! Now! Shut the ramp!" ordered Maksim, his voice barely audible over the rising turmoil on the ship.

The ramp's mechanism jolted into action and the metal incline started rising. A couple of soldiers hiding behind some crates stormed toward it. The first leapt up and rolled onto it, but the second only managed to grab onto the edge. Ubikor rose up to get a better view of the situation and noticed that one of the polymer boxes had cracked open and was filled with various tools. He tore the damaged lid off with ease and plucked out a large hand drill. He wound up and launched the tool like a missile at the mercenary, landing a headshot. The heavy fell like a stone and lay strew out.

"Nice throw!" praised Trent, taking a few more random shots into the shuttle before the ramp had a chance to seal up.

"Hey! We got to get back to our shuttle!" cried Anamara, pointed back toward their entry point where Phil and one of the nurses waved frantically to get their attention.

Noor had unlocked the ramp and it lay ready to receive passengers. With a quick glance to see if the coast was clear, Trent, Anamara, and Ubikor raced back to *Tethys*.

"Get in, go," urged Phil to Trenia, and she didn't hesitate for an instant. Phil watched as Ubikor flew into the lead and cover the half-football field length of the hangar bay in just a few seconds. "What kept you?" he asked as Ubikor slowed to climb the ramp, ignoring his comment.

"Hurry up you two!" he shouted, but his voice was drowned out by the thrusters of Makim's shuttle starting up. After a few more seconds of sprinting, Trent and Anamara arrived. Phil teased them, "About time!"

Puffing hard, the two ambled up the metal incline and sat down in the last row.

"Everyone, buckle up. Noor, shut the ramp," ordered Phil as he moved to the front of shuttle.

"Securing the ramp. Phil, I cannot pilot the shuttle," said Noor, shaking his head.

"That's all right, I'll manage. Would be quicker if I had two good arms."

"I will assist," Ubikor crawled to the pilot's seat, shoving Noor behind him and out of the way.

With the window shielding retracted, the passengers noticed Maksim's shuttle lift off and start toward its respective bay doors, which started to flip open. The thrusters of the craft hurled loose debris away from the vessel as it edged forward and pushed through the atmospheric containment field.

"Yup, we need to be doing that too," said Phil, looking over to Ubikor. "See those icons?" he pointed awkwardly with his right hand to a grouping of glowing symbols, "That one is the thruster selector, these allow you to control the power of each. I should be able to handle direction using these."

Ubikor grunted in acknowledgement and used the slimmest parts of his digits to tap at the icons. In a few moments, the shuttle jolted upward and began hovering.

"Great. Time to open the bay doors." Phil punched at some icons. Then he repeated the action. And again.

Phil's eyes opened wide and his breathing became heavy. "The doors aren't opening. Noor! Can you get'em open?"

"Not from here. However, I could from the console I used earlier."

"Yea, that's not gonna happen," Trent called out from the back, "The hangar is filling with smoke. Some panel just blew out and there are flames spewing out of it."

"Shit." Phil stared through the cabin window, his eyes trying to bore through the bay doors.

CHAPTER 34

"This is not a problem. We destroy them. This shuttle is equipped with missiles," announced Ubikor.

Phil thought for a moment. "Ok, not a bad idea, but we can't engage the missiles at this range. The shockwave will destroy us."

"Not these doors. Those," snapped Ubikor, pointing a large digit to the far end of the bay.

"Of course. I knew that," retorted Phil.

An enormous explosion ripped its way through someplace on *Hyperion*, causing even *Tethys* to reel and knock into the floor momentarily. Startled reactions came from the back of the ship.

Anamara had been watching the events unfold along the starboard side of the side and flicked her head back toward the front. "A large section of the wall just blew out in the hangar. Get us out of here," she said, voice still croaking from the physical exertion from a few minutes ago.

"On it." Phil yawed the ship to point toward the far hangar doors and gave it as much elevation as he dared to not impact the ceiling. "The missiles should clear the other shuttle."

Ubikor had been poking at the icons as best he could, then said, "As soon as I fire, face the shuttle at the far wall. If my assumption is correct, the destruction of those structures should collapse the artificial gravity. It will make it easier to ram the other vessel out of the way."

Phil gave a quick nod, "Understood."

"Firing," Ubikor struck an icon. Two small projectiles belched out of the shuttle and within a second careened into the bay doors at the other end of the hanger. A bright flash and resounding thud later, a gaping hole remained and the atmospheric force fields gave out. The sudden decompression sucked out anything that wasn't securely tied down.

"Ok, ready," said Phil, having turned the craft.

Ubikor fired another pair of missiles into the far wall, causing another bright flash. But without any atmosphere, it was eerily silent.

"There she goes," exclaimed Phil, as the shuttle before them slowly rose and rolled awkwardly. "Take us out. Just be careful not to ram the other shuttle too har—"

Ubikor had already powered up the thrusters to maneuver *Tethys* out of the hanger, jolting everyone in their seats as the nose of the shuttle came into contact with the other vessel.

"Never mind," Phil huffed.

"Less talk, more action," replied Ubikor. Phil raised his eyebrows and gave him a curious look.

Although weightless, the mass of the other shuttle slammed hard against the metal plating of the bay, and jarred *Tethys* intensely with every nudge. But the tactic was working and the ship neared the gaping hole in the bay.

"Perfect. Altering heading. Easy does it." Phil focused intensely as he oriented the ship without causing any major damage. "Almost... good, gun it!"

Ubikor tapped at a few symbols and *Tethys* lunged forward and sped out of the hangar, the darkness of space in full view.

"We should be able to fall into a high orbit to put some distance between us and that ship before she blows. Give me sec." Phil managed to set the new course with his good arm and *Tethys* responded. Its thrusters boomed and flung the craft over *Hyperion* in an arc.

"Oh the heavens of Iish'tehn!" murmured Trenia, her eyes glued to the view before them.

"Wow... now that's something you don't see every day," said Trent. He had already witnessed the rogue world, but not from this perspective.

The gargantuan planet sat less than six and a half million kilometers away, casting a subtle haunting glow into the shuttle, even though the disc was still merely a speck in the ocean of darkness. Also before them was *Keetovor*. The Vadokor battlecruiser was pitched at an unusual angle, bright green and fluorescent orange flames tearing through its hull at multiple locations.

"*Keetovor*. It's heavily damaged. Hail them. Inform them I'm on board," ordered Ubikor.

Phil punched in a few quick commands. "They're on."

The passengers could only understand the name of his ship and that of the commander's, but the rest was gibberish as Ubikor spoke in his native language. Upon finishing, *Keetovor* responded. Ubikor paused for a moment, inhaling a deep breath, then exhaling it. He dipped his head slightly and spoke again, his foreign words seeming solemn. His ship responded with a brief message, then the commander turned his head toward Phil.

"Thrusters to maximum. Activate shields. *Keetover's* reactors are going critical like Maksim's vessel. At this range we'll be destroyed along with them."

"Sorry about your crew and your ship." Phil eyed Ubikor sympathetically and quickly turned his attention back to the controls. "Shields going up. Let's get some mov—"

A proximity alarm blazed loudly, catching Phil's attention. "You've got to be fucking kidding me. Help me with evasive maneuvers quick," he shot a glance at Ubikor. "Maksim's shuttle just fired at us!" Phil punched the thrusters to maximum and *Tethys* jumped ahead.

Ubikor's large digits swiped as best as they could at the controls, the field of stars and strands of gaseous nebulae twirling and dancing through the windows.

"I cannot operate the controls and weapons systems at the same time. We need to return fire."

"On it," Phil responded.

"Can I help?" asked Trent.

"Didn't know you where an expert on how to use targeting systems and space-based armaments."

"I'm not."

Phil chuckled, "Thought so. Just hang on to your girl, buddy. This ain't over yet."

Trent turned his gaze to Anamara. His lips curled up at the sight of her face. She looked him in the eyes and returned his smile. Trent put his right arm over her and pulled her in close, taking her hand in his left. She leaned in and rest her head on his chest, feeling a kiss from his lips through her hair. Even with the missiles that Maksim fired detonating near the ship and giving it a rattle, the two remained unfazed.

"Shit. Think you can fuck with us Maxy? Think again." Although Phil could only manage the controls with one hand, he adeptly targeted Maksim's shuttle and unleashed a pair of missiles from the aft launchers. A pair of thuds rang from the rear as they fired off.

Maksim's shuttle veered randomly behind *Tethys* by less than a hundred meters. It dodged the incoming projectiles with relative ease and they exploded just behind his ship.

"Damn it!" exclaimed Phil.

"Keep firing. It will make it more difficult for them to target us," said Ubikor.

Maksim's vessel fired a series of shots, forcing the Vadokor commander to stray back toward the ailing vessels. Phil returned the favor and monitored their enemy's actions.

"They keep evading." Phil growled and angled his eyebrows in anger. The computer updated the tactical info and identified Maksim's shuttle as *Eris*. "Ok *Eris*, let's see how you like this." Phil programmed his next set of missiles to detonate just in front of their shuttle. "This might throw them off our asses a bit."

Tethys skirted the perimeter of *Keetovor*, flames licking at their exterior. Some of the shots from *Eris* missed them but instead ripped into Ubikor's ship, hurtling a cascade of hull debris in their path. The metal wreckage ricocheted off the shields, causing a ruckus and startling the passengers. Malerina reached over and held Michael's hand tightly, who grimaced at the pain in his injured leg. The nurses both white knuckled the arm rests of their seats, eyes shut tightly with their heads down. Noor, sitting in the first row behind Ubikor, couldn't take his eyes off the unfolding events, a sort of rage hiding behind his eyes. Trent and Anamara had straightened up in their seats, fingers interlocked between their shared armrests.

Phil saw his chance and launched the trio of reprogrammed explosives. He eagerly watched the output as the volley of missiles exploded in front of their pursuer's shuttle.

"Yes! The pilot freaked out!" Phil watched as *Eris* pitched up hard.

"Good. Re-establishing course to put distance between these vessels," informed Ubikor.

Tethys started to arc starboard and slightly below *Keetovor*, putting Circulum back into view. Phil noticed that *Eris* was maneuvering to fall in behind them to continue the chase, but before he could reset the targeting system, a frantic alarm signalled piercingly.

"*Keetovor*. It's critical. Are we far enough?" asked Phil.

"No. Redirect all available power to aft shielding. It might be enough to provide us with some defense."

"On it." Phil launched into action, swiping at symbols on his side of the console panel while keeping an eye on *Eris*.

"They're falling back. Changing course." Phil watched as Maksim's shuttle veered off and suddenly vanished off the radar. "They went into compression. They must've had a course set beforehand. Shit. We should have thought of that too."

Ubikor grunted, then boomed, "Brace for impact!"

Keetovor ignited with a ball of light brighter than the star in the system, with an energetic shockwave racing outward at immense speed. An instant later, it rammed into the back of the small shuttle jarring it violently. Everyone was forced back into their seats, and even Ubikor lost his grip. The explosion also impacted and rattled *Hyperion*, buckling its weakened hull throughout its length and sending it rolling awkwardly. Streams of energetic plasma spewed into open space through numerous ruptures in its metal skin.

Phil groaned, taking a few deep breaths. "*Hyperion's* had it. At least we've gained a bit more distance. But we're hurting. Everyone hold on!"

A few more colossal explosions billowed up along the battlecruiser, with a similarly large flash appearing from its aft section. The first quarter of the ship launched ahead, heading toward Circulum's atmosphere, whereas the rest of the craft merely vaporized. With close to twice the distance between them and *Hyperion* versus *Keetovor*, the shockwave took a few additional moments to arrive and didn't jostle *Tethys* as significantly.

Ubikor repositioned himself at his side of the console panel and examined the flood of blinking warning icons, with several alarms belting out their annoying blips simultaneously. "We have no choice."

"You gotta be kidding me. Fuck!" Phil unwilling gazed up at the planet they were trying to get away from. "We have to adjust our approach, we're coming in at far too steep an angle."

Anamara's eyes flicked between Ubikor, Phil, and the view of the planet through the fore window. "We're not going back. Are we? We can't go back again."

Phil looked over his shoulder. Anamara's mouth hung open in surprise and Trent looked like a vampire had sucked the soul out of him. "I'm sorry. It's either we land or burn up."

"Can you not redirect power to the thrusters and adjust course for a low orbit?" asked Noor, rapidly belting out his question, his head snapping between the two pilots.

"Not with one of the two main engines down and only three of the eight thrusters functional… barely. Three went into auto-shutdown, two are likely fucked up permanently. We'll be lucky if we survive the landing," answered Phil, not pausing for a second as he fiddled with the controls.

Trent looked over at Anamara. She turned to him after a moment eyeing his expression. At first his chest bobbed up and down a little, then his shoulders joined in. His mouth formed a wide grin, as Trent began a supressed chuckle, which transformed into a hearty, almost raging mad belly laugh.

"W—what…?" Anamara began to ask Trent what was going on, but his infectious guffaw tickled its way into her. She tried to restrain herself, but her occasional cough like outbursts took the better of her. Even tears collected in the corners of her eyes.

"They've officially lost it," said Malerina, an eyebrow raised high.

"Leave'em alone. They're just kids," responded Michael, not quite himself having lost copious amounts of blood and gesturing with a single wave to let them be.

Both nurses wide eyed them with stunned looks on their faces, still latched on to their armrests.

Phil peered back for a moment and smirked, then turned briefly to Ubikor. "Well I for one am glad someone is enjoying this trip. Honestly. I feel like that inside. But I'm also crying too. Just none of it's coming out." He shrugged and returned to the controls.

Tethys had entered a steep but manageable re-entry. Its compromised shields held, but the thickening atmosphere buffeted the shuttle more than usual.

"This area." Ubikor pointed a location on a topographical map nearly in the center of the control panel.

"Good as any at this point. Adjusting heading," Phil updated the instructions for the computer.

The shuttle yawed and rolled erratically as it descended, features on the ground becoming more recognizable. The small transport ship was headed toward a relatively large and flat plateau that spread across the perpetual terminator of the planet. Littered with some boulders, it offered a more suitable landing zone than compared to the eternally dark and frozen landscape farther into the dark side of the world. Albeit, the starlight reflecting off the incoming foreign world brighten up the landscape considerably in the next few hours.

"Tuck yourselves in. This landing might get a bit bumpy," Phil called out to the passengers. Everyone squeezed their knees together, placed their hands behind this heads, and hunched over. Everyone but Michael. He was zoning in and out of reality, so Malerina offered him some support with her arm.

"We'll flare up a bit, then fire the fore thruster at sixty percent at around fifty meters to go. It won't be a pretty landing, but we should be in one piece," guessed Phil, Ubikor grunting in acknowledgement.

Phil kept the landing pads retracted, as the forward momentum of the craft would likely rip them off. He mused that this tactic might also help keep them from getting lodged in a crevice, which could flip the ship over.

"Steady... now!" announced Phil.

Tethys angled its nose up and the fore thruster sputtered up to sixty percent power, give or take a few. The negative g-forces from the acceleration weighed everyone down, and the ship soon came in contact with the hard rocky plateau, sliding against the uneven surface. Without much commotion, the ship came to a grinding and screeching halt in what was essentially a dry and barren desert. Only a few of the smaller rocks along the vessel's path knocked it around a little. A moment after the ship came to rest, Ubikor tapped at a few icons and the engines settled down. Several flashing symbols lit the immediate area, along with the faces of the commander and Phil.

Phil breathed hard, sweat beading on his face. He looked through the window, observing the brightest of the stars many light-years away that managed to pierce through the glowing teal sky. After almost a minute of sitting in near silence, his heart rate calmed to a more reasonable pace and he proclaimed in an unsteady voice, "We're here!"

CHAPTER 35

"What the hell do you mean it'll take a few days? That planet's gonna hit in two! We don't have a few days. Do you not feel the tremors? Hell, I'm starting to feel the gravitational pull of *that*," shouted Phil, pointing in the direction of the titanic rogue world in the sky.

Shortly after landing, once everyone had a chance to unwind as best they could, Trent, Phil, Noor, and Ubikor, stepped outside to inspect their only means of transportation off Circulum. The few minutes they'd been outside in the minus seventeen degrees Celsius air, plus wind chill from a gusty breeze, had them shivering, their attire nowhere near appropriate for the conditions. Even the Vadokor commander appeared uncomfortable, regardless of his statue like façade.

The dull teal sky around them was cloudless as far as the eye could see, and the terrain mirrored the atmosphere in its own style. Waves of dust wafted and snaked along the seemingly endless gray-beige rocky plateau as the buffeting winds ushered the miniscule particles along. Large boulders loomed in the distance in one direction, and a mountain range many tens of kilometers away in the other broke the level monotony. Their landing site would have been in nearly full darkness year round, but the large invasive orb in the sky provided ample illumination, like that on an overcast day.

"To be more specific, I meant a few days to completely restore the shuttle, which includes the restoration of the second main engine, five thrusters, three requiring minor repairs, aft and starboard shield generators, long-range communications array, aft weapon systems, and inertial stabilizers. Of course I will endeavor to restore only the critical systems first," responded Noor.

"Is there any way you can get those nano things to work faster?" asked Trent.

"If I had my full supply of them then yes, but not with this miniscule amount. Technically they would not work faster, but there would be more of them to accomplish the tasks. It will simply take time for them to replicate and I must monitor them carefully, or else they might consume key systems and leave us stranded indefinitely. The cold temperatures are also playing a small part in the material synthesis. Above freezing is preferable, but there's nothing else I can do at this point."

Phil puffed out a long breath of air, the chilling air condensing it into a swirling apparition before vanishing.

"The Salapernean is correct. There is nothing that can be done at this stage. You humans need to learn more patience." Ubikor turned to Noor, "When do you expect both main engines and at least three thrusters to be fully operational?"

"You do realize I have a name?" huffed Noor. He looked away from Ubikor to no place in particular. His eyes seemed to be distant and flicked around seemingly randomly as he performed calculations to estimate a time frame. He responded a few seconds later, "Approximately forty-six hours, twenty-seven minutes."

"I'm probably gonna run out of my mind by then," murmured Phil to himself. "And you're sure that two engines and only three thrusters can get us to orbit?" he asked.

"I am certain, but you are just as able to run the calculations yourself if you don't believe me."

Trent thought for a moment, then looked at Noor. "Noor, you said we're tight on raw materials, right? So why don't we just give every seat to the bots? Along with anything else non-essential."

"Without all engines and stabilizers fully operable when we launch, the seats will provide additional safety for us."

"If we sit against the walls and use the tie-down straps, we'll be fine. We made it this far already," countered Trent.

"As long as you keep my seat," said Phil.

"Would there be a benefit for the nanobots to process these resources?" asked Ubikor.

"Of course. More raw materials," nodded Noor.

"Then take my seat. It's only in the way for me," grumbled the commander.

"Very well. I will update their commands and begin extracting them from my body." Noor headed quickly to the ramp, now hugging himself tightly.

"We're all getting cold," Anamara called out from the rear hatch, her arms crossed and being rubbed frantically. "The ship's heaters aren't doing much good against this freezing air rushing in. Are you coming in yet?"

"Yea," answered Phil. He scanning across Trent and Ubikor, "Let's go, we don't want the ladies getting cold." Phil started to march back inside.

Trent glanced at Ubikor for a moment. The commander nodded his head to the side, indicating Trent should go first. Trent flashed a brief smile and jogged up the ramp, the giant Vadokor right behind. Within ten seconds, the ramp sealed with a hiss and blocking the frigid atmosphere behind it.

"That's so much better," sighed Anamara in relief.

Noor had removed an access panel near the co-pilot's seat on the starboard side of the craft, and was in the process of extracting some nanobots from his body. Phil stooped over on his left and Trent joined them shortly after traipsing to his right side, arms crossed with hands shoved under his upper arms. Noor held the back of his right hand close to his face, his eyes scanning around the interface only he could see. In a few moments, a tiny slit in his skin appeared and miniscule device presented itself, not unlike some sort of mechanical proboscis. Placing it close to an exposed circuit board, the apparatus reached out and entangled nearly microscopic railings to the electrical contacts.

Trent leaned in more closely to study the curious event as it unfolded. "Whoa," he breathed. "You can actually see those tiny wires shimmering."

"Yes. Those are the nanobots migrating across the bridge connection into the ship's system. Within three to four hours, the machines will have occupied several areas of the ship and will begin to breakdown non-essential items. Most of the seats should be dissolved in about a day, then reconfigured to produce a large quantity of nanotech for various purposes, such as repairing the engine and thrusters and replacing any defective parts. If only I would have brought my case with me, this entire vessel would have been repaired within two days." The activity on the bridge connection ceased and Noor removed his hand. The structure that had manifested less than a minute ago began retracting and pulling back into his gray toned skin.

"Shoulda, coulda, woulda. At least we might be able to get out of here." Phil shook his head. "I swear, if we have to come back here one more time, I'm crashing the fucking ship. I love you, man, but I'm taking us down. Not even Ubi's gonna stop me." Phil flicked his thumb behind his back at Ubikor.

Trent couldn't help but chuckle, turning his gaze to Ubikor. "He's just kidding."

"Nope. No I'm not." Phil frowned and shook his head.

Ubikor just blinked a few times and made himself more comfortable against the port side wall near the control panel. Phil begun to wander back to the co-pilot seat, but a large backpack secured to the wall caught his eye. He started to fish around in it, dropping a small tablet and foreign electronic device on the ground. After managing to open a side pocket with his good arm, he rummaged around for a moment and pulled out an item. "Hey! I found a deck of cards. Who's up for a game? Losers get thrown off the ship to make it lighter."

About six hours had passed since Noor transferred some of his nanobots into the shuttle's systems. To help pass the time, Phil got several members of the group together for a game of cards, choosing one of his favorites, poker. Other than himself, the participants included the nurses, Miseth and Trenia, Anamara, Trent, and after some badgering, Noor. Malerina and Fezria looked on occasionally, but tended to Michael as best as they could under the circumstances. Michael had been zoning in and out of consciousness, but the bleeding from his wounded leg had at least been stabilized. The doctor was thankful for Phil's backpack curiosity, as aside from the deck of cards, a compact medkit he also came across, provided some painkillers and gauze. As for Ubikor, he chose to be a spectator.

Trenia leaned closer to Miseth and held up the cards she was holding. "Is this a good set?"

"I think Phil called it a, 'hand'. I think that's not bad," answered Miseth, eyeing her cards.

"You aren't supposed to show your cards to anyone," hushed Phil.

"Well I can't remember all these *hands*." Trenia pouted and shook her head.

Trent grinned. As his turn as the dealer, he took a card from the pile and displayed the river, then discretely eyed his cards. "I'm out." He slide them aside, carefully keeping them face down. "Turn'em over," he said to the remaining players, looking across each face.

Anamara and Noor folded after the flop, so only Phil and the nurses were now play.

A large grin grew over Phil's face. He slapped his cards down on the floor before himself. "Three of a kind."

Miseth lay her cards down. "From three to seven, various faces. I believe that beats your hand."

Phil's mouth dropped, "Ah—"

"Yes. Yes it does," quickly answered Trent before Phil could. "Trenia, how about you."

Trenia glanced at each member of the group, ending with Trent, then laid her cards down. "Here."

Trent chuckled almost silently, his body bouncing from the sight. "Well done, Trenia. You're a natural. That's called a Full House. That's a really strong hand."

Phil shook his head. "Man. It's like this contract. I'm not having any luck." He sighed loudly. He reached out with his right arm and shoved his cards toward Trent.

"I believe you've lost more than enough times. Do we throw you off the ship now?" Ubikor's voice broke the relative calm in the shuttle, his grumble of a laugh vibrating everyone's chest cavities.

The players broke into laughter. Even Malerina and Fezria sported wide grins. Their moment of glee was short lived though, as an alarm chirped excitedly.

"Hey. That's a proximity alarm. There's a ship nearby," said Phil, struggling to get to his feet.

"It must a ship here for the element," thought Anamara, turning her head toward Trent and flashing him a big smile.

Phil had reached the front of the ship and sat down at the console panel, Ubikor leaning in to get a better look. "It's a fairly big ship by the looks of it. They've just come out of compression and are performing braking maneuvers. No ID is being transmitted by their systems. That's a bit odd. Anyway, I'll hail them." Phil entered a few quick commands and started speaking, "This is Phil Sykes of the shuttle *Tethys*. We have crash landed and require immediate assistance. I repeat, we are in need of immediate assistance." Phil tapped an icon and eyed everyone in their small abode.

"*Tethyssh*. Intereshting. Are your enginessh operable?" answered a voice through the speakers after a lengthy few seconds.

"No. One main engine is functional and we only have three thrusters available. Can you assist us, please?" answered Phil, his eyes huge with hope.

The deep voice came through again a few seconds later. "*Tethysshh*. Unfortunately, we are indisshposshed at the moment."

Phil snapped his head to Ubikor, then to Trent. "The element. They might think that's what we came here for, or we want it." Phil quickly tapped at the comm symbol and responded, "We are not here for the heavy element. I repeat, we do not care for the heavy element. You can have all of it. We just need to be transported off this planet. You can drop us off at the nearest habitable world. That's all we ask. Please."

Several seconds passed again. "We are glad to hear you are not interesshted in the element." A grin widened Phil's cheeks and the nurses hugged each other. Trent reached for Anamara's hand and she did the same, eyes lost in each other's. "We're sshure you will be resshourshful in finding a sholushion to your predicament. You shtill have sshome time before the planet impactssh." The communication clicked off.

"Hey! Help us out!" Phil flicked at a few icons, then pounded his right fist onto the console panel. "Damn it!"

"Hynafol," said Ubikor, his piecing dark eyes facing toward Phil.

"I would not be surprised if they have something to do with Maksim's operation," Noor glanced at the commander and the others.

"Should we be concerned? Will they attack us?" asked Anamara.

"I doubt that, as they are unlikely to see us as a threat," responded Noor.

"But it's working," Trent chimed in with a hopeful smile on his face.

"What's working?" asked Phil? A confused look twisted Anamara's face and made Noor turn his head toward Trent, along with several other pairs of eyes.

"The message I sent out when Maksim's forces invaded, when I was stuck in the comm shed. It looks like the ships are coming in."

"This one was probably waiting nearby. But hopefully, others will arrive soon," added Noor.

"Both main engines online. Thrusters three, five, six, and eight nearly repaired. I estimate they'll need about four more hou—"

Another harsh quake suddenly rippled through the area, shaking *Tethys* vigorously. The deep rumble of the rocky surface reverberated throughout the cabin, with occasional high-pitched squeaks piercing ears as the ship scrapped along the ground, shards of the stony surface clawing at the vessel's belly. Everyone hung on tightly to the riggings on the walls, some of the group slumping to the floor to gain more stability. After about fifteen seconds, the quake subsided.

Noor took a few nervous breaths and continued, "Like I was saying, about four more hours and we'll be able to launch."

"That's something I'm very much looking forward to. And having four functional thrusters instead of three might just help us get out of here even faster. Plus I'm hungry as hell," said Phil, checking out another proximity alarm chirping away on his console panel. "Should I answer this one?"

"Might as well," answered Trent. "Maybe they'll be nicer than the last guys who threatened to blow us into little bits and take the element the ship uses." Trent shrugged a shoulder.

He sat on the starboard side of the shuttle near the co-pilots seat where Phil was. His right arm was intertwined and hanging loosely in a strap hung on the wall, and his left arm was around Anamara's shoulders. She was slumped lower against the wall and had her forehead against Trent's cheeks, several day old stubble tickling her skin. Their stomachs seemed to growl at the same time and they both shared an unkempt appearance.

Anamara's dust and dirt soiled hair drooped over her face, several strands tangled from an occasional quick venture outside for some fresh breezy air. She lifted her head up and adjusted herself to face Trent head on.

"Trent? I want to talk to you. But not here," she whispered.

Trent faced her and raised his eyebrows. "Everything ok?"

Anamara gave a subtle half-shrug of her left shoulder. "I just want to say something. It might be my last chance to do so."

"Don't say that. We'll make it out of here. How can it possibly get any worse?" Trent frowned and furrowed his brow. "Then again, I might have just jinxed it." He flashed a quick look over to Phil. He was attempting to communicate with another vessel, but it didn't appear to be going well. "Want to head outside for some privacy?"

"Too cold. There's no one at the back corner." Anamara indicated with her head in the direction of the starboard area.

At this point, almost all of the seats had been processed by the nanobots, along with some various equipment around the small vessel deemed sacrificial by the group. Phil still had his chair, and there was a pair of front row seats for Malerina and Michael. Everyone else had picked a spot along the port or starboard side. Noor was nearest Phil and next to Trent, while Fezria, Trenia, and Miseth sat opposite. Ubikor simply hunkered down before the pilot's console.

Trent and Anamara rose to their feet and took a few steps toward the corner. Anamara gently reached around her midriff, giving it a squeeze. Hunger pangs were setting in and the lack of nutrients made her feel lightheaded.

"Take it slow, Ana." Trent embraced her from behind and let her sink into him, even though he wasn't faring well either.

She turned herself around to face him, allowing his grip to remain around her body. A teardrop slid down her left cheek, leaving a partially cleansed track of skin in its wake. She paused for a moment, her eyes twitching back and forth over his.

"Trent." Anamara's voice cracked. She swallowed hard and continued, "Trent, I want you to know that in the short time we've known each other, you've been more special to me than those I've known for much longer. You are by far the most sincere. Your heart is pure. And there's something that transcends this reality with you. You are more unique than you know."

Trent felt his heart lodge itself into his throat, hints of upward curls on his lips. He reached up with his right hand and gently cupped Anamara's cheek into his palm, fingers sliding back along her neck and in between her hair. She pressed tenderly against the warmth of his hand and closed her eyes for a moment.

"I've fallen in love with you and I have no regrets. I only wish we could enjoy ourselves somewhere peaceful. Anywhere other than here." Her eyes, still managing to sparkle with life, welled up with tears, her lips trembling, breathing stuttering.

Trent had to let the moment sink in before he spoke. "If I knew this was going to be the outcome of this contract, but knowing I would meet you, I would have still accepted this job. You know I love you too. You're the strongest most resilient woman I know. Intelligent beyond your years. And beautiful." He leaned toward her, dipping his head, their foreheads meeting.

A strange feeling surged within Trent. He shut his eyes. For a brief instant, he felt weightless, like having an out-of-body experience. Anamara peered up at him quickly, taking in a quick shallow breath. A rush of emotions swelled throughout her mind, but she couldn't understand them. Her memory shot back to their escape from *Hyperion*, just before entering the hangar.

"Trent?" she breathed. "Are you ok?"

Trent's focus returned. His eyes snapped open and stared deeply into

Anamara's. "This is not going to end here. This is not our time. Not yet. I don't know how I know this. But you have to believe me. Do you believe me?"

Trent's glare intensified. But it was not one of anger, stress, or insanity. There was a sense of hope being conveyed through his being.

Anamara was taken aback at first, but a calm flushed over her. With their foreheads still in contact, she nodded softly. "I believe you," she murmured, then closed her eyes and pressed her lips to his.

CHAPTER 36

"Ok everyone, this better be the last time we see this damned planet," started Phil. "Stay in your positions throughout liftoff and until I…" Phil paused for a moment and flashed Ubikor a glance, "*we*, say so. Although we have that fourth thruster to rely on, I have a feeling things might get a bit rough. Sure as hell doesn't help that the weather's acting up."

The eccentric group was to depart from Circulum around an hour ago, but Noor's bots tangled with a few systems in unexpected ways, leaving them, mostly Noor, scrambling to take corrective action. The rogue world, nicknamed Malum by the group, was less than forty minutes away, and its presence was known incessantly. Gravitation tidal forces were wreaking havoc on Circulum's crust and mantle, as tremors were nearly persistent, and large quakes would rattle the small shuttle much too frequently for anyone's comfort. Even the gravitational pull of Malum could be felt, and the amount of light from the system's star reflecting off its surface was bright enough to make it through the thick blizzard that rolled in less than thirty minutes ago.

"Get ready!" Phil looked over to Ubikor and gave a hefty nod.

"Powering up main engines. Operable thrusters activated," announced the Vadokor commander.

Tethys wavered into the air, knocked back into the rocky plateau a few times by the strong gusts from the blizzard.

"There had to be storm." Phil's eyes were fixated intently on the flurry of activity displayed on his control panel.

Warning lights lit up the fore of the cabin, casting Phil and Ubikor's shadow on the ceiling, along with a gentle amber glow around their dark clones. Multiple alarms chirped and wailed, warning them of the hazardous conditions beyond the ship, as well as informing them of the multiple systems that were still either inoperable or only partially functional. The thrusters could be heard fighting against the gusty winds as the shuttle was buffeted hard.

"And we're off!" exclaimed Phil.

The main engines roared as the craft pitched upward. Everyone on the floor tensed their muscles in unison in response to the inertia, grabbing on tightly to what rigging was left on the walls. Malerina did her best to keep Michael stable, fighting the g-forces as best as possible. Michael had fallen unconscious over two hours ago, and the doctor wasn't as optimistic about his survival. Trenia and Miseth had their elbows locked together, both with their eyes shut tightly, heads firmly against the wall. Fezria, sitting closest to Ubikor's position, had her knees up into her chest, and had wrapped her arms in some straps to keep herself in place. Noor, behind Phil and on the starboard side, decided to stay standing during the launch to keep an eye on the controls and take action if needed. He wrapped a strap tightly around his right leg and had a couple more around his arms. Considering all the jostling, he managed to keep himself quite steady.

Trent and Anamara retook their chosen spots on the starboard side and held each other tightly, their eyes looking out the fore windows of the small craft. They watched the snow blast onto the window as the vessel picked up speed and broke the sound barrier around ten seconds after liftoff. The inside lit up from the whiteout conditions. It was a surreal scene. They could feel the shuttle accelerate, but could essentially see nothing but a blanket of thick white featureless clouds as *Tethys* tore through them.

For what seemed like several minutes, but was actually less than one, the shuttle shot through the cloud tops.

"Finally," breathed Anamara.

"Yea. I didn't think it would be nice to see space again, but I'm relieved. And look at that!" exclaimed Trent, his expression taking on both a surprised and awe inspired look.

Malum was terrifying close. The vast cities that once teemed with life were plainly visible, their gargantuan skyscrapers and other structures jutting into the planet's atmosphere and spreading out for hundreds of kilometers in all directions. Equally massive on their own scale, frozen rivers, lakes, and at least two oceans, could be seen from the vantage point of the shuttle.

"Strange how everything looks so... perfect," said Anamara. "It's like the world was put in stasis. Nothing seems destroyed or damaged. Look at that thick forest. Those trees must be hundreds of meters tall. This must've been a beautiful world once."

"You can even see the spaceports. At least I think that's what they are," mused Trent.

"Probably. They're huge. I've never seen ones that large though. How are the engines holding up, Ubikor?" asked Phil.

"Within parameters, but I've increased the coolant system output by three point five percent."

"Ok, that's not bad. But we're not going quite as fast as we should be."

Ubikor swiped at a few icons. "The weather system altered our course by a small amount. We are caught in Malum's gravitation field. We need to take corrective action. Recalculate escape trajectory."

"Shit! Give me a sec." Phil fiddled madly with the controls, his left arm still of no use to him. He shook his head and let out a frustrated laugh. "Ok. So we were going to swing around Circulum to the west and get whipped back roughly toward Ty'kape, but that's a no-go. We'll have to swing around the southwest end of Malum, and boy do we have skim its upper atmosphere to get out of here. That should give us enough speed, but it'll also hurl us in the opposite direction."

"We have no choice. If we stay on this course, we will either end up back on Circulum or possibly crash on Malum. Alter course quickly," stated Ubikor.

Phil dropped his head for a moment and sighed. "Updating instructions." Phil's fingers shuffled a few symbols around. "There. Done."

Now about fifteen-hundred kilometers above Circulum, the engines and thrusters were somewhat muted due to the lack of atmosphere. But their vibrations through the hull caused a rumble, and the change in course could be heard as well as felt, as *Tethys* veered just over twenty degrees to port.

"Noor. How are your bots holding up?" asked Phil.

"There's little concern for them. I am hoping the work they've completed will hold up. Are you reading any anomalies?" Noor's eyes seemed to be looking through the fore windows, but their subtle motion was a clue that he was communicating with his microscopic workforce or analyzing the data readout only he could see.

"So far so good. Engines seem to be performing within specs, especially after that coolant adjustment." Phil pried his eyes off the console and looked out the window. "Holy…"

As *Tethys* arced around Malum's south end, the rogue planet revealed more of its glory and vaguely hinted at its once rich history. Unlike Earth, its southern region mostly consisted of a frozen ocean, with two branches of large mountainous islands jutting out from the icy surface.

"Phil. Are those clouds?" asked Trent, bewildered at the sight.

"Yea, in a manner of speaking. It looks more like thick fog to me. The star is warming the surface and it's causing the frozen water to thaw and evaporate."

"Our speed has increased by eighteen percent," announced Ubikor.

"Good. We're still gonna skip along the atmosphere. Noor, how are shields?" asked Phil.

Noor took a moment to answer, his eyes dancing around. "The nanobots are still repairing the generator coils for the underside. However, the port side shield has ninety-three percent power and fore is at eighty-one. I would recommend facing the port side toward the planet if the shuttle can be successfully flown in that manner."

Phil mashed a few symbols, furrowed his brow for a moment, and then raised his eye brows. "Yea. I think that should work. Might get a little nastier, but ain't much else we can do. Commander Ubikor, what say you?"

Ubikor looked over to Phil and simply nodded once.

Phil returned the gesture with a quick nod of his own, then applied the changes. *Tethys* needed to gradually drop to within two hundred and fifty kilometers of the surface and was already around eight hundred and falling.

"We'll get out of this. I know we will," said Trent, giving Anamara's hand a squeeze and continuing to be mesmerized by the view.

Anamara's grip tightened in his hand. "I just hope we get back to civilization quickly."

A proximity sensor activated, catching Phil's attention. His eyes almost popped out of his head and his mouth hung wide open. "Fezria!" He turned his head to face her. "You won't believe this. It's the evac ship! Let me hail them before we disappear behind the planet." Phil swiped at some icons. "*Tethys* to *Mehn'tow*, do you read?"

"This is Captain Tellizra of the *Mehn'tow*, we copy."

Phil grinned from ear to ear as he listened to the static filled response from the evac ship. "Captain, we're survivors from the mining facility and we couldn't be happier to know you made it. Our systems have been up and down and didn't detect when you arrived. You can't imagine the hell that broke loose down there. Long story short, we managed to secure a shuttle, but it's damaged, and we're performing a slingshot maneuver to get us out of this system. Once we've stabilized, can you assist? And one more question, did you manage to rescue the miners?" Phil glanced over to Fezria, who looked on, surprise and anxiousness spread across her expression.

"By the looks of the facility, I too couldn't begin to imagine what you people went through. We arrived about two hours ago. We had a compression failure about three quarters of the way here and had no choice but to stop for repairs. Then we got a message from a... Trent. Is he with you? If he is, give him a thanks from us. We wouldn't have been the slightest bit prepared if it wasn't for his warnings. We've taken some hits from a few greedy bastards that wouldn't believe our message that we were here only for the rescue operation, but luckily its minor damage and nothing that can't be repaired once we get back to base. We picked up forty-three miners. Poor souls were hungry and thirsty as hell. Sorry to say, not all of them made it. One of them told us about a section of the mine that collapsed due to a quake."

Tears ran down Fezria's cheeks, a thankful smile beaming across her face. She had removed her hands from the rigging on the wall and wiped them away. Miseth unravelled her left arm from its strap and reached around her to give her comfort.

"We'd be happy to assist, but unfortunately we can't. The compression failure caused ruptures in several conduits, and we're low on fuel. We can jump home and that's about it." The static on the communication worsened and the captain's voice became more distorted. "But you have my word we'll contact... se... and have anoth... vessel sent."

"You're breaking up captain. Any support will help. Here's our trajectory. Hope this makes it through. Thank you for your assistance," answered Phil, pushing a few icons around on his console to send the evac vessel their course heading.

A surge of static sounded for a few seconds before the captain's voice re-emerged, "... your transm... ommunica... ood luck." The computer disconnected the transmission as the signal strength dropped below the usable threshold.

"Well, at least most of the miners made it," sobbed Fezria. She regained most of her composure, her expression one of relief.

"I'm really happy that turned out so well," said Phil.

"Me too," echoed Trent, nodding.

Fezria smiled, but it was short lived. She quickly ensnared her arms back between the straps, along with Miseth. *Tethys* shuddered and the vibrations jostled the metallic floor plates of the small craft as turbulence in the thick upper atmosphere of the planet beat at the hull.

"Already? At this altitude? We're just under four hundred clicks up," said Phil.

"Our calculations were based on assumptions. We didn't have the necessary data to take into account atmospheric expansion due to the star's energy warming up the planet," responded Ubikor.

"Compensating. At least as much as we can." Phil's seat harness tugged at him and he winced as his left arm slapped into his body.

Trent held Anamara tightly against hiself as the shuttle rolled and rattled against Malum's thick upper atmosphere. She reciprocated. Her right arm was wound around his back, and her left hand was clutching onto some netting on the wall.

An alarm sounded and everyone suddenly felt a lot lighter. Ubikor reached up with his long left arm and braced himself against the ceiling, keeping himself from floating away from the captain's console section.

"Shit! We're dropping fast! Thruster two lost power. Noor? Any help?" shouted Phil over the swooshing of air rushing over the hull.

Noor had dropped to his knees to give himself more stability, his eyes a flurry of activity. "The vibrations damaged the power couplings for that thruster. Nanobots have been instructed to repair them. It'll take a few minutes."

"Damn it! We need to slow our descent or else we're gonna burn up," exclaimed Phil.

"Roll to starboard and flare up. It should slow our descent," said Ubikor.

"Thermal shielding is hurting badly as it is. We're going to become a toaster."

"If we sink deeper into the atmosphere, we are not going to be able to escape it. It might become uncomfortable, but all of you should survive for the next six minutes it will take until we're free of Malum's gravitational pull."

Phil turned around to see the others. He shook his head. "I'm sorry. We'll divert as much power as we can to internal cooling systems, but I have feeling it'll become really hot in here."

"Not your fault, Phil," started Anamara. "Just get us out of this system."

Phil could see Fezria nodding and nurses followed suit. His gaze found Malerina, who shrugged her approval, as there wasn't much she could do anyway. Then he looked over to Trent.

"Just do it, man. I know we'll make it. I know you and Ubikor can do this. You will." Trent's words seemed to carry more weight than ever before.

Phil regained some of his usual enthusiasm and whipped back around in his seat to face the console. "We sure as fuck are going to do this. We're not giving up. Ubikor, help me stabilize thruster output."

Ubikor grunted his agreement.

The view beyond the fore window changed as Malum rolled around to the starboard side of the window. The superheated air striking the thermal shields glowed orange, with occasional wisps of maroon skirting over the ship. With the angle of the nose up relative to the surface of the giant world, *Tethys* rhythmically skipped along like a flat stone on water.

"Two minutes and thirty seconds until this shit show is over, and would you look at that!" Phil exclaimed excitedly, pointing with his right index finger toward the view.

All eyes in the shuttle, except for Michael's, would witness a spectacular event. Malum's crust began to scrape along the surface of Circulum. The incredible force of the impact lit up white hot around the area with the release titanic amounts of energy as the air and rock of both worlds collided. Shockwaves tore through the atmospheres and crusts of both planets in a surreal display that looked like some sort of slow motion special effect seen in movies. Massive plumes of dust and debris scattering violently across their landscapes, but what appeared like boulders were actually sections of the ground the size of small mountains. Bodies of water on Circulum and the frozen lakes and rivers at and near the impact site on Malum burst into superheated steam.

Anamara watched, her mouth open slightly, eyes unblinking. "If only I could visit that site when it cooled off to see what has formed."

Trent slowly turned his head toward her. "That would mean going back to Circulum."

"You know what I mean. I'm a geoscientist after all."

Trent smiled and pecked her on the cheek. "As long as I get to go with you." Anamara's eyes met his for a moment, before returning to the calamity unfolding before them.

"Escape velocity exceeded by forty-six percent," announced Ubikor, who also seemed to be enjoying the once in a billion year chance to see such an occurrence.

Phil took his eyes off the show for a moment and scanned his readouts. "Yup, we're moving at an impressive thirty-nine thousand clicks a sec, and rising. Backing engines off to seventy percent. That'll get us right out of this system." He silenced a few alarms with a few well-placed jabs, then released a big sigh.

"I will personally ensure that you are treated with the utmost respect and care if a Vadokor vessel arrives before any other ship," said Ubikor.

After over an hour of coasting in the vastness of space, the Vadokor commander had sent his homeworld a distress signal. Their system was slightly closer to this region of space than the Ty'kape Empire was, which meant they might be rescued sooner. The main engines had to be shut down shortly after the slingshot, as instabilities developed in their reactors. As for the three operable thrusters that remained, it was decided to keep them offline unless emergency maneuvers needed to be performed, and to conserve what fuel was left.

"Thanks, Ubikor. Hopefully someone will hear our calls and get over here quickly," answered Phil. "We'll maybe last for another day or two without water, and I swear I'm going to pass out from this hunger."

"If we all agree, I can instruct the nanobots to breakdown engine and thruster components, which should provide us with unique raw materials in order to keep life support active for another day or two. I believe that a small water purification system could be constructed within a day," said Noor.

"The main engines are useless and so are all non-operable thrusters. I would say that is a wise suggestion," responded Ubikor.

"I'm sure as hell in," agreed Phil.

Trent flashed Anamara a look, her eyes indicating agreement. "We're in too."

"Yup," nodded Trenia, Miseth, and Fezria.

"The sooner the better. We're all severely dehydrated, and it didn't help we had to go through such physical exertion," said Malerina.

Anamara looked concerned and stared at Michael for a moment, noticing his shallow slow breathing. "What about Michael?"

The doctor placed her hand on Michael's arm and gently squeezed it. Her lips rolled inward and a deep frown formed. Her eyes welled up, looked over to Anamara, and she shook her head. It took her a few moments and some deep breaths before she would answer. "Even if I had immediate access to our medical bay, I doubt I could save him at his point." Her voice cracked and ended in a whisper.

Anamara lay her head next to Trent. The two sat side by side, mirroring each other's seating position, backs against the wall with knees bent and close to their chests. Trent's left arm was outstretched and resting on his kneecap. Anamara reached over and intertwined her fingers with his. Trent turned his head and gave her a loving look, his eyes caressing the elegant features of her face.

She was about to say something when a proximity alarm sounded from the console. And not an instant later, an imposing angular vessel materialized before them. The impressive and bulky, mostly bright white ship, raced toward their tiny shuttle.

Phil forced himself back in his seat, right arm out stretched and pushing against the edge of the console. "Fuck. Are they gonna ram into us?"

Trent and Anamara braced themselves together, squeezing their hands tightly. Noor leaned back as he anticipated the collision. Trenia turned away and hid her face in her hands, letting out a scream. Miseth grabbed her shoulder from behind but couldn't pull her eyes off the unfamiliar vessel. Fezria braced her back against the wall and clenched her teeth, while the doctor white knuckled her armrests and glared through the fore window. A louder and more annoying proximity alarm kicked in, repeating its call over and over.

Then just before everyone thought this would be it, the extraordinarily large ship slammed to a halt a hundred or so meters from *Tethys*. The group eyed the huge vessel that took up almost the entire view they had.

"The Shenki," said Ubikor in an unusually withdrawn manner.

It was apparent from his almost non-existent expression that he seemed to dread the sight before them.

"The... who?" Phil asked. His eyes ate up every aspect of the foreign craft before them.

"The Shenki," Ubikor repeated. "Not a single Vadokor ship has ever returned from their region of space."

Trent's eyes shifted to Ubikor, then back out to the vessel.

"Trent? What is it?" Anamara sensed his mind was at a distance. "Trent?" she whispered again.

"They're not here to hurt us," he paused for a moment or two. "They're here for something else."

Trent and Anamara will continue their journey.

ABOUT THE AUTHOR

Imre Zsolt Balint is one of those people who would like to become one of the most interesting in the world. He has a love and desire to learn almost anything, and the perseverance to actually accomplish many of those things.

He has self-published two books. Circulum (a sci-fi novel) and Concepts of Photography and More (non-fiction) are available on Kindle and Kindle Unlimited. In addition, he's almost done writing a book on how to make longboards and has started preparations for another novel.

Overall, Imre's career has been focused in the areas of information technology and education. For the former, he specializes in Web application and database development, and for the latter, he has worked for some post-secondary schools in various roles. He currently finds great pleasure as an instructor for computer technologies and business mathematics in a prominent polytechnic institute. Imre's education includes a Bachelor of Science in Computer Information Systems (Summa Cum Laude), Master of Project Management (with Distinction), and an MBA (also with Distinction).

Aside from teaching, Imre continues to delve deeper into his love of music by teaching himself to play the violin, ukulele and other instruments, along with continuing to fine tune his woodworking skills.

Keep up to date with Imre's world by visiting his website and following him on his various social media accounts:

https://imrezbalint.ca

https://www.facebook.com/ImreZsoltBalint

https://twitter.com/ImreZBalint

https://www.goodreads.com/imrezbalint

Manufactured by Amazon.ca
Bolton, ON